Pearl by the Sea

Regina Mouradian

outskirts
press

Pearl by the Sea
All Rights Reserved.
Copyright © 2024 Regina Mouradian
v2.0

This is a work of fiction. Names, characters, businesses, places, events, locales, and incidents are either the products of the author's imagination or used in a fictitious manner. Any resemblance to actual persons, living or dead, or actual events is purely coincidental.

The opinions expressed in this manuscript are solely the opinions of the author and do not represent the opinions or thoughts of the publisher. The author has represented and warranted full ownership and/or legal right to publish all the materials in this book.

This book may not be reproduced, transmitted, or stored in whole or in part by any means, including graphic, electronic, or mechanical without the express written consent of the publisher except in the case of brief quotations embodied in critical articles and reviews.

Outskirts Press, Inc.
http://www.outskirtspress.com

ISBN: 978-1-9772-7387-1

Cover Photo © 2024 www.gettyimages.com. All rights reserved - used with permission.

Outskirts Press and the "OP" logo are trademarks belonging to Outskirts Press, Inc.

PRINTED IN THE UNITED STATES OF AMERICA

This book is dedicated to Joanne Boldi and all the people who have shared their joy of books with me.

Odessa Odesa

Kiev Kyiv

Let's Call the Whole Thing Off

Love is the emblem of eternity; it confounds all notion of time, effaces all memory of a beginning, all fear of an end: we fancy that we have possessed what we love, so difficult is it to imagine how we could have lived without it.

Anne Louise Germaine de Staël

Chapter 1

She loved to make lists. Since she was a kid growing up in Medford, Massachusetts, making lists comforted her. In fourth grade, her favorite list was the presidents. She would run through them in her head while attending church, sitting through one of her brother's baseball games, or getting a cavity filled to take her mind away from the here and now.

She would stop on Obama since he was last on the list, having been president the last two years in 2010. Then when she finished the list, she would start over again, trying to complete it faster from beginning to end.

She expanded her repertoire from presidents to medical lists while studying in college. Caterina used the typical mnemonic technique that her classmates and teachers used for, say, learning the metacarpal bones, the Krebs cycle, and cranial nerves. Sometimes, she made up her own acronyms for fun. Science came easily to Caterina. She has always had a good memory and was genuinely interested in majoring in exercise physiology. She was hoping her undergraduate degree would lead to an advanced degree in physical therapy or physician assistant, but the thought of more student loan debt crippled her ambition and put that dream on hold.

After four years at Boston University, she kept the same job she worked at all through school as a personal trainer. She enjoyed working with all ages and fitness levels and found satisfaction in her success stories. The recently widowed man, who was unsteady on his feet, showed quick progress. He returned every week for his sessions and became one of her favorite clients. At first, he could not talk about his deceased beloved without tearing up, and he would slow his bicep curl to a standstill, looking forlornly across the gym. After a year of consistently attending Caterina's training sessions, he transformed into a man steady on his feet who could recount memories of his wife with laughter and joy. He was very popular with the older women who would jump on an elliptical next to him so they could chat during their workouts.

She loved working with the shy girls who lacked confidence in their bodies and soaked up her advice like sponges. Caterina never had to struggle with weight when she was younger because she was always naturally skinny. She always felt awkward, though, like a newborn giraffe with unsure legs. She would get tangled up during speed drills on her sports teams. She fell more than her fair share when her legs crumbled beneath her. Caterina would be surprised each time her body didn't cooperate with what her mind thought was a spectacularly coordinated move.

Caterina never excelled at sports. She was always a bench hugger and received awards they gave to participants who never quite got the ball in the net. Her childhood bedroom was lined with ribbons that said, "Best Spirit," "Team Player," and "Most Improved," and not the "MVP" shiny trophies like her four older brothers accumulated throughout their sporting careers. Caterina should have taken the easy route to stand out among her siblings. She could've had it easy as the only girl in the brood and thrilled her mom with talk of makeup, dresses, and dance lessons. Her mom was a knockout, and when baby Caterina was born into the world, a girl after four boys, her mother treated her like an American girl baby doll, sometimes changing her outfit three times a day for home photo shoots. Her mom and dad loved her, and she could convince her parents of anything with the words "Mommy, Daddy" said in a coquettish tone. She could have easily glided through life partaking in her mom's vision of her, rising to the top of the litter as the only princess, but the siren of her brothers' laughing, playing in the dirt, was a call she could not ignore.

Instead of dance costumes, hair ribbons, and makeup, she dove into the world of soccer cleats, hockey pucks, and any hand-me-down sports equipment she received from her older siblings. Her brothers, Aldo, Dom, Anthony, and Giovanni, were six years apart from oldest to youngest, and she was three years younger than Giovanni, making her competition strong. Her brothers let Caterina join their games, with no one caring which side she was on since she added nothing to the odds of winning. She tagged along on all their lessons and joined Little League baseball when she was age-eligible. Her mother gave up trying to lure her away from her brothers' recreational activities. It was easier for her mom to lump her in with boys from a logistical and financial standpoint.

The advantage of loving sports and years of roughhousing made her fearless on the fields and ice, but this didn't exactly translate into athletic success. She would come home from a soccer game with a twisted ankle, having to hobble on crutches for a week before slowly weaning herself back into running. In her junior year, she was well into the ice hockey season when she sustained her worst injury. Her gangly legs got twisted in an opposing player's stick, and she felt a sickening noise in her knee as she landed hard on the ice in tears. The MRI showed a terrible triad tear, a three-area injury that would require extensive surgery. She knew her hockey season was finished as she read the report of medial meniscus tear, medial collateral ligament strain, and anterior cruciate ligament tear. Once again, she was in a brace, this time, a knee immobilizer, and contemplating her options.

She only knew sports. She would get the ACL repair surgery and try to return to the ice better than ever. She ran through her list of US states in her mind as her physical therapist strengthened her leg in preoperative therapy sessions. She ran through the list of presidents as she slowly came out of anesthesia, trying to orient herself to the bright lights in the recovery room. She ran through the list of planets while sitting on the bench watching her teammates win the championship, trying not to feel bad for herself that she couldn't participate.

"Things happen for a reason," her mother would say, trying to get her interested in dress shopping for the junior prom even before a boy asked her to go. Her mother would nudge her to put on a little lip gloss or say, "It wouldn't hurt you to put a little curl in your hair," but Caterina would ignore these suggestions and head off to class with her hair pulled back in a ponytail, no makeup, and her long, skinny frame hidden under track pants. No one ended up asking her to the prom. She promised her mom she would go "all out" senior prom, which was a bread crumb her mom cherished to play dress up once again with her baby Caterina.

She didn't make the cut for the senior lacrosse team, and the coach smiled at her rather condescendingly, patting her on the shoulder, explaining that not everyone is cut out for sports. After tryouts, she removed her custom-made ACL brace and threw herself on the bed, running through some type of list in her head, trying to soothe herself from her disappointing performance. She never returned to sports and started applying just a little bit of lip gloss occasionally. It seemed like an easy way to make her mom happy. She would head to the gym after school and enjoy the atmosphere of being a gym rat, a way to be athletic at her own pace, away from the fierce competition of brothers and girls more coordinated than her. She even got asked to the senior prom, although her date was much shorter than she was, disappointing her mother. She went wearing flats and not the rhinestone high heels her mom spotted at the Glitterati dress shop. Senior year transitioned into college, and she kept going to the gym, adding on a paying gig there helping others set up workout routines and navigating exercises after an injury.

She loved her exercise physiology classes, understanding how using executive functions such as making lists could successfully diminish the body's interpretation of pain. The sensation of aches traveling the spinothalamic tract was interpreted in our brains, which we had the power to control. She dived into classes and workouts and competed for top grades. She was competitive, trying to earn straight As or running a bit faster along the Charles River to improve her mile time. She sharpened her edges not to be last in a 10K, to be less awkward, and graduated summa cum laude from BU.

Who she was competing with was a bit complicated. Boys? Her peers? Her past self? She had only one serious boyfriend in college, but she frightened him off with her need to compete with him on every level. If she lost the first game, she would take a simple dart game at the bar and turn it into a must-win, two-out-of-three series. She would find the Facebook group he made about travel by noticing the travel group was liking his personal Facebook account. She thought it was great investigative work that she could study him and uncover his secrets. He thought it was just creepy and the final straw of a relationship that felt more like a competition and less like a couple.

After graduation, she kept working as a personal trainer, and her applications to take the GREs were getting pushed out year after year. She made decent money and also started working another job on the side to keep up with bills. She put her study and research skills to work as a private investigator. It sounds more exciting than it was. Geico insurance would hire her for auto accident claims that would always be settled in arbitration before they went to court. Fraud was rampant in claims, and she would be hired to research the case and add some layers of information about the insured that the insurance company outsourced to private investigative firms. She got involved in this side gig from her uncle, who also did PI work for a national insurance company. He was kind of lazy and called it in with lame dossiers of the claimant. They were scant of any real juicy tidbits of fraud.

Conversely, Caterina would produce facts worthy of an opposition research team on a presidential candidate. She treated it as a game, a competition she would win against an adversary who was frauding the system. She fell into the routine of personal training, investigating, and the occasional date to keep her mom happy, snapping a photo of herself in lip gloss with her hair down and a little curl. She would text the picture to her mom with a whimsical remark about her wiping the dirt off her face before taking the selfie.

Her mother stopped bothering Caterina about her looks and would reply to Caterina's selfie with a quick heart emoji. Her mother found her princesses, lots of them, in her grandchildren. All four of her brothers were married, with her oldest nieces taking dance lessons, shopping, and letting their grandmother curl their hair. Two of her brothers, Aldo and Dom, followed in their dad's footsteps, working as police officers, and the other two, Anthony and Giovanni, took the trade route, working HVAC in their uncle's business. They married their high school or college sweethearts and stayed local. Caterina should have been relieved that the pressure was off her to please her parents, as they now had everything they dreamed of, but for some reason, it made her feel discarded.

She ran through her lists, old lists, college lists, and now, new lists of other topics. She was thinking about bilateral injuries on her way to work at the gym this morning. She had been a personal trainer for seven years, three in college and now four postcollege. Categorizing gave her comfort and control over a somewhat unpredictable life of the unexpected ACL tear, her boyfriends' misunderstanding her motives, and her mother no longer caring about her lip gloss color. Lists centered her, her bilateral injuries list. Let's see, there was Muhammed with the bilateral posterior cruciate ligament tears he sustained from standing between two taxis at the airport when one got rear-ended. There was poor Jackie with two broken shoulders from slipping on the ice while taking her doggy out for a walk last winter. Marco's was a crazy bilateral injury. Two broken patellas that required internal fixations. He was vague about the details when he showed up for a personal training consultation. A baseball bat was involved, and that was all he would say about the matter. The list was about six people long, certainly not one of her longer lists, but it was compartmentalized into her memory cortex filing system. Joanne was on the list, and what a fluke injury she had. She tore both Achilles tendons playing pickleball. A quick turn to return a serve and, "*pop, pop.*" Joanne felt like she was shot in both calves as she went down like a ton of bricks on the court. Let's see, Muhammed, Jackie, Marco, Joanne, her bilateral injuries list was filed into her brain next to her "My Very Educated Mother Just Served Us Noodles" song for the planets. The planet list was truncated after Pluto was reduced to a floating rock.

She pulled into the Life Time Gym parking lot in the Boston Seaport district. It was a swanky health club that had a wealthy, diverse clientele, primarily residents from affluent condos in the Boston harbor neighborhood. She grabbed her gym bag from the backseat, waving her phone under the scanner to sign in at the expansive front desk that looked more like an upscale hotel lobby than a gym entrance. Another day, another list of clients to serve. A routine that she enjoyed, yet her subconscious knew she was missing something. Something that no workout challenge or time shaved off her mile would fulfill. She wanted love like her brothers had. She wanted the love her parents shared as they doted on their grandkids. She wanted to let her hair down and relax with someone she didn't have to compete with. She wanted someone who accepted her with lip gloss and dirt on her face. She didn't know who he would be. Maybe she already knew him. Maybe he didn't exist. Maybe she would be alone forever.

She threw her bag into the corner of an office she shared with the other personal trainers, then took a big swig of her iced coffee before heading down to see her seven a.m. client near the circuit training equipment. She didn't know it that morning, but she would see him today . . . the man who would capture her heart. A man with a bilateral injury story that would be added to her list. An injury that changed his course of life ten years ago and would bring her into his world soon. She would love this man with all of her being. She would use her research skills and competitive nature to save his life. She would see him today, and her world would never be the same. Caterina was meant for this moment in time.

Chapter 2

Petrov Leonidovich Geller loved to make lists. Always had since growing up along the coastal city of Odessa. His lists were mostly about soccer facts. He and his brother, Alexsei, who was two years older, would run through the roster of their favorite local soccer team, arguing who were the top three most important players. Their dad often brought them to see their hometown team play at Chornomorets Stadium. These were his happiest childhood memories.

When Ukraine was under Soviet Union rule, the biggest shipping company in the world sponsored the Chornomorets. *Blasco* was emblazoned on the soccer players' uniforms. Petrov was born in 1995, four years after Ukrainian independence, so he would see *Pony*, an American sneaker company, across the players' shirts.

Petrov's mother would send her husband and two sons off with a backpack of sandwiches and drinks, and they would take the train three stops to Sobornaya Square and walk over to the 34,000-seat arena. They would eat in the park, and Petrov and Alexei would play an impromptu game of soccer with other young boys, waiting for the gates to open for the game. After the match, they did not loiter as the attendees tended to be rowdier after two hours of drinking. They would hop back on the train to their apartment near the Azov port. The boys would talk nonstop, rehashing the game.

Not much changed for the Chornomorets transitioning from competing for the Soviet Union Cup and now playing for the Ukrainian Cup after 1991. Now, though, all English-speaking sports media had to spell Odessa, Odesa. This was a big deal for journalists to understand they needed the Ukrainian spelling and not the Russian spelling to appease Kiev, which also had to be spelled Kyiv. Otherwise, you might be accused of being a Putin sympathizer. These subtle changes festered under the surface, rearing their need to control speech slowly at first, but then nuance and subtlety flew out the window.

Soon, the politics of Russia versus the West consumed all aspects of cultural events. Electing a president was when the country felt most divided. Eastern Ukraine would vote for a Russian-speaking politician, and if he were positioned to win, Western Ukrainians would take to the streets demanding a do-over. In 2004, the Orange Revolution demanded the leading candidate, Yanukovych, be removed from the ballot, and Yushchenko became president after the successful color revolution. Yanukovych fought back and won in 2010. History repeated itself after another revolution built momentum in 2014, and Yanukovych was removed from office when much of Western Ukraine demanded his resignation.

Pearl by the Sea

Twenty-three years after Ukraine split from the Soviet Union, 2014 would be a tumultuous year for a fledgling country still trying to navigate its independence. Corruption was rampant, and the government and oligarchs could sway big decisions. All Alexsei and Petrov wanted to do was watch their hometown team play soccer. They cared not for the rumblings of dissatisfaction with the Pro-Federalist movement that was popular with the Russian-speaking youth in Odessa. They cared not for the Pro-Unity movement, which was becoming a mantra for some Chornomorets fans and players. They weren't choosing a side in politics. They wanted to enjoy being eighteen and twenty.

In the last few years, they would go to the soccer games without their dad and enjoy their freedom. They would take the train three stops and run to avoid missing the beginning kick. They were good kids. After the game, they didn't join the rowdies that would wander in and out of the bars until closing. They would take the train back home for dinner with their parents. Alexsei was studying engineering at Odessa National University, and Petrov was taking his exams to apply to the same college for the following year. Commuting would keep costs low, and working part-time would help pay for tuition and books.

Their mother told them not to attend the May 2, 2014, game. She listened to the news religiously for the past few months since President Viktor Yanukovych resigned after the successful revolution in Maidan Square in Kiev. She saw the revolution ripple to all parts of the country. The news would lead with stories about fighters in the Crimea and Donbass regions of Ukraine that did not recognize the color revolution and felt their votes were betrayed. Politicians in the capital city would ramp up their hateful rhetoric toward any Ukrainian citizen who disagreed with the results of the revolution. The punishment was not proportional, for many innocent citizens were lumped into being guilty of just being Russian-speaking citizens. Their churches were closed by the police, their media was outlawed, and any cultural references honoring the Soviet Union were considered against Kyiv.

Petrov's mother heard a story that the police beat an old veteran, and his St. George medal that he hung from his rearview mirror was taken from him. Who knows if this was true. Ukrainian-speaking news would say it was a lie pushed by Russian propaganda, but the Leonidovich family only spoke Russian, so they listened to Russian-speaking news.

The tensions of the last few months continued to escalate since President Yanukovych fled in a helicopter to Russia seeking asylum. The Pro-Federalists, who brazenly carried orange and black flags, the colors of the St. George ribbon, demanded the right to decide their own local governance in Odessa. These same demands were popping up in other regions of Eastern Ukraine, including Crimea, Donetsk, and Lugansk. The Pro-Unity group supported the ousting of Yanukovych and wanted better relationships with Europe. Some Chornomorets soccer fans went to the extreme with their Pro-Unity support. They began identifying themselves as the Azov Battalion and started brandishing weapons publicly, insisting they were only for defense. Recently, it was said a Pro-Unity extremist launched a hand grenade at a checkpoint, injuring nine people.

"You shouldn't go near that area for the game. I don't care if you can't sell your tickets or get a refund. That area is bringing out the crazies," Mrs. Leonidovich would warn her sons, who brushed her off as a paranoid woman who listened to the news too much. Even Mr. Leonidovich tried to downplay his wife's nervousness, assuring her that the Pro-Federalist camp was very small and everyone ignored their protest. However, none of their reasoning diminished her concerns. Perhaps she sensed something that she herself could not even understand.

After the soccer game, Alexsei and Petrov streamed out of Chornomorets Stadium, walking straight to the train to get home to assure their mother everything went smoothly. When they arrived at the train platform, they heard all trains were canceled because a bomb threat was called in. They wandered away from the train down Shevchenko Ave. as many of the soccer crowd converged in the area. It was around seven p.m. on May 2nd, so the sunlight from the day was still present, and the air temperature was comfortable. They weren't concerned it was a real bomb, just an inconvenience to getting home. The police told those waiting for the train to go to the Trade Unions Building for help. Years later, this detail would be disputed, like hundreds of facts that day, but the brothers followed the crowd.

When they arrived at the Trade Unions Building, they saw the protest camp of the Pro-Federalists staked near the front steps. The Pro-Federalists and Pro-Unity were brandishing weapons of all types, but they were not fully displayed yet. Alexsei saw a classmate wearing an orange and black St. George medal in the camp, but Alexsei kept his head down, not wanting to be associated with either side. If this was cowardice, he didn't think so because he was just avoiding controversy. Petrov and Alexsei entered the Trade Unions Building to look for a bathroom. Pro-Federalists were wandering around but also train passengers, trying to find information about transportation. The building was closed, but the protestors had taken it over and opened the doors.

Their timing could not have been worse. Who started throwing the petrol bombs is determined by who wants to frame the narrative, but the video showed both sides taking part in throwing Molotov cocktails at each other. Alexsei and Petrov exited the bathroom and wandered down the hall, but the entrance to the front of the building was on fire. Bewildered, they rushed down the hall but could not find an exit. The flames grew higher, and the smoke was choking them. They saw some stairs and descended a stairwell, but the basement doors were locked. They climbed back to the first floor and had no choice but to go to the second floor. Frantic people surrounded them.

"Go to the roof," someone shouted, but they did not know if they should follow. The building was formidable, with Greco columns aligning the entrance and high-vaulted ceilings on each floor of the five-story building. However, their instincts said to climb, so they climbed.

"Go to the roof," another panicked interloper shouted, but they did not listen this time. They entered a room where half a dozen people opened the windows to scream for help. The smoke engulfed them. They saw a man climb out the window, hang from the ledge, and let go. They ran to the window to see his fate, but the black smoke engulfed the front of the building, blinding their view. They heard the crash of glass as a petrol bomb was thrown through a window and exploded next to them. Pain seared through Petrov's mind as he smelled the burning hair and flesh of his body and quickly hit his arm with his jacket to put out the flame. They had no choice. They ran toward the window. They were on the third floor, which was much higher than they thought.

"Let me lower you down, Petrov!" screamed Alexsei. He grabbed his younger brother, helped lower him out the window, and let go. Petrov hit the pavement hard. The burning of his forearm was nothing compared to the sharp pain he felt in both of his feet. He tried to stand up but was unable to. He looked up and saw his brother releasing his grip and landing with a sickening thud near him. Alexsei's body did not move after contact. The world stood still in that moment, like a skip of a record, and then noises around Petrov came into hyperfocus . . . glass shattering, popping noises like gunfire, and screaming people filled his ears.

"Alexsei!" Petrov screamed in a voice he didn't even recognize. "Alexsei!" was the only word he could form. He dragged himself on his forearms toward his brother's lifeless body. He wasn't aware of the gravel scraping his left forearm that had burned. He wasn't aware of his bilateral heel pain. His only thoughts were to touch his brother. He was within a foot of reaching out to him when he felt the force of a boot hit his stomach, a hard kick that stopped his slow crawl toward his brother and caused him to grab his middle reflexively. The kick came again, landing on his arms that protected his stomach. This time, he felt the searing pain of the gravel on his arm being pushed deeper into his burnt flesh. "Alexsei!" he screamed once more, and another quick kick was administered to his wounded body. Petrov turned his eyes toward his assailant, confused about his beating.

His eyes were met with a sinister snarl of a Pro-Unity punk. His shaved, sweaty head shone in the light of the flames. The punk leaned closer to Petrov's face and whispered with a sadistic laugh, "Burn, Colorado, burn." Petrov grabbed him by his shirt as other Pro-Unity activists pulled the punk off him. Petrov saw a black sun tattoo on the assailant's chest, the last thing he remembered before he passed out. Forty-five minutes would go by before emergency vehicles finally arrived.

Ten years later, Petrov would still relive May 2, 2014, like it happened yesterday. He lost his brother that day and his childhood. He ended up attending National University just like his brother, but he changed his major from engineering to philosophy. He wanted to understand evil. He wanted to understand how neighbors could kill neighbors who were cheering for the same soccer team just hours before. He wanted to make sense of the world, but searching for answers only brought him more questions. He made lists. Lists of philosophers, lists of former Soviet Union countries, lists of events his brother had missed the last ten years. Lists helped dull the pain. They were an executive function that allowed the memory cortex to interpret his anguish in a more palatable way.

He made lists while the physical therapist stretched his legs. He made lists when he stared at the recovery room lights after surgery. He made lists while exercising at the gym and never played soccer again. Lists gave him some semblance of control.

He receded into a routine of studying and eating dinner with his parents. He attended the university year after year until he received a master's in philosophy. He got a job teaching Soviet Union history at the university. Finally, one day, he was offered a job as a guest lecturer abroad at UMASS Boston. He hesitated to leave his parents but assured them it would only be for a year. He needed to be there for them. He was their only child now.

He was halfway through his second semester teaching in Boston when she saw him that day. He walked into Life Time gym for his workout when he passed Caterina and her friend. He did not notice her, but she noticed him. He wasn't looking for love, and neither was she. He wasn't looking to be saved from his loneliness. Sometimes, events unfurl without a plan, and we are very much in the wrong place at the wrong time or in the right place at the right time. How events are retold is based on who is telling the story.

Chapter 3

"I'M TELLING YOU, Cat, if I can't get this weight off, I'm never going to fit into my wedding dress," Kimmie complained while pedaling furiously on her Peloton bike at the Life Time gym.

Caterina leaned against the bike beside her roommate and listened to her concerns. Caterina wore her Life Time personal trainer uniform, a royal blue T-shirt with its logo emblazoned on it, and black track pants with a royal blue stripe down the side. Some trainers preferred yoga pants or shorts, but old habits die hard, and Caterina always felt at home in track pants working out. She nodded her head for the tenth time and reassured her friend she didn't need to lose a pound, reminding her she fit into the dress just last week and the wedding was only six months away.

"You look fantastic, Kimmie. Don't turn into a bridezilla. If you do, I'll move out early before Jack moves in to take my spot," Caterina sighed dramatically. "Who am I kidding? Jack will have to drag me out kicking and screaming from that apartment. I will never be able to live a rich lifestyle vicariously through you again."

Kimmie took a quick swig of her water and looked at her bike screen to keep the pace. "Why can't you stay? It's a two-bedroom, and me and Jack will be in one. It's going to be so weird not being together. Besides, you know my mom and dad will still subsidize my lifestyle. My salary and Jack's salary together could never pay that rent, but my dad insists it's an investment." Kimmie grinned. "Who am I to complain?"

"Well, it was a good run. I'll probably end up back at my parents if I can't find anything decent. I really don't want to live in Medford and commute into Seaport. I might find a gym closer to the burbs."

Kimmie raised her arms in the air when her video screen displayed "Finish" at the end of her cycling time. Caterina handed her a small royal blue Life Time towel that was available in dispensers. "Thanks, Coach," smiled Kimmie.

Caterina laughed, "I'm not your coach if you're not paying me. I'm assigned to the cardio room from eleven to one, but I can whip your butt into shape for a nominal fee."

Kimmie took another sip of her water. "I'm good. I used my freebie personal training sessions last month. I know I just need to lay off the mint chocolate chip ice cream."

"You look great," Caterina said fondly to her best friend and roommate. "You are going to be a beautiful bride."

"Aww, thanks, luv. I hope you bring a date to the wedding. Who knows? Maybe you and Jason will rekindle your romance. He's been asking about you, y'know."

Cat rolled her eyes. "I doubt it. I think that ship sailed after I freaked him out by stalking his Facebook Travel Group Page.

Besides, him being Jack's best friend would just be awkward. He'd be hearing all the complaints about you. How you wait until the dishwasher has not one square inch of empty space before you run it, or how you do not hang up your coat but throw it over the couch. That would just be annoying."

Kim laughed. "Ha! You're probably right! We'll find you another guy."

Just then, a striking man walked past the Peloton bike section with his gym bag in one hand. He wore a basic red T-shirt and black shorts. Caterina followed his stride until he disappeared around the corner and went to the locker rooms. After a minute, Kimmie raised her eyebrows and commented on her roommate's interest in the gym member. "Who's that?"

"Who's what?"

"Who was that? That man who looks like a younger, better-looking Daniel Craig. I could see his gray eyes from across the room. He's gorgeous."

"I don't know who you're talking about. All I see all day is athletic men here. It's one of the perks of the job."

Kimmie raised her styled eyebrows again. "I'll say, but you had that look in your eye when you checked him out. I know you too well."

"Believe it or not, I actually have a date in an hour. A guy I met on Hinge."

"No, Cat. You go on a lame date every few months to satisfy everybody to say you're dating, and then you never go on a second date. I swear you only do this to tell your mom you're dating and have an alibi."

Cat's eyes opened wide, and she became animated when she spoke. "I'm super interested in this date." She walked with her friend to the mats, where Kimmie did her cool-down stretches, and Cat continued her story. "So, this guy Sidar asked me on a date. Well, I checked him out and—"

Kimmie interrupted, "You mean you like googled him?"

"Sure, sure. Of course, I googled him. But I also, y'know, did other stuff too, like checked his criminal records, previous addresses, court filings—"

"Oh God, please, don't give me angina, Cat. Why are you doing this to me?"

"It's fine, fine. You know me. I only do lunch dates in a very public place, no drinks, and seat myself first, so I'm in a visible spot."

"Cat, why do you treat dating like your private investigator job? It's called a date." Kimmie stretched into a lunge position. "So? So, is this guy a sketch? What did your research show?"

"Well," Caterina looked around, a habit she acquired with her stalking skills. "This guy has no criminal indictments, but I saw a civil case was filed against him, I believe, by his ex-wife. They shared the same address last year, but the case was sealed and dismissed, so electronic records didn't give me much info." Cat stretched a little and continued her story. "So, I went on Court Listener and used the Wayback Time Machine app to read the complaint before it was sealed. You can do this sometimes to circumvent what has been sealed. Anyway, his wife was suing him for a million dollars because she said he killed their cat. Wild, huh? Like, what happened? Why would he do that? I want to find out why. Kind of profile him to test out if I get some hints."

Kimmie just looked at her friend strangely. She had known this woman since Medford Middle School, but some parts of her would always be an enigma to her. Her interests would veer off in ways Kimmie could not understand or relate to.

"What is wrong with you, Cat? Are you going to go on a date with a cat killer? Are you insane? I'm not going to let you do that. Do I have to inject common sense and basic safety into you like you are five years old? I forbid you to go."

"It will be fine. I'll text you later and tell you what happened. I don't know. I go down these rabbit holes, and my curiosity gets the best of me, and now I have to find out what happened."

"You said it, not me. Curiosity killed the cat. And do I have to remind you your name is 'Cat'? Please, be careful." Kimmie threw her towel at Caterina. "Could you please stop treating dating like some puzzle you must solve? Could you just turn off that weird competition thing you have with guys to outsmart them or whatever the hell you do?"

"It'll be fine. I'll bring you home some dinner, and then I have a PI case tonight, so I'll probably be home around nine."

"You're killing me, Cat. Why can't you just stick with teaching people how to do push-ups? This private investigator job is giving me gray hairs, and I don't want to start dying my hair before the wedding."

Pearl by the Sea

Chapter 4

CATERINA ARRIVED AT the Mexican restaurant fifteen minutes early and seated herself strategically to watch the entrance when her blind date arrived. She changed into jeans, a light knit sweater, and flats. She never wore heels on these dates in case the guy fudged his profile height by a few inches. At five foot eight inches, she was actually in the eighty-fifth percentile for height for women in America, with the average height being five foot three and a half inches.

She sipped her water as she observed a man enter the restaurant by himself, and the hostess moved her arm in Cat's direction. Caterina gave a small wave, and the man walked toward her table, then confused, walked slowly past her seat and looked around, somewhat bewildered.

"Sidar?" inquired Caterina.

Sidar looked in the direction of his name being said and stared for a moment. He whispered more to himself, "Caterina?"

"Yes, hi. Nice to meet you," she said, shaking his hand firmly and gesturing to him to sit in the seat opposite her at the table.

He did not take his eyes off her as he pulled out the chair and sat down. "Thank you. I . . . I'm sorry if I'm staring. It's just, well, you are stunning. Your profile picture does not do you justice. It's usually the opposite reaction I have when reality sits across from me on these encounters."

Caterina smiled and looked down at her menu to avoid his stare. She was used to this reaction. She purposefully kept a blurry photo of her in dark frame glasses wearing a flannel where you can't really ascertain her features. It weeded out the dates only going after looks.

Sidar continued to stare until she looked up from her menu and caught him in the act. Then he looked away quickly and then went back to staring again. "I'm sorry if that was blunt, but you really are a very beautiful woman. You look just like Cleopatra. This is a pleasant surprise."

Sidar wasn't too bad looking himself. He was wearing a dark green Polo shirt with khakis and dress shoes, a typical look for a casual young professional in the area. He was probably around her height, so a wise choice for the flats. He opened his mouth to repeat something about her beauty again, and she cut him off with small talk.

"Have you eaten here before? I work a few blocks away, so we often come here after work. It's probably the cheapest restaurant in Seaport. If you can call twenty-dollar tacos cheap."

"I don't come down this way often. I live in Cambridge, and we have our fair share of overpriced taco places too," he smiled.

He had a nice smile and dressed nicely. Caterina was

interested in what would possess a man to be a cat killer. She studied him and the menu. The waiter took their orders and without the prop of a menu to avoid eye contact, made the pressure of conversation increase.

Caterina took a sip of her water as they exchanged pleasantries. She never ordered alcohol on a lunch date, wanting to keep the bill cheap and also to treat the date like an interview.

"You know," Sidar smiled bemusedly, "I would have probably scrolled by that blurry picture of yours if it wasn't for your name. It's a great name, Caterina. I love cats."

Ah, this was her moment to begin questioning. "Oh, you do? Do you have a cat?" She watched his reaction closely. She noticed an irritation in his face—a quick flare of his nostrils and a flash of hate in his eyes.

"No, I don't," he said curtly.

"Oh?" Caterina said innocently. "What happened to your cat?"

His eyebrows raised quickly, and he crossed his arms. "What do you mean? Why would you assume I had a cat, and why would you assume something happened to it?"

Caterina realized her line of questioning was flawed. She wasn't as good at this as she thought. She took a sip of her water and tried for honesty. "Well, I have a habit of 'overresearching' my prospective dates." She raised her fingers to place air quotes around the word "overresearching." "And I came across a strange lawsuit from a woman I assume was your ex-wife. I have to admit, it made me curious about the circumstances."

Sidar slammed the table loudly with both hands. The

silverware rattled, and she had to reach out to stop her water from spilling.

"Who are you? Did that bitch set you up to this? Who the fuck are you to snoop around in my business?"

She was ready for him to be defensive. After all, she was quick to bring it up. "Well," she sheepishly mumbled, "I sometimes get carried away in my predate googling. I know you probably googled me. We all do that stuff on these setups, don't we? I'm a private investigator as my side job, and I admit I go a little over the top with my googling skills. Forgive me." She smiled again as if her proclivity for being a stalker wasn't off-putting.

"Did she put you up to this?" Sidar shouted. "Is it not enough that she torments me and makes my life miserable? She now has to throw some honeypot wannabe spy in my face? She's crazy, and you're crazy." He slammed the table again, and his voice started to rise. "You know nothing, *nothing* about the circumstances of my poor Mr. Bond. He was happy with me. I had him before I even *met* that bitch. She knew how much she could hurt me and torture me, taking Mr. Bond from me."

"Mr. Bond?" Caterina said quietly to get him to bring his volume down a bit. It worked, somewhat, but his voice still rose loud on the bitch enunciation, which caused many heads to turn toward their table.

"I love Mr. Bond," Sidar said dejectedly.

"Then why did she accuse you of . . . of killing him?" she said hesitantly.

Sidar slammed the table again. This time, Caterina's fork

Pearl by the Sea

flew off the table, and she pushed it out of foot traffic with her shoe. She leaned in to listen. The reason why she found this conversation entertaining was the researcher in her. She treated her questioning like a sparring session, with her competitive nature bubbling to the surface in odd ways.

Sidar leaned in and pointed a finger at her with his eyes full of anger. "I didn't kill him, you bitch. You know nothing—*nothing* about the situation. Who are you to throw this at me when I don't even know you? She didn't accuse me of killing Mr. Bond. She accused me of killing his spirit—his *spirit*. Do you understand? I had Mr. Bond declawed when I first got him, and he had a great life as a housecat with his cat toys and cat house. When I moved out, my lease had a no-cat clause, so she got to keep Mr. Bond. She wanted to let him go outside defenseless, and I told her I'd sue her if she put Mr. Bond in harm's way like that. He's a house cat, and she says I killed his spirit for removing his claws."

Caterina quickly realized she misinterpreted the case. How quickly was she to take his ex-wife's side when this certainly was a more complicated situation. She tried to switch gears, lighten the mood, and change subjects.

"I mean, technically, you should have got the cat if it was a 'no-cat claws' lease," she laughed somewhat high-pitched.

"Excuse me?"

"Get it? No-cat claws, claws as in c l a w s, not clause. If the cat had no claws, you weren't breaking the no-cat claws lease."

Her joke fell very flat. He stood up abruptly. "There's something very wrong with you." He turned around and walked away. He didn't say goodbye or say that she was beautiful any longer. He just left.

The waiter came by the table with Sidar's margarita and their fish tacos. Caterina asked for some to-go containers and the check. She paid the bill, sipped his margarita, and carried the meals two blocks back to her apartment.

She ate her tacos at the kitchen island and left a note for Kimmie that there was a meal if she wanted it when she got home from her 3–11 shift at the hospital.

Caterina felt terrible when she upset poor Sidar, who did seem like a nice guy who just loved his cat, but she thought she was honing her investigative skills, learning as she went. A more introspective person would wonder why anyone would go on a date with these motives, but Caterina was already unto the last part of her day. It was a real PI job she was hired to perform.

Chapter 5

CATERINA'S ADRENALINE WAS already pumping when she set off for her private investigator job. She hopped into her tan Honda Accord and drove over to her suspect's apartment, pulling into a spot where she had a good view of the front door. It was a triple-decker house in Somerville, and Derek, the guy she was tailing, rented the first floor with other students from Tufts.

This was Cat's first gig that wasn't an auto accident case, and she was excited about new possibilities. When Derek's dad inquired about investigating his son, the landlord's rental insurance company gave the landlord her contact information. The landlord had called Derek's dad a few months ago after Derek stopped paying his rent and ignored all notices tacked to the door of threats of eviction. Derek's dad was venmo-ing his son the rent money, but Derek wasn't paying his rent. When his dad confronted him, Derek was evasive, saying, "I did pay him," or "Maybe I sent it to the wrong address." Now, he just ignored his father's questions.

Fed up with his lies and excuses, his dad went the unique

route of hiring a PI to find out what the hell was going on with his son.

Caterina turned off her car and waited, hoping Derek would leave the house. Derek's dad, Mike, had given her photos of Derek, his car color and license plate number, and his habits of sleeping late and going out in the evening when living at their home in Long Island. All Caterina had to do was get lucky on one of these stakeouts, and he was leaving the house when she arrived.

She sat in her car, staring at the house and watching pedestrians on the street come and go to see if any entered or exited the apartment. She didn't find it boring. She'd go through the list of facts she knew about the case to figure out why an intelligent young man going to such an elite college would be such a screwup. She didn't have to wait long as she watched Derek leave the house and jump into his silver Nissan Altima, a car Caterina was sure his dad bought. He was an easy tail. Caterina was a city driver who had commuted from Medford into the city for many years. She could weave her way through Mystic Valley Parkway cars with ease. She followed the Nissan out of Somerville, driving north until it pulled into the casino in Everett, where the word *Encore* was brightly displayed on top of the building. She pulled in a few spots away from him and watched him enter the elevator, noting what he was wearing. Then she took the stairs to arrive in the casino at the same time.

Derek went to the sports betting area, placed a few bets, and then headed to the roulette table. He quickly went through

Pearl by the Sea

one hundred dollars of chips and dug three twenties out of his pocket for more chips before those were quickly scooped up by the dealer. Derek hung his head and returned to the sports betting area, watching the Celtics vs. Knicks game, screaming at the wall of TVs when Jayson Tatum landed a three-pointer. At halftime, he stepped outside for a smoke, and Caterina followed him closely behind.

He hung his head down, leaning against the railing that overlooked Boston Harbor. He watched the Encore boats that were crowded with passengers motoring from Everett into Boston.

Caterina bummed a cigarette off a group of Asian men that were outside smoking, asking for a light too, and sauntered over to Derek.

He kept his head down until he looked up for another drag on his vape. It smelled like street pot, a skunky smell that made Caterina take a step away. She took a drag of her cigarette, turning her head away to blow the smoke out quickly, trying not to inhale as she wasn't a smoker, and then turned back in his direction.

"Not my best night on the slots," she remarked casually. "I'm hoping to turn it around."

He nodded but didn't respond.

She tried again. "Any luck for you?"

"I'm just here for the free toaster they're giving away tonight," he replied sardonically.

Caterina laughed hard and smiled at him, inching closer. "That's hysterical."

He took another hit on his vape, took out his phone to check the basketball score, and went back inside. She quickly put out her cigarette in the sand ashtray, following him inside. She watched him linger at the roulette table until returning to the televisions to sit at the bar. She sat a few empty bar stools down from him and ordered a seltzer with cranberry that could pass as alcohol. The Celtics were up by ten in the third quarter, and Tatum sank another three to expand the lead to thirteen. "Shit," he spit out, and Caterina knew his money must've been on the Knicks to win. She knew he was from Long Island, so it made sense he was a New York fan.

"Hey, you again," she smiled down the bar, raising her glass.

He gave her a slight acknowledgment but started to play on his phone. She figured out his flaws tonight and could go back to the dad with the dossier and get paid. She could tell Derek's dad he was smoking pot, losing money at roulette fast, and betting on sports. Derek's dad could draw his own conclusions from that. Done. Cased closed. But Caterina could not be satisfied with being stealthy. She felt the need to inject herself into the drama.

She picked up her drink and sat beside him and looked at him with an expression of part disapproving mother and part concerned sister. He ignored her and made a motion to get up from his seat, obviously a bit freaked out that this girl was flirting with him.

"You aren't rooting for the Celtics?" she remarked at his responses to the game.

He ignored her.

She tried again. "Hi, I'm Caterina."

"Uh-huh," mumbled Derek, rising from his seat to exit.

She blurted out, "Derek, we need to talk."

He stared at her, wondering how she knew his name, and sat back down. "Do I know you? Do you go to Tufts?"

Caterina was twenty-five, and Derek twenty-one, so it wasn't a stupid question. "No, I went to BU but graduated a few years ago. I know your name because I was asked to do a well-check on you by someone who loves and cares for you very much." Caterina paused for effect, then continued. "Your dad hired me as a private investigator because you are lying to him and not paying your rent."

Derek looked shocked and defeated. He put his head down on the bar momentarily, then lifted it again. "That prick," he scowled, picking up his beer and finishing it, then pushed it down the bar. Caterina broke all the rules of an investigator. She should protect the person who hired her, keep their name a secret, and certainly not tell the suspect you're tailing them, but she couldn't help herself.

"Listen, Derek, don't blame your dad for just caring. You are obviously going through something. You are spending the money your dad sent you for rent. He just paid the past four months directly to the landlord to prevent you from getting kicked out, so it's not the money he cared about. It's you."

"Why are you so nosy? Why don't you mind your own business?"

"This *is* my business. I was hired to find out your issues, and I did."

"Oh, really? What are my issues? You think because I smoke pot and make a few bets, you know my problems? You don't know *anything* about me."

Caterina winced a little at his statements. They sounded very familiar to her conversation earlier when she assumed the worst of Sidar. Maybe there was more to the story than meets the eye.

"Derek, you're right. I don't know you, and I'm not judging you. All I know is I will tell your dad about what I observed tonight. I'm giving you a chance to be honest with your dad about your struggles and why you are losing money. Don't you think you should face your dad like a man instead of me tattling on you? Don't you think it's better he hears this from you and not from me?"

Was she overstepping? Totally, but she felt that it would be better for the father-and-son relationship if Derek brought it up first because he would act defensively and shut down more if his dad confronted him.

"He's just worried about you. Should he be?"

Derek looked up at the basketball game with the Celtics widening their lead to twenty points. He waved to the bartender for another beer and asked Caterina if she wanted anything, but she declined.

"Y'know, I have three hundred dollars on the Knicks to beat the spread. I thought Tatum was in a funk. You go by instinct on these games, and I used to be better at predicting outcomes." He grabbed his beer from the bartender and took a swig. Not looking at Caterina but up at the television, he said

Pearl by the Sea

quietly, "I used to win."

Caterina nodded sympathetically, saying nothing, and he continued. "All my friends gamble. All my friends smoke pot and drink. I don't know why I just suck at life. I can't face my parents on my screwups. I'm supposed to graduate next year, and I'm flunking my classes this year. I can't . . . I can't tell them. They'll be so disappointed."

Caterina touched his forearm and said kindly, "They will find out. You are procrastinating on the inevitable. It's okay to mess up. We all do, but you need to acknowledge the screwups to get past them, or else they turn into bigger screwups. Your parents will be disappointed, sure, but they will help you figure it out and love you. Let them help you." Caterina paused and asked Derek, "How do you want this resolved? What do *you* want?"

Derek smiled sheepishly, "I want the Knicks to win." He took another drink of his Sam Adams. "I don't know. What I really want is to go home and finish school on Long Island. I'm tired of the struggle. I'm tired of pretending to my parents that I am succeeding when I miss New York and want to go home. I want to work my summer job year-round to pay off my debts and start fresh. I want a do-over."

She pulled out her phone and switched to her PI line. She had two lines on her iPhone with different ring tones . . . one for personal use and one for PI work. "Listen, I will delay giving this to your dad for one week, and then I will tell him what I witnessed tonight. You have a choice to have him hear it from you first and just be honest with him. You can tell your dad you talked to me. That's up to you. I'm not going to ask you to lie. I'll probably get sued by your dad for breach of contract," Caterina nervously laughed, "but I just feel like it's worth it for you to set stuff straight with your parents." She asked the bartender for a pen and wrote her PI number on a napkin. "Let me know if you ever need anything, Derek. I wish the best for you." Caterina pushed her napkin toward him. "And good luck to the Knicks."

Chapter 6

"Mmm, this is so freakin' yummy," a mop of blond hair in a messy bun said to Caterina through FaceTime. "I forgot how good Temazcal fish tacos were. Thanks, Cat."

"You are seriously eating fish for breakfast, Kimmie? I could never."

Kimmie's face came into view after she took another bite and answered with her mouth full. "I was so tired after work last night, so I just ate a bowl of ice cream and went to bed. I was famished this morning. I just wanted to call and say thanks for breakfast." Kimmie took another bite of her taco and washed it down with some water. "Also, I was happy you were safely tucked into bed last night when I got home. Thanks for texting me after your stakeout." Kimmie laughed. "I feel like I'm living with Shawn from *Psych*. I used to love that show." She leaned in so her blond hair was out of the frame, and Cat instinctively pushed the laptop back. "So? How did the date go? Any chance of a second date, or was he really a creepy cat killer?"

Cat sighed. "No and no. If you ever see me on a dating app again, just throw my phone across the floor. I suck at dating.

I've decided to be a crazy cat lady from here on out."

"You already are crazy. We need to find you the right guy. Let's have a party on Saturday night. Jack can bring over Jason, and it will be like old times. You know, just invite our friends over and all hang out. Always keep the door open for possibilities. That's all I'm saying."

"We'll see. I'll talk to you more when I get home from work. Thanks for caring about my well-being, luv."

Caterina switched tabs on her laptop and continued clicking on exercises to set up a program for a client. The fitness models alternated from male to female, and she typed in reps and sets to do for each exercise. She thought about what Kimmie said about a party Saturday night. She wasn't sure how she felt about it. Maybe Jason was asking Jack about her. Perhaps she could dial back her crazy. She shook her head at the memory of her stalking Jason's Facebook Travel Group and chuckled. She hit print on the screen and walked over to the printer.

She heard a knock of three taps on her door. She smiled and said, "The door is open for possibil . . ." She then turned toward the door and saw him. Well, the first thing she saw was his beautiful gray eyes. ". . . for possibilities," she whispered to herself, finishing her sentence.

"Good morning. I hope I'm not bothering you. I was told you were the person to see to solve my problem."

Caterina was caught off guard. "Who told you that? Who gave you my name and where I worked?"

It was now his turn to be caught off guard by her reaction to a simple statement. "Um, the guy at the front desk. I believe his name is Kenneth. If this is a bad time, I'll stop by later."

Caterina had to pull away from his eyes. She felt like she was being rude, staring at them for too long, but where else did you look when you talked to someone? She wrinkled the exercise sheets in her hands and shook her head, slightly laughing. "Oh my God, I'm so sorry. No, now is fine. I just, I just for a moment thought you were asking about my other job. My coffee hasn't kicked in. Sorry. No, now is good. Sit down." Cat sat in her office chair, and he sat in a chair next to her desk. "I need to learn to compartmentalize better. My head is sometimes in ten different places."

The gorgeous eyes smiled politely. He sat calmly with his arms on his thighs, waiting for her to speak. "Hi, I'm Caterina. Did you want to set up some personal training sessions? You get six complimentary one-hour sessions to use in any way you choose that expire twelve months after the first day you signed up. If you want additional sessions, we have different packages. We have a lot of great trainers here."

"What if I want you?" he said with a coy smile. Coy? Shy? Bold? Cat wasn't sure what kind of smile it was. Maybe it wasn't even a smile. Was he flirting? She couldn't quite tell. No, he was just asking a question. Cat was not one to blush, but she felt like she was as red as a strawberry.

"Um, sure. I mean, I can set up your initial consultation, and if I'm here at the time that works for you, that's no problem. You can have a lot of flexibility in scheduling. What time is good for you?"

"How about now?" he responded. Cat clicked on her

schedule tab and saw she didn't have to go to the cardio section for another half hour.

"No time like the present!" she said, a little too singsongy in a voice she didn't even recognize. It's those eyes. They were making her quite giddy.

"Okay, so we have you fill out this questionnaire to find out your strengths and weaknesses and what you want to work on. We can run through it together, or you can fill it out yourself. Up to you." She handed him a clipboard with one sheet of paper and a pen attached. "I'm so rude," she averted his eyes. "I didn't even catch your name."

"It's Peter," he said as he filled out the beginning section of his name, age, how long he'd been a member, and other basic facts.

He stopped and put down the pen. "My main reason I want a trainer is I'm having a lot of elbow pain." He roughly rubbed his left elbow with his right hand like he was trying to rub the pain away. "I don't usually run for help, but this thing is getting so aggravating."

She listened to Peter speak. His English was excellent without much hesitation on words, but his accent was very thick, and she had to concentrate on his words to understand what he was saying.

"Well, for any acute injuries, we really need you to see an orthopedic doctor, and I'd recommend physical therapy. We do more fitness routines here. I don't diagnose or treat acute injuries."

"Oh, okay. Well, we will skip that then. You can show me

a fitness routine." He said, "fitness routine" very clearly and smiled. "But what do you think a doctor would say about my elbow?"

Well, she supposed it wouldn't hurt to look. He described what aggravated it, where the pain was, and how he was treating the pain.

"Well, like I said, I recommend seeing a doctor, but I believe they may say you have tennis elbow."

"That's funny. I don't play tennis."

She laughed at his joke. Other clients have said the same joke, but it sounded different coming from this handsome young man. He had a thin, muscular build and wore black shorts and a red T-shirt. Was it the same clothes from yesterday? She made a note of this to see if he had a hygiene problem. No, he smelled nice. He had a touch of a sandalwood scent to him when she leaned over close to him. Subtle. His dark hair was not as dark as hers, but it was styled with a little gel in a natural way. His face was clean-shaven, but she could imagine stubble would appear quickly on his chiseled chin.

"It's a common injury called lateral epicondylitis. Tendonitis occurs with overuse, and your extensor carpi radialis brevis and/or longus muscles can be a real stubborn pain to calm down. It's hard to get a handle on sometimes because if you don't stop the activity causing the problem, it doesn't get a chance to heal. Gripping a mouse, bike handles, or using tools exacerbate the problem. You see, if you overuse the muscles, then the firing rate has to go into overdrive either by recruiting more muscle fibers called spatial recruitment or firing at a faster rate called temporal recruitment." She realized she was droning on. Why did she have to do that? Was she trying to impress this handsome stranger and compete with him somehow? My God, she was annoying herself.

He nodded politely as she geeked out in her explanation, and he seemed to appreciate the detailed response. He sat silently for a moment as if he were translating her words again in his mind. He nodded again and spoke. "I believe this is the problem. I do two out of the three activities you described. I bike to work and use the mouse quite a bit. Power tools are definitely not the problem," he laughed.

She liked his laugh. It was pleasant, "pleasant" meaning it was a laugh you wanted to hear repeatedly, and you wanted to get him to laugh.

She wheeled her chair over to sit beside him, reached for his arm, and caressed the outside of his elbow. She wanted to help him with his injury. She gently rubbed her fingers along the scar that looked like a bad burn. "Are you left-handed?"

"Yes," he reached for his elbow with his right hand, brushing against her hand in the process. "I think I brake more with my left arm, and I use the mouse on the left side, so I think I'll make a conscious effort to use my right hand more."

She gently put her hand in his and continued to put her other hand near his elbow. "A tennis elbow brace works well too for some people. They place it here." She rubbed the area an inch below his elbow.

"Thanks," he said, looking into her brown eyes and not averting her return gaze.

Pearl by the Sea

She let go of his arm abruptly. "Also, this might sound weird, and there's not much in the scientific papers on this, so it's more anecdotal, but I find that people who use an iPad a lot have been complaining about elbow pain. It's not just the prolonged use of holding it, but some say it's the aluminum on the casing of an iPad. I know, it sounds stupid, but I've had patients put a case on their iPad and their elbow pain goes away." She tilted her head side to side, shrugging her shoulders. "Like I said, just anecdotal, but throwing it out there."

She wheeled herself back over to her desk and picked up his questionnaire. Then she saw he really didn't fill out much. Maybe she interrupted him. She was unsure, so she picked up a pen to finish the form.

"Any other orthopedic problems I should be aware of?"

"No, I don't think so."

"Any surgeries?"

"Well, a couple." His mood seemed to change, and he was now averting her eyes and looking down at the questionnaire. "Um, well, I had some graphing done for a burn on my arm, and I had surgery on my feet," he answered vaguely.

Caterina did not pick up on his hesitancy to discuss either of these injuries. "Well, the scar tissue can affect your elbow too. I could Graston the area if you wanted. Those are tools to help break up the scar tissue."

"Sounds good," he said softly, rubbing his hands together in his lap.

She still had her pen in her hand while filling in the paperwork. "What kind of surgery did you have on your feet?" It was a simple question. He paused with his answer. Maybe he didn't remember the medical terminology and was struggling to explain. English wasn't his first language, it appeared.

"Hammertoe? Bunions?" Cat was throwing out terms he might remember from his procedure.

He shook his head and, with a solemn face, answered. "I had my heels fixed after I broke both of the calcaneal bones."

Caterina's eyes lit up. "No way! That's wild. I'm going to add you to my bilateral list. I have never had a bilateral heel fracture client. Cool." She realized her response was not appropriate. She had to remember no one cared about her lists. She needed not to blurt stuff out and keep it in her brain. "I mean, that sucks. I'm really sorry. How'd you do that? Did you fall off a ladder or something? That's a common way people break a heel."

"Something like that," he said evasively.

She looked at the questionnaire and was satisfied it was filled out completely. She asked him to sign the bottom, and he scribbled his signature.

Caterina opened a new tab on her computer and typed out some stretches for his forearm and an article about lateral epicondylitis. She walked over to the printer to hand him the paper.

"I have to head down to the cardio room now, so let's set up a session this week to review your workouts and goals."

He took the handouts and was relieved she didn't ask him any more questions about his burn and heel injuries. The event was ten years ago, and he tried to bury the memory of that day from haunting his days and nights. Who would imagine that in America, a country so far from Ukraine, the events of that day would soon consume his world and bring him right back to the dangers of that fateful day?

Peter stood up and placed his palm over his heart. "See you soon, Caterina." It was a simple gesture, but it melted Caterina's heart. She stood silently, not quite knowing how to respond to his parting words, so she just smiled a half smile and watched him exit her office.

She placed her palm over her heart after he left and whispered to herself. "See you soon, Peter."

She stood there watching the doorway in a trance until she was stirred awake by a couple of patrons passing by and talking loudly.

She picked up his questionnaire to study his writing style. She knew left-handers sometimes had a tighter grip because they had to push the pen left to right as opposed to a right-handed writer that pulled. She will have to tell Peter about this. Maybe he didn't know. She found an article about left-handed people and tennis elbow and copied the link. Then she picked up her phone and sent it to the cell phone number he had written down. She hit send quickly without explanation. *That was stupid*, she thought. She needed to add something else to the message.

What was she doing? She never gave her clients her personal cell phone number. She always used her work email for communication. She watched the three dancing dots in the bubble on her phone screen. Was he typing a response? She waited as her heart began to race.

The bubble went away. *Shit*, she thought. *I should add to the message*. She stood and thought what to say. Then the bubble came back, and her heart skipped a beat. A thumbs-up emoji was attached to the article. Her heart sank just a bit. She wanted more. Then another bubble popped up to indicate he was in the writing area.

"Thanks, Caterina . . . I'll give it a read. Thank you for your expert advice today. I appreciated it very much.—Peter."

She found her palm at her heart again, and she read the response a few more times before heading out to the cardio area with an extra bounce in her step.

Chapter 7

"Honey, I'm home!" shouted Cat as she ran her key over the keypad and opened the door to the apartment.

"Hi, Cat!" shouted Kimmie from the kitchen. "You are going to love this salad. It's arugula, goat cheese, glazed walnuts, and sliced pears."

Cat wandered into the kitchen, "You even made your own vinaigrette?"

"I've been watching way too many TikToks lately, all about food."

"Are you still up for *Love Island* tonight? I could use a lazy couch night snuggled in blankets."

"You read my mind. You haven't been sneaking episodes without me, have you?"

"Never," responded Cat. She opened the cabinet and got out some plates, humming an old tune of "*someone's knocking at the door, someone's ringing the bell. Do me a favor, open the door, and let 'em in.*" She must've hummed the bars a few times before she realized Kimmie was just observing her.

"You're in a good mood."

"Just thinking about the advice my wise sage roommate gave me."

"What, like don't date murderers?"

"You said, 'Keep the door open for possibilities.' I just want to let you know I do take things you say to heart."

". . . okay . . ." Kimmie responded, unclear what Cat was referring to.

After they ate dinner, they cuddled on the couch, watching their favorite reality TV show. Cat seemed extra receptive to the over-the-top drama from the Australian millennials trying to figure out relationships.

"I love a good accent," Cat added her own commentary to the show.

"One more? I will watch something else if we don't watch another episode. I don't have to get up at the crack of dawn like you."

Cat pulled her blanket up close to her chin, smiling with her eyes closed. "I think I'll go to bed. I have a new client tomorrow morning. I don't want raccoon eyes."

"Okay, g'night," Kimmie said as Cat headed to her bedroom.

Caterina lay in bed thinking about Peter. She had so many questions about him. She was about to pick up her phone and google him when she heard her phone buzz.

A text message from Peter popped up on her phone. Her heart began to race. She opened up the message.

"I'm in bed thinking about you . . ."

Her heart began to beat faster. Was she dreaming? Was she

Pearl by the Sea

reading this right? This is kind of creepy, right? Or not? What is going on?

She put her phone down and reread it. She saw his three-dot dancing bubble pop up several times and disappear. What was he doing? Waiting for a response? She put her phone down. The phone was silent. She thought her heart was going to burst through her chest, it was beating so loud and fast. She put a pillow over her head, then tossed and turned in the bed. She lay on her stomach thinking about those beautiful eyes. Then she heard her phone buzz again and tried to slow her breathing before reaching for the phone to read his message.

"I'm in bed watching Netflix on my iPad and I realized . . . no case. I just ordered one from Amazon. Thanks. See you tomorrow at nine a.m.—Peter"

She smiled. He's teasing her. He's flirting. She knew it. She could feel him smiling on the other side of the phone, knowing his first text was fresh. He liked her. She put her phone down for a minute, then picked it up, rereading his two texts and analyzing how much time passed between them. He gave her time to have her thoughts go in ten different directions with the first text. He did it on purpose. She put her phone down, then picked it up again, rereading his first message. Finally, she got some courage. She felt bold. She put a heart emoji next to the first message and put her phone down. She could not fall asleep, though. Did *Love Island* get her in the mood for love or his gray eyes? One thing she knew for sure: she was opening the door wide for possibilities.

Caterina was debating every decision the following day.

She wasn't sure if she should get her usual large, caffeinated coffee because her heart already felt like it was skipping beats. She also didn't want to have a caffeine headache at nine a.m. She decided on a large half-caf, half-decaf. She arrived at work at seven a.m. and reviewed her equipment inspection checklist. She had an eight a.m. client, a friendly, wealthy woman who just liked the company when she went through her Nautilus weight machine workout. Caterina documented her progress on her iPad chart and showed her how much stronger she was from when they first began training a few months ago.

They were hanging out on the leg press while her client told her about her daughter's bridal shower this weekend when she spotted Peter lingering on the other side of the gym. He was wearing a blue T-shirt and black shorts. Thank God it was not the red T-shirt again. She tried to hurry along the story about centerpieces, bridal shower games, and other details, and finally just said, "Oh, I see my next client. Have a great time this weekend, and I'll see you next week."

"Well, wish me luck. I'm wearing a sleeveless dress thanks to you. My arms have never looked this good."

Caterina was wearing what she wore every day: a royal blue T-shirt and black track pants with a royal blue stripe. She wore her bright blue Hoka brand sneakers and quickly walked over to greet Peter.

"Right on time," she smiled a big smile, her black hair pulled back in a ponytail, looking fresh and awake.

He smiled. "I made a vow today . . . No more Netflix in bed. I think I've been aggravating my elbow gripping the

Pearl by the Sea

device. You fixed me in one session, Caterina. Bravo."

"I wish it was an easy fix. It can take awhile to go away, but that's a good start. We get into routines and overuse our muscles. They might start calling it 'Netflix elbow' instead of tennis elbow."

He smiled. She smiled. They stared into each other's eyes, looked around at their surroundings, and then looked at each other again, waiting for the other to speak.

"So," they both began speaking at once.

"So," Caterina continued the sentence, "let's go over those stretches I gave you and see if you have any asymmetry in your upper body strength. Strengthening the core muscles, the ones more proximal to the spine can really benefit distal injuries."

"You're the boss," he smiled. They reviewed his stretches, and she showed him some mid and lower-trap resistance exercises. She found his strong areas from biking and swimming and his weak areas from not doing any strength training.

"Are you from around here, Caterina? What made you want to be a personal trainer?" They were sitting on the mat after she timed his single-leg planks.

"I grew up in Medford, a fifteen-minute drive from here. I lived there my whole life up until a couple of years ago when I moved in with my best friend to a condo in Seaport. Her dad bought it, and believe me, I know I have a good thing going. I could never afford the rent." He sat cross-legged, listening intently, not rushing her, and appeared genuinely interested in everything she said.

She realized he asked two questions. "Oh, and being a

trainer? I don't know. I just kind of fell into it. I hurt myself in my junior year of high school and never played sports after that, so I became a gym rat. I always thought I would be a physical therapist, but you have to get a doctorate for that now, and who has that kind of money? So, yeah."

He listened and did not speak. She thought he wanted her to keep talking, but then he said quietly, looking at his hands, "I hurt myself in my junior year too. I never played soccer after that."

"Sucks, doesn't it? I tore my ACL. What did you do?"

"Broke my heels." He was surprised he was telling her this. It certainly was a subject he wanted to avoid, but something about how she inquired made it feel like she cared about his story and wasn't just asking to ask.

"That doesn't sound like a soccer injury."

"It wasn't." He kind of shrugged and gripped his mouth taut.

He wanted to open up to someone, to her. "Do you have brothers and sisters?"

"Four older brothers. I was such a tomboy growing up. My mother fought me to wear dresses my whole life. All I wanted to do was follow my brothers around. How about you?"

"I know what you mean about wanting to follow in an older brother's footsteps. I did everything my older brother did . . . played soccer, sailed, and went to the same university in Odessa he went to. I was like a mini he."

"Odessa? Where is that?"

"Ukraine, along the coast. It's a beautiful city. You should visit."

Pearl by the Sea

Caterina answered, "Not now. I mean, you guys are at war with Russia. Did you escape from there?"

He smiled a tired smile. "No, I can come and go as I please. I've been teaching here for a year. I was not eligible for the military because of my heel injuries. I have very mixed feelings about not being able to fight. It's a terrible war." He did not want to talk about the war in his country but wanted to talk about the beautiful parts of Odessa. "You really should visit after the war. Do you like oysters? My favorite restaurant is Di Mare on the coast of the Black Sea. Watching the sunset sitting on the deck with a glass of white wine and a dozen oysters is paradise."

She wondered who he was sitting with. This sounded like a romantic scene, certainly not something he would do with his buddies. This guy was out of her league. Who was she kidding? She invented some relationship in her head when he clearly could have any woman in this gym—if not the city.

Her next clients shouted her name to let her know they were ready. "That was a quick hour. I'm going for a run on the boardwalk with my next clients. Do you want to come with us? It's beautiful outside."

He stood up so they could stand close together. He was about five inches taller than her. "I haven't run in ten years. I can't run." It was an emphatic statement. She didn't press him to clarify.

"What are you doing tonight, Caterina? I get out of class at four, and we can get a bite to eat if you like. I would really like that."

Her mind raced. He was interested. Her disappointment quickly turned into excitement. "That'd be great."

"We'll go to Oysters on the Bay, then watch the sunset. It'll be . . ." he teased her using the same phrase, ". . . great."

She smiled and turned to walk away. He touched her shoulder to have her turn around again toward him. His touch felt good.

"I'll text you later, Caterina. Have a good run."

Chapter 8

"You never call me at work, Cat. Is everything all right?"

"Guess what, Kimmie? I have a date in two hours."

"I thought you told me to destroy your phone if you ever went on a Hinge date again. Does this guy have a criminal record?"

"No, not Hinge. You will never believe with whom, though. The young Daniel Craig guy you told me I was checking out. I acted dumb then, but I knew exactly who you talked about. He even wore the same outfit yesterday when he booked a session. He has an accent. Well, not a British accent like Daniel Craig, but like a thick Eastern European accent. He's from Ukraine."

"Slow down, Cat. He asked you out after his workout? Don't you have a policy not to date your clients?"

"He'll fire me then," Cat laughed. "That'll be easy to fix."

"So, what about Jason? We're still planning to have people over Saturday night, right? I told you Jack said he's been asking about you."

Cat thought for a second. "I don't know, Kimmie. Besides, I think I'm working that night. I have some loose ends in an ongoing case."

"Who works on a Saturday night?"

"You do, Kimmie. We all have crazy hours. So I don't know. Just cancel the party. We can rebook if we want."

"All right. Just be careful. You know nothing about this dude."

"I know, right? Kimmie, I haven't even googled him, and I'm gonna try really hard in the next two hours not to go snooping. For once, I want a little mystery."

"I have to get back to work. Thanks for giving me a heads-up. I know I said to keep the door open, but maybe we should cut back on binge-watching *Love Island*. I have never known you to sound . . . I don't know how to say this quite right . . . girly," Kimmie laughed.

Caterina returned the laughter. "Smitten might be the word you're looking for. Ta-ta!"

Peter said the Uber would arrive around five o'clock, so she waited outside her apartment. She could've easily walked the few blocks to the oyster bar in the neighborhood, but he insisted he would pick her up and to wear a warm jacket. That was thoughtful. It did get chilly when the sun went down along Boston Harbor. She wore jeans, a three-quarter sleeve cotton shirt with her favorite jewelry, and some flats in case they did some walking. She wore her hair down with a little curl, put some colored lip gloss on, and decided to spray on a little perfume at the last second.

The Uber pulled up right at five o'clock, and he stepped out of the backseat to greet her and gave her a little peck on the cheek. He looked handsome, and she detected the hint of the sandalwood scent she smelled in her office. He smelled really nice. He wore a dark blue long-sleeve shirt with a paisley imprint of the same color, dark jeans, and nice dress shoes. Okay, maybe not too much walking was planned.

They sat in the back of a black Altima with soft leather seats. She sat close to him and listened quietly while he resumed the conversation he must've started with the driver on the ride over. After the driver dropped them off, he apologized for monopolizing the discussion on the five-minute drive to the restaurant.

"I didn't care. I could have driven around another hour listening to you two talk. Where do you live? It sounded like you guys were already chummy from the drive."

"I teach at UMASS Boston, so I rent a room near campus. I'm on Dorchester Ave., about a mile bike ride to work. Not the best area, but the best price I could find for rent. This city is prohibitive with rents."

"Tell me about it. I have to find housing in September when my roommate gets married, and so far, my only option is my parents' home, which, thankfully, still has my bedroom. My brothers' rooms have been converted to an office and my mom's extra closet. She's a clotheshorse."

"She rides horses?"

"What? No, she doesn't ride horses."

Oh, he looked perplexed. He took out his phone, googled clotheshorse, and read that it was an idiom based on someone who liked clothes. A clotheshorse was a structure on which clothes would be "mounted" to display clothing; hence, the word "horse."

"I had no idea what that meant. I guess there are things you just say and don't think twice about them," Caterina chuckled as she read the idiom explanation on his phone.

Peter responded, "Like, 'think twice.' I had to stop and understand that it must mean 'think carefully.' I do miss words here and there when people talk. I've watched countless English-speaking movies, especially as a kid growing up, and I learned that people from Boston talk fast. Growing up, I spoke Russian, but I would practice English any chance I could get."

"They speak Russian in Ukraine? I didn't know that. I'd assume Ukrainian. That's a language, right?"

He smiled. "Yes, Ukrainian is the official language of Ukraine, but my region of Odessa has many Russian speakers. Some people can speak both languages, and it's not uncommon to be out and hear both languages, but I don't speak much Ukrainian, strange as that may seem. Even President Zelensky spoke Russian and had to learn Ukrainian when he ran for president. He had a TV show for three seasons, a very funny show, where he played the president of Ukraine, and it was all in the Russian language."

"Well, your English is excellent. If I'm talking too fast, just tell me to slow down. I know I'm a fast talker."

"I love to hear your voice," he said in his thick accent and motioned to walk toward the restaurant. It was above-average temperature for a late April evening, and the sun was still high in the sky at five o'clock. Oysters on the Bay was a small, lively restaurant catering to the Seaport district's wealthy residents and tourists walking along the Fan Pier Marina. A wide

Pearl by the Sea

staircase outside the building brought you to the top of the restaurant and showed an expansive view of Boston. A steel drum player positioned himself on the stairs, and people were sparsely seated on the wide pavilion steps, listening to the music and enjoying the scenery. The world felt alive after so many cold months during the winter. Everyone was craving some sun on their faces.

They enjoyed the view, climbed down the wide stairs, and entered the noisy bar, finding a small table for two near the floor-to-ceiling windows. The waiter took their order of two chardonnays and a dozen oysters to start, and they settled into their surroundings. "In Odessa, we have a famous staircase called the Potemkin Stairs. It is the formal entrance into the city at the port. It's very striking and impressive. Many tourists also take pictures on the stairs because it was in a famous scene in a movie called *Battleship Potemkin*, so Potemkin Stairs became the unofficial name of the stairs."

"That name 'Potemkin' sounds familiar. Potemkin village? I've heard that phrase, or am I making that up?"

He smiled. "Yes, it's a phrase that means 'propped up' or 'fake.' As if something isn't as it appears. I don't really believe the story as I think it's a myth. Still, the story goes that Grigory Potemkin was in charge of the military region of Russia's empire in Crimea and also a lover of the Russian Empress, Catherine the Great. They say that to impress his lover and his empress, he concocted a fake village of happy villagers with cutout facade homes that she could view along the water. Then the military dismantled the fake village and set it up downstream with the same two-dimensional houses and the same villagers. It's certainly not proven, but it shows how far lovers will pretend to impress you, I guess."

Peter took a sip of his Chardonnay and leaned toward Caterina as if he had a secret to tell. "But he wasn't Catherine the Great's most useful lover. One of her lovers, who was also in the military, rode his horse to the castle to visit the emperor, Catherine's husband, and told him that his services were no longer needed. Catherine took over ruling the Russian Empire. Her husband renounced his crown to save his life, and without a shot fired, she became the leader."

Caterina smiled and wanted to continue listening to her date. It gave her an excuse to stare into his eyes, listen to his accent, and hope he would laugh so she could hear his adorable, unpretentious laugh again.

"The country initially loved Catherine. She came to Russia as a curious sixteen-year-old German girl in an arranged marriage. She was brilliant and a big fan of Voltaire and philosophers in the Age of Enlightenment. She believed in giving the poor more rights and started out very promising, but then she watched the common people rise up in France and use the guillotine freely on those who ruled, and it changed her philosophy. It gave her pause to implement some of the freedoms she planned to give the poor. When your neck may be next in a guillotine, enlightenment looks a bit different." Peter swirled his Chardonnay at the stem. "Maybe she regrets kicking her husband, Peter, out of the top spot. It's a tough job being in charge."

Pearl by the Sea

Caterina giggled. "Peter was her husband's name?"

He slowly smiled, realizing she had connected his name and her name, Caterina, which is Catherine in a different form. He had not made the connection himself until just now. It was something neither could say out loud. He just raised his eyebrows whimsically and laughed, which made her laugh. She stared into his translucent gray eyes that were more striking with the lowering sun shining directly on them. He never seemed to be the first to break from eye contact. Was it an American thing that we didn't have the attention span to even converse, or was he just so comfortable in her presence? She wasn't sure and did not care. She liked the attention; no one had ever looked at her like he did. She could never get enough of this man.

"You know a lot of your history. That stuff was my least favorite subject. I was all science; still am."

"Well, it is my job to know all about history. I teach about the Soviet Union, especially its dismantling in the early nineties. That's the course I teach at UMASS. I was a philosophy major at a university, but getting a job teaching history is easier. When I . . ." Peter paused for a moment and took a sip of his wine, "when I broke my feet, I couldn't stand for months and just read everything I could about my country, Ukraine, and our role in Soviet Union history, and before that, the Russian Empire. When America was fighting to throw the British out, Odessa was being fought over by the Ottoman Empire and the Russian Empire. The Ottoman Empire ruled Odessa, and Catherine the Great started the war to kick them out of Odessa.

Back then, Odessa was mostly Jews and Russians. Many Jews fled to what is now called Israel to still be under Ottoman rule. Sounds crazy to say now, but they didn't feel protected by the Russians. Back then, Jews made up a third of the population. Odessa had the second-biggest Jewish population region in the Russian Empire. Now, it's .5 percent. Point five. There is a lot of sad history in my country. Eighty percent of the Jews in Odessa were killed by the Axis occupation during World War Two." Peter looked down at the table. "We had a group of Ukrainians led by Stepan Bandera that sided with Hitler over the Soviet Union." Peter squeezed his napkin tight and appeared to be somewhere else in time at the moment. "We still have white supremacists who are big Hitler fans. It's sometimes an ugly minority that can cause so much havoc." Now, it was Peter who could not make eye contact. He studied his napkin closely where he was gripping it tightly and carefully smoothed it out and folded it back into a square.

He subconsciously rubbed his left elbow along his scar with his right hand. "When I was in that wheelchair for six months, I made lists. I loved to make lists. Sounds silly, but I made up songs about the ex-Soviet countries to remember them all. There were fifteen of them: AA B E G KK LL M R TT UU. I would remember the beginning letter of each country and then make up a song about each letter to make it easy to keep track. Armenia was Anastacia, and Azerbaijan was the word 'arrived.' Well, it's tough to translate into English, but you get the idea. I would do this a lot to help remember facts."

"Oh my God, I do that all the time too. Almost obsessively.

I did it to you the first day I met you. Remember?"

"Guys that bore you with a history list?"

She laughed. "No, my bilateral list. You told me you broke both heels, so I immediately blurted out I was adding you to my list. I apologize for being so insensitive. I geek out on lists too." She reflexively touched his left arm in the same spot he rubbed with his right hand, and he took a deep breath as if her touch gave him life. He looked out the window and grabbed her hand on the table. "C'mon, our adventure is just starting. Let's get down to the water."

He paid their bill and strolled to the dock, waiting for a free water taxi to arrive. They traveled between all the restaurants owned by Charles Larner. Caterina was glad she wore a warmer coat and understood why he told her to plan for the weather. He held her hand as she stepped into the boat, and they sailed along the Boston Harbor toward East Boston and then to Charlestown. The sunset was glorious. The fiery orange and bright pink expanded as the sun lowered, and the lights of the city's buildings blended into the reflection of the sunset on the water to illuminate the whole landscape. Caterina had never seen Boston from this viewpoint, and it was indeed the best way to enjoy the evening. She saw many sunset cruises traveling their same course, capturing twilight in the passenger's photos but never doing the real thing justice.

They stayed cuddled on the boat when it stopped in East Boston as passengers disembarked who were eating at the Reelhouse or The Tall Ship, which had just opened up for the season. Other passengers took their seats to continue traveling to Pier 6, another Charles Larner-owned restaurant. Free water transportation was just one of Larner's innovative ideas, and it was a favorite for his guests.

They decided to have another drink on the rooftop of Pier 6 overlooking the boats and the city. They sat side by side to enjoy the views of Boston. It felt natural to snuggle close together and talk, watching the full moon shine in the sky to contrast the darkening night. She would point out landmarks and give him some history of Boston, but she had a feeling he knew more about its past than she did. At twenty-eight, he seemed to deeply understand world events, far more than she thought she could learn in a lifetime.

"You are fortunate to live in Boston, Caterina, a city without war. Living here, I can almost forget about the fighting, but I fear the war will never end. Ukraine has always been a pawn between Russia and the West. It will forever be torn apart."

"I'm glad you broke your heels and didn't have to fight. Sometimes, there's a silver lining in events. That's what my dad always says to me."

Peter put his arm around her, and she pulled in closer to him.

She continued, "Was your brother recruited? He's what, like thirty?"

"My brother is dead. He died ten years ago," said Peter matter-of-factly without much expression. Caterina was shocked by this. She had no idea. He talked so fondly about following in his brother's footsteps to the university so she would, naturally, assume he was alive.

Pearl by the Sea

"I'm so sorry, Peter. Oh my God, that's awful. Your only brother? What happened?"

She felt his whole body take a deep breath and let it out slowly until he expelled all the air. He removed his arm from around her, leaned forward on the table, and then turned in his seat to look at her. She felt his gray eyes that turned to blue steel in the dark, trying to look into her soul to determine if she was ready for this story and his world.

"He fell from a high surface and broke his neck. He died instantly, which was the only blessing. There is no silver lining in this story. Sometimes, a tragic event is just that . . . a tragic event."

Caterina did not turn away from his pain. She wanted to absorb some of it somehow if it helped him. "I'm so sorry, Peter. You were so young, eighteen. I can't even imagine losing my brother that way." She thought carefully about his timeline. Ten years ago was 2014, the year he said he broke his heels. "Your injuries, your feet, and your burns, you were with your brother when he fell."

"Yes," he said sadly, thankful she could form the words and connect the two events. She didn't want to pry and waited to see if he would tell the story, and he did. He talked forever about the bond they shared traveling to soccer games with their dad and the events that unfolded that tragic day. It was as if ten years of grief came flowing out of him that had been bottled up for this caring woman to capture. They realized they were the last ones on the rooftop after the waiter had walked by several times to get their attention and pay their check. Caterina paid.

She felt it was a small gesture to help this young man in his pain.

They took an Uber back to her apartment and did not converse with each other or the driver. Peter did not expect himself to indulge in his sorrow. He prayed his intensity did not scare her away.

She reached for his hand as the Uber inched to the curb. She pulled him close to her and kissed him passionately. Then, without a word, she opened the door quickly and walked away. She had so much emotion bubbling up inside her she didn't know if it was from too much wine or such intimacy with a stranger, but her head was spinning.

He returned to his apartment in the Uber, his head spinning from the kiss. He had no idea why he poured his heart out to this stranger, this beautiful woman he met just yesterday. They seemed connected as if they had known each other forever. That kiss. His lips still seemed to tingle from her touch. He desperately wanted to turn the car around to feel her warmth again. He felt as if she understood his pain and his loneliness. He immediately thought of an old song by Nat King Cole. He loved to watch old American movies and listen to songs. He would spend hours on YouTube watching videos of Frank Sinatra and listening to Elvis songs. He searched YouTube and found a recording of "I Remember You" with the lyrics written out.

He hit copy and paste and messaged it to Caterina. She felt her phone buzz in her pocket and nestled in bed to read his text. She clicked on a song she never heard before, but it was beautiful. The lyrics were about endless love between two people. A kiss reminded one of the lovers of their time in the distant past. Was it in Tahiti? Or was it on the Nile? "I Remember You." It was incredibly romantic. She listened to the whole song a few more times and read the lyrics repeatedly.

"Arrghh!" she screamed into her pillow with delight. She was happy Kimmie wasn't home yet from work, or she would be drilling her with questions about her date. She wanted to cherish the moment and this song. "Peter and Caterina," she said aloud as if they were a couple from yesteryear in the Empire of Russia.

"I remember you too, Peter," she texted back, throwing caution to the wind.

"Good night, Queen," he quickly texted back. "I will call you tomorrow. Thank you for a wonderful evening."

"Same," she quickly texted with a heart emoji. "I will see you for your training session Friday."

"Looking forward to it. What are you doing this weekend?"

She sank farther into her blankets, smiling. "Hopefully, seeing you," she boldly texted.

"Good . . ." popped up as his response.

"G'night, Peter . . ." was her last text before closing her eyes and dreaming of kings and queens and faraway lands.

Chapter 9

Kimmie walked at a quick pace on the treadmill, and Caterina stood on the treadmill next to her, leaning against the rail.

"I'm in love."

"You're not in love; you're in lust. The guy is gorgeous and foreign. You love that type."

"I'm serious. It was amazing. He really trusted me and confided in me. He's been through so much with the war in his country and the death of his only sibling. It was a real connection."

Kimmie pressed the buttons to add an incline. "Are you sure you're not overcompensating for your disastrous Hinge date? I know how competitive you are. Maybe you're trying to compete with this guy for who has the worst spring fever. Lust, yes, I believe that, but not love at first sight."

A tall, good-looking man walked by in a red T-shirt and black shorts. Caterina drew a breath in and exhaled when she realized it was not Peter. Kimmie observed her expressions and shook her head, laughing. She lowered her incline and pace to cool down.

"Excuse me," said a woman working out in the gym, "could you help me with the elliptical? I'm hopeless with the newer machines. I want to do some interval training."

"Sure thing," answered Caterina as she hopped off the treadmill and turned to Kimmie.

"Are you working tonight? *Love Island*?"

"Sorry, working. Don't watch without me. You promised."

"No worries, I'm thinking of starting that Netflix series about Catherine the Great with Elle Fanning. I heard that was good."

"Speaking of lust, don't they make fun of Catherine's insatiable sex drive in the series?"

Caterina turned as red as a tomato. "What? Okay, now I am *really* curious about this show," she laughed.

The woman looked impatient as she waited for Caterina's attention. This made the girls laugh silently even more with each other.

Peter jumped on his bike, humming the Nat King Cole song he sent Caterina. He biked the mile down busy Dorchester Ave. to the UMASS campus. Then he locked up his bike and helmet and untucked his pants from his socks to teach his class. He taught two classes that each met several times a week, so it certainly was not a rigorous schedule, but with office hours, preparing the lecture, and grading papers, it filled up his day. Eastern European History was the broad name for his course, and his students were a diverse group. He had many international students taking his course from China, South Korea, and other countries worldwide. American kids majoring in international studies and political science also took his course.

This was Peter's second semester teaching at UMASS for a predetermined, one-year teaching job. The original professor was on sabbatical in Poland, writing his book about Poland's first democratically elected president, Lech Walesa, after Soviet rule.

Peter felt fortunate for the opportunity. Ever since his brother died, he felt like doors had opened for possibilities that he was not worthy to enter. Perhaps it was because people felt bad for him after the accident and were charitable. He knew he didn't get this chance to teach abroad on merit alone.

After his brother died jumping out of the fire that engulfed the building, Peter realized he was a witness to a horrific event in Ukrainian history. The Pro-Unity skinhead who kicked him while he was coiled defenseless was arrested. It was a slam-dunk case. Peter was able to describe the black sun tattoo on his chest and his hateful words of "Burn, Colorado, burn" to the police. The reference was to the Colorado Potato Beetle that was black and gold, the same colors of the Pro-Federalist movement.

Peter and his brother were certainly not part of any separatist movement. They were Ukrainian and knew no other life but to be citizens of Ukraine. They didn't care about who the president was. They were too absorbed in playing soccer and watching their favorite professional soccer team.

At the trial, the Pro-Unity punk, whose name he learned was Dmitry Panchenko, sat with his defense team with a mountain of evidence against him, including video from multiple witnesses' phones recording the beating. The judge would be backed into a corner to give some type of sentencing in this high-profile case, but a crazy event happened. While Dmitry sat in his prison garb, a mob of his Pro-Unity supporters entered the courtroom. Hundreds of them surrounded their comrade to escort him out of the building. The handful of police were useless, with the swarm of young men dressed head to toe in black outfits and waving Azov Battalion flags and Ukrainian flags. The Azov flag was red and black and represented the Bandera supporters who had links to Nazi symbols. Their patch was a double Z with a stripe in its middle and the black sun in the background, the same tattoo on Dmitry's chest. No judge would sit for the case under death threats, and thus, the case was dropped.

Of course, Peter knew nothing of the symbolism at the time. He just described the tattoo he saw on the punk's chest. A professor from his brother's university visited him several times during the summer of his convalescence to interview him extensively about what he witnessed on May 2, 2014. The official May 2nd Committee also interviewed him but did not seem to want to hear anything negative about the Pro-Unity movement. Their bias was evident to Peter, even for a naive eighteen-year-old. They despised the Pro-Federalist movement and associated Peter with the group, which was absurd. Peter was simply in the wrong place at the wrong time.

Peter remembered Professor Kanovsky as kind and nonjudgmental. He was sympathetic to Peter's grieving and was not accusatory in his line of questions. He upset some people with his academic paper, which countered the May 2nd Committee paper accounts of that day in the fire of the Trade Unions Building. He was labeled as "Pro-Federalist," and the media dismissed the paper, but quietly, some honest peers would congratulate him for his unbiased account. Ivan Kanovsky was now teaching computer engineering at Boston University, an opportunity he took advantage of during the upheaval in his war-torn country. Ukrainians were deemed "good guys" in the eyes of the West, and "Russians" were no longer being offered teaching positions abroad.

Peter heard Professor Kanovsky was in the area but was too shy to try to track him down, so he was thrilled to receive an email from him this morning to stop by his office. Peter tucked his pants into his socks and plugged in a bike-friendly route toward Commonwealth Ave., approximately five miles from his campus, being cautious about braking more with his right arm to give his left arm a rest. He was still humming the Nat King Cole song, thinking about the kiss, and his mind was far away from Dmitry Panchenko.

Peter locked up his bike and entered an impressive new engineering building on BU's campus. A sleek, all-window structure with a modern overhang adorned the Star Trek-like doors. The professor met him in the lobby with a firm handshake. "Petrov, so good to see you. Thank you for taking the time to stop by."

"Professor Kanovsky, it is an honor to see you again," said Peter.

"Petrov, please call me Ivan. We are both teachers now. I was happy to see you taking the academic path, and what an excellent course to teach. I would love to audit your class."

Peter laughed modestly. He knew Ivan could write the curriculum for his course. Peter admired the man's mind.

"Okay, Ivan, and you can call me Peter if you want, although it is nice to hear my real name being said. I've been homesick for Russian; always speaking English is exhausting."

"Wonderful, we will speak Russian. Come up to my office, please."

Ivan waved his key over the keypad to the elevators and pressed the button to the fourth floor. His office lacked the old-school charm of some Bostonian college buildings but was outfitted with the latest technology. He had two large Apple PCs on his computer desk and his credentials framed on the wall. Peter studied the framed pictures of him with friends and family. He picked up the large oyster paperweight shining with a thick resin coating. "This is a great paperweight. I have something similar. It reminds me of home."

Ivan took the oyster from Peter and opened the latch to the glued pearl on the inside. "'Pearl of the Black Sea.' Only a fellow Odessite would get the reference," laughed Ivan. "I miss Odessa too. I miss the old Odessa before the uprising." Many Ukrainians don't view the war as beginning when Putin invaded in February 2022 but eight years earlier during the Maidan and the ousting of President Yanukovych.

"Odessa, Pearl of the Black Sea . . . That is how I will always view our beautiful city. A pearl was said to be teardrops from heaven. Sometimes, all I have for Ukraine lately is tears." Ivan ran his hand over the pearl and continued, "A pearl represents purity, humility, and innocence. That was all taken away from you the day your brother died. I want you to know I have not forgotten Alexsei. I never got to be his teacher, but I know colleagues in the engineering department who said he was a good student and was serious about his studies." Ivan closed the oyster and returned the shell to the pile of papers on his desk. "Your brother would've been an outstanding engineer. I know it." He compassionately tapped Peter's shoulder. He motioned Peter to sit in a leather seat facing the desk, and Ivan chose the matching chair beside him.

Ivan was in his forties, but the strain of the war and his research aged him quickly from the last time he visited Peter's home. He leaned forward in the chair with his hands rubbing together, then sat up with his thumb pressed hard to his temple, anticipating his following words would cause him pain.

"Studying May 2nd and the war has been an obsession of mine. I never stopped digging into evidence, and as hard as it was for others to understand, I just wanted the truth with no narrative. Spin muddled the truth with omissions as large as the Azov Sea." Ivan studied the oyster paperweight and continued. "I want to tell you a story about an event surrounding 2014 but also understand the story continues to this day. I can't tell you everything yet, but you will hear the story when my paper is published soon enough. I wanted you to be one of the first to know that when my paper is released, it will stir up some pain for you about this war. I want to prepare you and have you understand how I will be smeared in the public arena. However, I am prepared for the arrows coming for me."

Peter was solemn. "I have lost three classmates in the fighting, and many more were injured. I feel guilty that I was spared, yet my brother and friends are dead. The wheelchair I used was just for a summer. My friend is in a wheelchair for life from his injuries. I know you despise war like the rest of us, Professor. I would never find fault in your character. I know you love Ukraine, like all of us in Odessa. We are Ukrainians."

Ivan extended his sympathy to Peter's losses. "No family in Odessa has dodged tragedy from the war." Ivan pressed his temple again. "I released a paper a year after my May 2nd paper that circulated on the internet but never made it to the papers or the Justice Department. I identified Dmitry Panchenko as the Pro-Unity extremist who threw the grenade at the checkpoint that injured nine people. CCTV cameras at the checkpoint showed the man's face, and digital forensics identified Dmitry Panchenko. I knew at that moment, I was certain, when no one had charged him with his crimes, that he had connections. People like to downplay the influence the Banderites have on the Ukrainian government, but it appeared Dmitry has a carte blanche in this ugly war. I followed his career after he got away with those two heinous crimes in Odessa. I—"

Ivan got up abruptly, walked around the desk to his computer, and paused with his fingers hovering over the keyboard, debating how much he should divulge today. "I know of more crimes. That is all I can share today, but I have spoken with a senator on the Intelligence Committee who is very interested in my work. He is a proponent of bilateral talks and a ceasefire, which most politicians will not publicly discuss. Even uttering the words 'ceasefire' will get you labeled a pro-Putinist and ruin a career. There is serious money in war, from all angles, and any negative information about an Azov member like Dmitry is throttled."

Ivan continued, "My motivation is not against Ukraine. You know this, Peter, but I cannot stand to watch cover-ups for the sake of a chosen narrative. We must see the good, bad, and ugly from all sides and draw conclusions from there." Ivan ran his shaky hand through his hair. "My career will be ruined after this, but the truth is more important. As you said, we may not be on a battlefield, but we can still help Ukraine by not shying away from truths."

Peter was concerned for his friend. He knew how seriously he took his research. "Where is Dmitry Panchenko now?"

"You will learn everything you need to know in a few weeks. I will send you a link when my paper is put online. I don't want any prerelease to have the media ready to pounce on me. I want Ukrainians to read for themselves and draw their own conclusions."

Peter nodded, appreciative that the professor was preparing him for the release of more bad news about the punk who kicked his burning flesh while his brother lay dead inches from him. It was a foreshadowing of a heinous war that continues to rage. His friends know tragedy far worse than his own. "Thank you for the time, Ivan. I was always very thankful for the kindness you showed me. You were the only person I could confide in and trust. I very rarely share my thoughts about Alexsei with anyone." Peter looked at the oyster and smiled, remembering last night's sharing oysters with Caterina along Boston Harbor. "Well, I've met a special American who shares my love of oysters, and I told her. Her name is Caterina, and she is also fixing my elbow pain. There are some pretty cool people in this city."

Ivan smiled as well, proud to see the young boy so broken ten years ago, grow into this handsome man who could still enjoy life. "Peter, come with me sailing next weekend. My cousin Tatiana is driving up from New Jersey for the weekend. I belong to a yacht club and can commission a sailboat for an afternoon. We deserve some fun. Bring your friend Caterina along. She sounds lovely."

"I will. Thanks, Ivan. *Dosvedanya*, Professor."

"*Dosvedanya*, Petrov."

Chapter 10

FRIDAY MORNING DRAGGED by at work, and Caterina checked her Apple watch constantly to bring the time closer to two o'clock. She hadn't seen him since that glorious kiss, but they had been texting, Facetiming, and getting to know each other. Peter would scan around his lonely, rented room in South Boston, and Caterina, in contrast, would scan around her beautiful condo in Seaport with an ocean view. The surroundings in their late-night chats were vastly different, but their interest in each other was the same.

Finally, it was two o'clock, and she rushed upstairs to an agreed-upon spot outside her office. He was sitting on a bench playing with his iPhone when he felt her slide next to him and gently brush up against his side.

"You know, just for fun, try scrolling and switching hands. Hold the phone with this hand and scroll with this hand," Caterina switched his hands and watched him attempt her instructions.

He laughed. "That feels very strange. You are always working on improving me." He tried a few seconds more scrolling, then gave up.

She held onto his left forearm, noticing his elbow strap. "Oh, you got your tennis elbow brace. Good for you. I hope it's working."

He smiled back at her, and she noticed his teeth for the first time. They were slightly crooked in an authentic way. Americans always have nice teeth from braces, but she realized other parts of the world had not gone this route of early orthodontia.

"My tennis game has never been better." Peter swung his arm to pantomime using a tennis racquet. Caterina laughed, knowing he didn't play tennis.

Peter then openly stared at Caterina and felt a bit overwhelmed to be in her physical presence after talking to her for many hours through a screen. All he wanted to do last night was jump through his phone to be with her and resisted the temptation to ride his bike to her apartment. He fell in love with her on their first date and was helpless to change that the more he looked into her caring, brown eyes.

She broke the trance by standing up and walking toward the workout area. "Ready?"

He walked along beside her. "No. Can we get some fresh air instead? I know you run with some of your clients. Maybe we can walk?"

Caterina smiled and felt the same need just to be with him and not surrounded by coworkers and gym members. "Perfect."

"Kenneth, we're headed outside if anyone is looking for me."

Kenneth at the front desk smiled. "Sure thing." Life Time staff came and went, but Caterina and Kenneth had worked together for years and were both hard workers. He liked to see Caterina interested in someone. He knew she acted tough, but she couldn't hide her smile today.

They were quiet as they walked along the boardwalk, just enjoying the views of the harbor. They observed their fellow strollers that were enjoying a sunny Friday afternoon. Caterina unzipped her sweatshirt and wrapped it around her waist.

Peter broke the silence. "I canceled my next trainer session with you. I hope you don't mind."

Caterina laughed. "I was going to tell you the same thing today. Kenneth said he'd do your next workout, but I must warn you, he shows no mercy, even with your injury."

"Okay, on second thought . . ." Peter comically rubbed his chin. "If I have to choose between dating you or a trainer, I pick a trainer. You need to fix me."

Caterina hugged his arm. "I'll do you pro bono. That's what I do all the time anyway with people. I give unsolicited advice, regardless of whether people want it."

They turned around at the fifteen-minute mark and wandered back toward the Life Time building. Caterina continued to hold onto his arm, and he had his hands in his coat pocket. "What are you doing tonight, Peter? Do you want to grab dinner?"

"I would love that, but I don't have much time this evening. My classes are turning in their ten-page papers by midnight, and I have a feeling I will be fielding many emails from panicked procrastinators. Maybe we can do a quick bite tonight and go out Saturday night?"

"That sounds fine for tonight. I have something to do Saturday night, but also . . ." Caterina spontaneously blurted out, "do you want to go to my brother's house Sunday for a cookout? It's going to be super informal. It's one of my niece's birthday, and my mother would be thrilled if, for once, I didn't show up alone."

"That is a very generous offer, Caterina. I have not had a home-cooked meal since I have been in Boston." Peter suddenly felt apprehensive that they were going too fast. The last thing he wanted to do was disappoint this beautiful woman. He didn't plan to fall in love and had to tread lightly. He was only in Boston for a few more months, and then he would be returning to Ukraine. Love came at inconvenient times, but how could this feeling be squashed? He never felt this good in his life with another person. She was a grown woman. He wasn't tricking her into liking him. It just happened. He should enjoy feeling happy.

"If I get through a chunk of my grading on Saturday, I would be honored to go to your brother's house with you. Thank you so much, Caterina."

She loved the way he said her name. She felt loved and sexy. Caterina knew he was returning to Ukraine in a few months, and there was no future, but how could she ignore how she was feeling? It happened. She should just enjoy feeling happy.

"So, how about Sweet Greens?" she smiled.

"Shake Shack?" he responded.

"I would lose my reputation if I got caught with greasy fries and a hamburger a block from work," Caterina laughed.

"Okay, I get it. Let's do an early dinner of healthy salad, and I will stop for fries after."

They both entered the gym after their walk, waving to Kenneth. Peter went swimming in the pool while Caterina finished her workday. They then walked the short block over to Sweet Greens restaurant for salads. He hadn't asked her what she was doing Saturday night, and she offered no information. She wanted to tell him about her private investigator job but didn't want to make a big announcement. She wanted it to pop up in a conversation casually, but it never seemed like the right time. It wasn't a big deal. It was just some side job, so she was unsure why she kept it quiet. He also avoided talking about his recent discussion with Professor Ivan Kanovsky and the unsavory assailant Dmitry, whom Ivan was still exposing. Peter had spent so much time trying to ignore the war at home, but that was the thing about living in Ukraine . . . The war came to find you even if you didn't look for it.

Peter wondered what the professor was referring to. He liked Ivan a lot and respected his academic work. He was a decent man who helped Peter while grieving his brother's loss. Peter remembered the invitation Ivan had extended to Caterina for sailing the following weekend.

"Do you like sailing?" asked Peter.

Caterina was munching on her salad and sipped her unsweetened iced tea. "You know, I've never been sailing, and I've always wanted to go. I love seeing the sailboats in the harbor. It looks like so much fun."

"My friend invited me to go sailing next weekend. Would

you like to join me? Next Sunday?"

They were already plotting out their next weekend together. Was this going too fast, or was this what couples do? Caterina was wondering. She didn't care. Her cheeks were sore from smiling so much, and it felt good. After dinner, they walked back to the Life Time bike rack, taking the long way on the harbor walk.

He unlocked his bike and left it on the rack so he could turn his full attention to Caterina. He pulled her close by the shoulders and kissed her gently. He brushed a loose strand from her ponytail, tucked it behind her ear, and whispered in Russian, then translated to English. "You are my *perla* by the sea, my pearl." He kissed her again. "My perla."

She closed her eyes and savored his lips on hers. She wanted to stand there forever, kissing him.

"Can I walk you to your car?"

"I didn't take my car today. I walked, but I'll be fine. Good luck with your papers this weekend, and I'll see you Sunday."

"*Dosvedanya*, my perla," he said again in a husky tone that left her a bit light-headed.

She watched him bike down Northern Ave. and felt the need to sit down. She closed her eyes and felt the warm breeze on her face as she replayed his words and his kiss in her mind. Honking car horns on a Friday afternoon traffic brought her back to earth. She shook her head dramatically to reset it back to reality. This was so out of character for her to leap into a man's arms. She hadn't even googled him.

She got so caught up in this fantasy that she resisted the

urge. She felt she was betraying his trust by snooping, but that was her nature. She felt compelled. Finally, she googled his name, "Peter Geller UMASS Boston professor," an easy task she thought. Nothing came up. She didn't want to jump to any conclusions. She shouldn't ruin the moment. She googled again. "Peter Geller, Odessa, Ukraine." A bunch of responses to this came up, but no one that looked like Peter. She stopped and put her phone away. She shouldn't jump to conclusions on a quick search and assume he was a liar. She didn't believe that. Look how her bias about the Hinge date with Sidar was wrong. She needed to trust her instincts more than search engines.

The sun lowered fast behind the building. Twilight sometimes would play tricks on the eyes with reflections off the glass buildings. A gust of wind replaced the gentle breeze. She untied her jacket and put it on, hugging herself to get the chill of the wind out of her body. Finally, she stood up and walked toward her condo. Was Kimmie working tonight? She always knew Kimmie's schedule and was mad at herself for not knowing. She texted Kimmie, but she didn't respond. She tried to replay earlier conversations in the week if she said she was working Friday night, but all their talks revolved around Peter.

She waited for the "walk" sign at the crosswalk. Halfway across the street, she felt like someone was following her. She turned quickly over her shoulder, but no one was there. The countdown to get out of the street flashed to red. And she quickened her pace to get safely to the sidewalk. She flashed her key on the keypad to enter the building. Before opening the door, she took a quick look around. She observed a shadow cast on the brick wall that grew bigger as a pedestrian rounded the corner, walking past her building. She closed the door, feeling unsettled and not sure why.

She pressed the elevator to their eighth-floor condo, and her phone buzzed. It was Kimmie. "I'm home. Jack's over." The text filled her with joy, and she felt so much emotion her eyes teared for no real reason.

"Hey, guys," Caterina shouted as she entered the apartment feeling more composed.

"Hey, Cat," said Jack, lying on the couch and flipping through his phone. "Kimmie's getting dressed. How's things with you?"

Caterina plopped in a chair next to the couch. "Good. I'm dating some cute guy from the gym. I even asked him to go to my brother's house on Sunday. I know, completely out of character for me, but I don't know."

"You what?" shouted Kimmie as she exited the bedroom. "You are bringing this dude to your brother's house, and I haven't even met him?" Kimmie teased Caterina. She was delighted her friend was happy.

"Well, maybe bring him. Let's see what Google says. Mystery was fun the first week, but let's see if he is a cat killer or something." Caterina walked to her bedroom and opened her laptop to try some advanced searches on the love of her life.

She clicked around for a while but hit dead ends in her research. She opened her personal investigator emails, that were usually all from employees at Geico Insurance with new car accident claims cases, but there was one from an email sender she didn't recognize. It was from a woman requesting an investigator about a personal matter. She was unsure how this woman had her email. Maybe the same way the Tuft's landlord received it, from Geico. She was excited to take on a new case, especially if it wasn't an auto claim. She emailed the woman back, and they agreed to meet at Starbucks tomorrow morning at ten a.m. They each described what coat they would be wearing to make it easier to identify each other.

She closed her laptop and slipped into bed. She wanted to text Peter but knew he was busy communicating with his students. She resisted for an hour and tried to sleep, but she ended up picking up her phone to text him.

"Hi . . ."

"Hello, my beautiful perla. I have missed you. What are you doing?"

"I'm lying in bed thinking of you."

A bubble with dancing dots popped up, disappeared, and reappeared several times. Finally, after a full five minutes, he typed out.

"That's nice, very nice. I'm doing the same . . ." He sent several links to love songs, making her scream into her pillow for falling into this romance.

"*I remember you . . . a few kisses ago . . .*" She typed, referring to the Nat King Cole song.

"Good night, Caterina, sweet dreams."

She heard his voice saying those words and drifted off, listening to her growing playlist of love songs.

Chapter 11

CATERINA SAT DOWN with her venti dark roast, watching the door ten minutes before ten. She wore the red jacket she promised to wear to be visible to her potential client. She looked over her business card, a sleek black card with an obtuse silver logo, and her name, title, and work email. She was excited to hand out her card for the first time. She had five hundred she recently ordered.

A woman matching the coat color description she had given Caterina opened the coffee shop door and walked directly over to Caterina's table. "Caterina Antonucci?"

"Yes, Justine?"

"Yes," said the woman somewhat nervously, touching the frame of her sunglasses that she had yet to remove.

"Please, sit. Can I get you a coffee?"

"No, thank you," the woman stammered. "I'm a bundle of nerves as it is. Thank you for meeting with me. I got your name through a friend of a friend." She touched her sunglasses again. "I've never done anything like this before, but I just have to know . . ." She took a deep breath in and out. "I have to know if my husband is having an affair."

Caterina listened to the woman tell the tale about how her husband had been making excuses that he would be late for dinner, and he recently took up golf and turned off his iPhone tracking. He will not tell her what golf course he is going to or who he is going with, and she has not confronted him about him turning off his locator.

Caterina waited until the woman paused her story. Justine seemed put together as an attractive woman in her forties. She was Irish-looking with a Bostonian accent. She wore jeans, sneakers, and a pretty blouse under her blue jacket. She obviously was flustered about asking for help to find out the truth.

"I'm sorry for your situation, Justine. I just want to let you know I wouldn't be right for this job. I have minimal experience and have mostly done insurance claim work. I think you need a more experienced PI."

Justine nodded. "It's just that I really wanted a woman to help me with this. I don't want to hire a guy. I'm willing to overlook your inexperience. You seem," she took off her sunglasses, and her eyes were red. "You seem nice. I want answers. My husband had always been a good husband. If it's nothing or something, I just need to know."

Caterina handed her a Starbucks napkin, and she blew her nose. "Okay, I'll get on this right away. Here's my card. Give me your cell phone number. I can text you my business cell number. I don't do encrypted emails. I feel that if anyone is interested in my communication, they will figure out how to read anything.

"Let's start from the beginning. What is your husband's name?"

"His name is Ivan. Ivan Kanovsky. He's a professor in the engineering department at Boston University."

Caterina and Justine agreed on a fee, and Justine opened up her wallet and gave her five crisp one-hundred-dollar bills to start. Caterina folded them and put them in her front pocket. "I'll update you as soon as I find anything out, Justine. Thank you for trusting me with this job."

Justine left first, and Caterina finished her venti while looking at Google Maps and studying Kanovsky's home address, 136 St. Paul Street, and the surrounding neighborhood.

Soon, Caterina returned to her apartment and retrieved her tan Honda Accord. It's the perfect car for nondescript surveillance. She drove past Ivan's home several times, then settled into a parking spot down the street. It was a large house next to other large houses, but it was hard to figure out how these big houses were chopped up into smaller units. She scanned the recent listing and description of the house on a real estate website. His was Unit 2. "*A sun-filled duplex in a Victorian style nestled in the heart of Coolidge Corner. His unit was worth 1.5 million or a convenient 10,000 a month on a 30-year fixed mortgage at 7.25 percent.*" Caterina shook her head at the absurd prices. She knew she was doomed to move back home in September. The world was too expensive, and she could just imagine what Kimmie's condo value was.

After several hours of no one entering or exiting the building, Caterina left to grab something to eat. It wasn't unusual to have no success in surveillance. It took patience. She decided to switch gears and pursue another target tonight, albeit this case finished long ago. She drove over to the Holiday Inn in Waltham, Massachusetts. Tonight was the regional qualifying round for the New England bodybuilding championship, and she didn't want to miss it.

The parking lot was full, and the hotel's ballroom was set up with a stage, a panel of judges, and chairs for the audience. She settled into the back row, watching the competition. The categories were endless, with top winners announced for wellness, classic physique, bikini, bodybuilding, and overall winners. She lingered in the lobby with sponsors from airbrush tanning salons, gyms, and personal trainers when the competition was over. She had never entered this world of bodybuilding and was fascinated by the dedication and popularity of the participants.

She spotted Alda talking to some other contestants and loitered close by so she could see her.

"What do you want, Caterina? Come to gloat on how much I sucked tonight?" Alda was cranky and appeared disappointed in her performance. Caterina knew she didn't place in any category, but other contestants were just happy to compete.

"No, Alda, not at all. I thought you looked terrific out there. You looked fantastic." Caterina smiled a soft smile. "I have just been thinking about you and am curious about how you've been doing."

"Is that even legal, Caterina? My stupid insurance company hired you to follow my ass everywhere I go, and you want to rub it in my face that I lost out on my settlement after my car accident?"

"Come on, Alda, you know I just wanted to see how you were doing. That's the truth."

Alda softened a little. She said goodbye to the other contestants and turned her attention to Caterina. "Do you want to grab a drink or something? All I've eaten this past week is unflavored rice cakes. I'm about to faint from starvation."

"Sure," said Caterina, "I'd like that."

The bar at the Holiday Inn was filled with bodybuilders and their friends and family. Caterina and Alda sat at a table in the corner to find a spot away from the music. Caterina ordered a chardonnay, and Alda a rum and Diet Coke. They order two tomato, mozzarella, and basil appetizers, the only healthy thing on the menu.

Caterina shouted a little loud so she could be heard over the music. "You know I had nothing to do with you losing your case, Alda. Anyone could google your Facebook and Instagram pages. It wasn't rocket science to know you were bodybuilding and still claiming ongoing back disability payments from getting rear-ended. Don't blame me."

"I'm not mad at you, Caterina. The whole ordeal just pissed me off. I really did hurt my back, and bodybuilding saved me. I won't give up what I love because some judge tells me I'm not hurt enough."

Caterina smiled. She always liked Alda and felt like she got to really know her, stalking her for months, then finally introduced herself after Alda lost her case. She knew Alda would be mad at her, but Caterina always felt compelled to place herself in the case. Helping the insurance company was one part of the job, but she wanted Alda to know she didn't have it out to "get her."

Alda took the tiniest bite of her tomato and mozzarella and pushed the plate away. Caterina had already finished hers and was still hungry. "I'm going to lose my disability insurance now too. I don't know what I am going to do."

Caterina spoke. "Why not go back to working as a nurse? You are only thirty-eight and have your whole life ahead of you. Don't you miss it?"

Alda pulled her plate closer and took another tiny bite. "I do," she softly said. "I do, but the system punished me for working. I had to file for disability if I had any chance with my court case. I guess I just got caught up in the system with my lawyers and played the role. I mean, to a certain point." Alda looked at Caterina curiously. "Why do you even care? You won. You probably got some bonus showing the insurance I was just working on improving myself. Why are you even here?"

Caterina thought long and hard about why she was here. She didn't have to be here in a musty Holiday Inn bar on a Saturday night when she could have gone out with Peter. She guessed she was here because she just cared about Alda as a person and wanted to check on her.

"That's a good question that deserves an answer. I felt compelled to see you after talking to one of my clients. She reminded me of you. She also has spinal problems from a car accident and is trying hard to get stronger."

Pearl by the Sea

Alda laughed. "I forgot you were a personal trainer. I just think of you as some creepy girl who likes to stalk people. You're a strange bird. Is that why you are here? To drum up some business for your fledgling trainer career? Most of these bodybuilders are personal trainers themselves. I'm sure they could run circles around your workouts."

Caterina laughed. "I'm sure they could. No, it wasn't her back pain that brought me here. It is what she said. As you know, my two jobs are completely different. As a PI, you are never supposed to talk to your target. As a trainer, all I do is talk with my client. I was talking to her about the struggles she had taking care of her dad, who had multiple sclerosis. She told me it was a difficult but right decision to put him in a nursing home. She said the nursing home staff were fantastic, which helped with her decision, but she said there was one nurse in particular she would never forget. She cared for her dad for years and was with the family on the night he passed away."

Alda nodded, listening to the story and understanding what Caterina was trying to say.

"She said she would never forget the nurse, Alda, who cared for her dad. She was like an angel to her father. That's all, Alda. That is the only reason I'm here to tell you that story. I just thought you would like to hear something positive about your job."

Alda took a big sip of her rum and Coke. "You could've messaged me on Facebook or something, Caterina. You didn't have to drive all the way over here."

"Do you think you would've accepted my friend request on Facebook, Alda?" Caterina laughed.

Alda joined in with her, laughing. "No, you're probably right. I would've had great joy deleting that request." They both giggled and finished their drinks as Alda gobbled up her appetizer.

Chapter 12

CATERINA WAS IN bed awake Sunday morning. She was recapping her day yesterday of meeting her new client Justine, dinner with Alda, and, of course, thinking about Peter. No matter how much she tried to keep her mind on other thoughts, he floated back to center stage. She shouldn't have googled him. She felt like she had betrayed his trust, but now doubt lurked in her mind. He was too perfect. He must be lying about who he is, and his fake name proves it. Why was she so stupid to fall for his lines?

She threw on her running shoes, shorts, and T-shirt for her weekend run around Castle Island. Usually, she liked to run in silence, but today, she popped in her AirPods and put on her playlist of love songs she created with songs Peter sent her. She could not get enough of listening to the old crooners sing about love and thought she might be going mad. She had become obsessed with Peter in such a short period of time, and today, she was going to bring him to meet her family.

Caterina didn't even cool down or slow down her stride and ran straight to her apartment door. She had to talk to him.

She had to find out exactly who he was. She dialed him on her phone, listening to the phone ring through her AirPods, and he answered immediately. His voice made her weak in the knees. She turned around to walk out of the building, ignoring the elevator. She needed air.

"Good morning, Caterina. You sound out of breath. Everything all right?"

"Hey, yeah, I just went for a run. Sorry for the heavy breathing." Her heart was racing from the run and the anticipation of confronting Peter. She wanted to sound casual and not like some crazy stalker, which she had been accused of in the past. She procrastinated. "So, did you have a good night?"

"Pretty boring. Just graded papers. How about you?"

"Good. I visited a friend of mine and got a bite to eat." She took out her AirPods and switched to putting the phone up to her ear, pacing around outside her apartment.

"Yeah, so, just checking in for today. I can pick you up at around twelve. Does that sound good?"

"I'll bike to your apartment. It will be easier to drive from there so you don't have to go south, then north. It will save you time."

"Are you sure, Peter?"

"Riding my bike to see you today will make me the happiest man on the planet. There is no greater joy than biking to a pleasant destination."

Caterina raised her eyebrows. He was too perfect. Doubt was creeping in. She got up the courage to ask him.

"I just thought of something. What's your real name?"

Pearl by the Sea

He was surprised at this off-topic question but answered nonchalantly. "You mean my full name in Russian?"

"Yeah, I guess. Peter Geller just sounds, well, you know, so American."

"Sure. Sure. My name is Petrov Leonidovich Geller. All Russian names use their dad's name as a middle name, so my middle name means son of Leonid. My dad's name is Leonid Petrovovich Geller because his dad's name was Petrov. Ovich means 'son of.' If I were a girl, my middle name would end in 'ovna,' meaning 'daughter of.' Leonid is actually derived from the Spartan King Leonidas. Remember him?"

Caterina was silent because she felt so stupid and just listened.

"Leonidas was the one who stopped the Persian army in Athens. He was called 'Son of Lion' because of his bravery in fighting. My dad loves his name. He's big into Greek history."

He paused, waiting for her to say something, and she knew she had to respond. "That's cool." She felt so dumb. He was so knowledgeable about the world. She felt like a third-grader about her facts. Now, her lists felt so amateurish. She didn't know what to add. "Cool," she repeated. "So, I'll see you around twelve?"

"One more thing," Peter said, excited about her question. He liked inquisitive people who wanted to learn. "Catherine the Great named my city Odessa after a Greek colony Odesso that supposedly was in the area. Catherine loved art and literature and wanted to build Odessa as an elegant European city to rival Paris. That's why they call Odessa 'Pearl of the Black Sea' because of its beauty."

"Cool, cool," said Caterina, hanging up and sighing. He really was perfect. She walked back toward her apartment, hitting play on her love songs.

As Caterina waited for Peter to text her that he was downstairs, she googled Petrov Leonidovich Geller on Yandex. She had Yandex translate to Cyrillic, and sure enough, his face popped up as a graduate of the National University in 2017 with a degree in philosophy and a minor in Soviet Union history. There was a picture of him in the book of professors at National University teaching Soviet Union history. She smiled at his slightly crooked teeth and piercing blue eyes in the photo of his younger self.

Her phone buzzed, and she texted she'd be right down. She met him by the door. He grabbed her hands and kissed her on the cheek lovingly. She held his hands, looked into the eyes she was just staring at on the computer, and gave him a nice kiss on the lips. He smiled a big smile with his slightly crooked teeth, and she felt happy. Happier than she ever felt in her life.

Caterina drove her Honda to her brother Anthony's house in Wakefield, about half an hour north of Boston. He was having a birthday party for his daughter, Gianna, and all her family would be there, including all her brothers, sisters-in-law, parents, nieces, and nephews. Even her grandmother would be there to meet Caterina's new boyfriend. Caterina floated into her brother's kitchen with her arm on Peter.

"Auntie!" squealed a handful of nieces and nephews who approached her to hug her. She let go of Peter to give each of them big bear hugs and wished Gianna a happy eighth birthday. The kids ran back to the backyard to play. Caterina introduced Peter to the inside crowd, then wandered outside to introduce him to the family who were gathered outside, grilling and playing cornhole. Caterina wore jeans, sneakers, and a pretty pink blouse with her hair down and some colored lip gloss to match her shirt. Peter wore a dark blue Polo tucked into crisp jeans and sneakers. They were a stunning couple, and Caterina's sisters-in-law, one by one, whispered in her ear, "His eyes," "Dear Lord," and "My God, he's gorgeous."

Caterina and Peter were quickly recruited for a cornhole game, and Caterina's brother taught Peter the rules. Caterina encouraged him across the lawn, standing next to the other cornhole. Peter threw his beanbags, which all missed the target, and Anthony got a couple on the board for two points. Next, it was Caterina's turn to throw toward Peter's cornhole. She took her hairband off her wrist and put her hair up in a ponytail. Then she concentrated on the hole in the middle of the inclined wood, sank two in the hole, and got two on the board: eight points. Caterina danced a jig and pointed her hand toward her brother Anthony. "Beat that, Tony!" It was easy for Caterina to fall back into the competitive nature with her brothers, and the playful teasing the five siblings had with each other was a sight to behold. They had inside jokes and stories of childhood that each would tell in their own colorful version.

Soon, Peter got swept into the brothers' crowd, and Caterina sat with the women, listening to her mom tell stories about her grandchildren. Gianna, wearing her princess outfit, sat on her grandmother's lap as Arlene, Caterina's mother, hugged Gianna.

The adults entered the big family room after the barbeque, presents, and cake. Most of the kids descended to the basement to play video games. Caterina's dad, Aldo, enthusiastically grabbed Caterina's shoulder to turn her around. He had his arm around Peter.

"Hey, you know what this guy's been telling me? His city used to have a load of Italians in it. He said they would come from Genoa, Italy, and all sailed over there. Did you know that? It's up near Parma and Bologna. Did you know that? That's where our family is from, and he's been there!" Aldo gave Peter another big hug around the shoulder.

"You couldn't find any of those places on a map, Aldo," Arlene, his wife, laughed. "All you know about Genoa is salami, and Parm is the cheese you put on your chicken parm." Aldo laughed as well. He and his wife had never been to Italy, and raising five kids and eight grandkids later, they neither had the time nor the money to travel.

Caterina was about to talk to Peter, but he got pulled into another conversation with her brothers, so she plopped on the couch to talk to the women some more. As usual at any Antonucci family gathering, a couple of wireless mics were passed around the family room, and Aldo, Caterina's dad, started off karaoke with some Frank Sinatra. His overly dramatic interpretation of "My Way" was very off-key but well received, giving others the confidence to sing. Some nieces wandered upstairs to sing their favorite Disney songs from movies like *Moana* and *Frozen*. Gianna handed Peter the microphone after the girls finished their singing.

Peter received the mic like a good sport, pointed the clicker to the smart TV search bar, and typed out Nat King Cole.

Uh-oh, thought Caterina to herself. This could be a disaster. He scrolled to "Autumn Leaves" and clicked to play. Caterina sighed, secretly glad it wasn't "I Remember You," a song she had not stopped listening to since he sent it to her after their first date. She had never heard of the song he picked or heard him sing, and she held her breath. He started to sing, and everyone laughed and cheered as they did for all those who began their songs to encourage. Many laughed because his thick accent sounded funny to them. However, after the first line of the song, the audience settled down and listened to him sing. His voice was tender, and his singing was excellent. He continued, occasionally looking at Caterina and back at the lyrics scrolling on the television even though he knew every word by heart.

The song talked about a couple in love and how one person had to go on living after the other was no longer with them. The seasons would come and go, but the lover would miss their soul mate the most when the autumn leaves started to fall.

When he finished, the room was silent. There was something beautifully sad in his voice. Caterina observed her Nana rise from her sturdy seat next to her mother and walk slowly and carefully over to Peter. She had tears in her eyes and held his hands, smiling. "That was wonderful, wonderful. My husband would sing that song around the house. Thank you for that." It was such a precious moment. So many "Awwws" came from the audience. Peter was encouraged to sing again, but he passed the microphone back to Gianna and her cousins, who picked out a Taylor Swift song and danced around.

Families said their goodbyes one by one, and soon, it was just Aldo's family and Caterina's brother Dom's family. Dom and Aldo encouraged Peter to have another beer while Caterina's sister-in-law tried to hand her a wineglass. Caterina waved her off since she was driving. "I can drive if you want to enjoy some wine," Peter quietly said to Caterina.

Dom chimed in, "This guy's a keeper, Cat! Don't scare 'em off like you did that Jason guy." He turned to his brother. "Remember Cat freaked the guy out by stalking his Facebook page?" Dom laughed some more. "I guess that's what you get for dating a private investigator. They're gonna know all your secrets."

Peter looked confused at Dom's comment and at Caterina, who grabbed the wineglass. "Maybe I will let you drive," she said, trying to laugh off her brother's comment as frivolous.

After another awkward half hour, they all said goodbye, and Caterina handed Peter her keys. "Can you drive? Do you even have a license?"

"Not here, I don't, but I'm a good driver."

"Wait, what side of the road do they drive on in Ukraine?"

"Right, same as here," he said, taking her car keys.

They jumped into the car and drove until they were stuck in traffic on 128 South. Both were lost in their own thoughts. A fantastic day turned awkward at the end when he found out she was a PI from her brother. She didn't mean to keep it a secret. It just never came up, and it was certainly hard to explain that last night, she was visiting a woman in a bodybuilding competition that she used to stalk for months to let her know someone said something nice about her. No, that was impossible to explain. It was just easier to say she had dinner with a friend. Technically, that was true, she supposed, even though Alda would hardly categorize Caterina as a "friend."

Peter broke the silence. "I had an amazing day today. Your family is so welcoming. I want to say thank you for inviting me. Truly."

Caterina smiled. "You made quite an impression on the crew, especially my grandmother. I never hear her talk about him. It was so nice you stirred up memories for her. I didn't know you were such a good singer."

"And I didn't know you were a private investigator."

He wasn't upset or angry. It seemed to deepen his awe of a woman he fell in love with, and if anything, it scared him just a little. The whole day frightened him because it felt so right, and he wanted to be nowhere else and with no one else. He reached over to grab her hand and stroked it tenderly with his thumb. He hummed his original Nat King Cole song "I Remember You" as he paid attention to the car braking in front of him. She closed her eyes and rubbed his hand with her thumb, listening to his song.

He parked the car in her designated parking at her apartment. It was six o'clock, and both were tired from a busy day. Caterina's phone buzzed. It was Kimmie. "**I'm working until eleven. I'm pissed I'm the last to meet Peter. We better be**

doing a double date this week." Caterina showed him the text. "She's pissed."

Caterina realized Peter had not seen her apartment, and it would be quiet without Kimmie home.

"Do you want to come see my apartment?"

Caterina thought he would jump at the question, but she noticed hesitancy in his response. He rubbed his hands through his hair, and his expression turned to what she thought was anguish.

Caterina spoke, "Listen, I'm sorry I didn't tell you I'm a PI. It's just that it never came up in conversation. I wasn't holding back, well, maybe I was holding back a little because it's a crazy part of my life, and I wanted to be normal to you. It has frightened guys off in the past."

He pinched his nose hard and silently exited the car, and she followed. He held her hand tight as they walked down to the water. The sun was setting, and the sailboats and sunset cruises began their nightly ritual of touring the harbor at sunset. He closed his eyes to draw in a breath and let it out slowly. He didn't turn to Caterina but stared out into the sea.

"It's not the job. If anything, it makes you more fascinating to me. I love you, Caterina. I have never felt such joy and pain at the same time. I feel happiness because you are the most amazing woman I have ever met. All I can think about is scooping you into my arms and laying you down on your bed. But I know this will be short-lived. I will move back to Ukraine in a few months, and we will be worlds apart. We cannot blend our worlds. It's not possible."

He turned to look at her with sadness in his eyes. "I don't

want to hurt you or me in the future. I was dumb to start this, but I never felt pure contentment as I do with you. It was selfish to lead you on. The longer we see each other, the worse our pain will be. I have felt enough pain in my life. I see how losing my brother has turned my parents into different people than I knew." He continued. "You, your family, you are good people. You deserve someone who can go back year after year to events and grow old together. I love you enough to say goodbye because that is all I want for you, Caterina. I want you to be fulfilled. I can't give you that."

Caterina shut him up by kissing him hard on the lips. She didn't care about the future. She loved the man standing in front of her. She was always different from her brothers, searching for more, and she found it. She didn't know what it was, but she wasn't going to sacrifice her happiness now for some amorphous pain later. She found someone who was not scared of her crazy and fell more in love with her the more he learned about her. She hugged him as tightly as possible, tears streaming down her face. She wasn't sure if she felt joy or pain at that moment, but it was a feeling she welcomed and embraced.

She held his hand and led him into her apartment. They kissed on the couch, and he picked her up and laid her on the bed. "I love you, Caterina, but I will not make love to you, even though it is all I can think about. I love you too much."

She could not understand his logic. He kissed her forehead. "We weren't meant to meet in this lifetime. I remember you a few kisses ago." He gently stroked her hair. "My darling."

He went to leave, and she grabbed his arm. "No, Peter, please, stay. Stay. Did you ever hear, 'Don't mourn what is gone, but be glad that you had it in the first place'? Please, stay."

Peter stayed.

Chapter 13

"**What? He's here?** Like *now*? In your bedroom?"

"Yes, I told him to take his time leaving because he doesn't have to teach class until eleven." Caterina's phone buzzed, and a selfie picture of Peter with a Starbucks coffee in his hand near his bike came up. "Never mind. He already left. He just texted me." Caterina became absorbed in his photo and forgot Kimmie was still on the line.

"Cat? Are you still there?"

"Yes, sorry. I have to get back to work. I'll see you tonight. Oh, and he's up for double-dating Friday night. We can do drinks and apps at the apartment and then go out or just stay in and make Jack and Peter dinner to keep it low budget; up to you."

"You better give me a good hour tonight for all the details. Things are moving so fast. This is not like you, Cat."

Caterina laughed. "I know. I'm not used to feeling like this. It's lust and love, Kimmie, wrapped up into something lovely."

Caterina was extra attentive to her clients all day at work and then jumped into her car to head over to St. Paul's Street to stake out her new target, Ivan Kanovsky. The guy had a class called "Digital Forensic Analytics for Big Data" at four, and she wanted to catch him leaving the house. She saw a man who met his description lock the first-floor unit door and get into an old-looking silver Toyota Rav4. Not the kind of car a guy with a midlife crisis would drive, but it was best not to jump to conclusions and overanalyze. She learned just to observe as much as you could. She tailed the car several miles to a parking lot on the BU campus that required a parking permit. She parked near the engineering building, waiting for him to walk in that direction. Soon enough, she saw him walking quickly with a backpack a block away. There was nothing unusual about him; she was already losing interest in this case, but the money was good.

She paid the meter and walked around the BU campus, waiting for class to be over to tail him again. She texted Justine some pictures but told her before not to communicate over the phone. They'd talk at their next meet-up. At six o'clock, she returned to her car and watched the door. She never saw him reemerge after an hour, so she thought it was enough time for a stakeout. Maybe he was a hard worker. She knew if she were having an affair, she would have raced out of work to meet her lover. Her mind wandered to Peter, and her phone rang, breaking her daydream.

"Caterina? This is Mike, Derek's dad. I haven't heard from you in a while and, well, I just wanted to let you know I no longer need your services. You see, Derek called me, and we had a good heart-to-heart talk. I was right to have voiced concerns

Pearl by the Sea

over his well-being. I was right to have helped him." Mike's voice cracked, and he gave a slight cough to regain composure. Mike sounded like he was trying to convince himself more than Caterina that hiring her was the right thing to do. "I will send you the final payment through Venmo."

Caterina interrupted him. "No, you don't have to do that. I hadn't even provided you with any information."

Mike ignored her rebuttal. "Derek is dropping this semester at Tufts University. He will work full time until the fall and then enroll in Stony Brook College near our house." Mike's voice sounded more optimistic. "You know, he's a good kid, a good kid. Things are going to work out. Well, okay, bye, Caterina."

"Bye, Mike. Good luck with everything."

Caterina held the phone in her hand. She knew she had crossed the line to have approached her target, but it was something she felt compelled to do. Same thing with Alda. It was the helper in her, and she sometimes thought she was in the unique position to be a mediator for those just trying to muddle through life. Derek needed a mom or a friend to guide him. Giving him the ultimatum to tell his dad his problems, or he'd hear them from the private investigator felt right to Caterina. She was also relieved Derek didn't mention their interaction. She didn't need a complaint to the Better Business Bureau either.

Caterina's week continued with purpose. She felt energetic, and even her clients commented on how great she looked. Kenneth at work knew the reason but did not tease her because he was happy for her and felt she deserved it.

On Friday, she ran to Trader Joe's to prepare for the soiree. She wanted to make a charcuterie board. The extra money in her Venmo made picking out the specialty meat and cheeses for her tray easier. They decided to stay in and have a bunch of appetizers. Their harbor view was as good as any restaurant's in town. Caterina dressed up more for this night of staying in than she ever did for going out. She put on a cream-colored light-knit sweater with black linen pants and black heels. She wore her hair down and put on her favorite perfume, Eternity. She never wore heels on dates but felt more confident on Peter's arm and embraced her height. She looked stunning. Jack and Peter hit it off, and Kimmie approved of this new man in her roommate's life. They all felt like dear friends by the end of the evening, and Kimmie was already asking for his address so she could send him a wedding invitation. Peter stayed the night. There was no talk of pain and sadness in the future, just the joy of the present. They were both in the right place at the right time and wanted to enjoy every minute of each other.

Caterina woke up in the middle of the night to use the bathroom and found that Peter was not in bed. She panicked. She was not sure why her first emotion would be distress. She heard a noise in the kitchen. Fight or flight will emerge in a person without warning, and her heart decided now was the time to race and the hair on the back of her neck to stand up. She was scared to leave the room but overcame her fear to find out what made the noise. The night heightened some senses, like hearing, and dulled others like vision. She heard the hum of the fridge and the ticking of the clock, but she had a hard time managing the door threshold using her hands to guide her safely through and not hit the frame. She saw the shadow of a person flash across the wall. It was probably the reflection of clouds passing by a lit building, but in her paranoid state, she felt the presence of a person. She stood in the middle of the room, too frightened to move, but her bleary eyes scanned the room for clues.

A hand grabbed her by the shoulder, and she let out a quick scream.

"Are you okay?" said Peter, standing in his T-shirt and boxers. Where did he come from? Was he in the kitchen, or did he emerge from the bathroom? She felt childish for her skittish reaction. "I'm fine, fine. I just thought I heard something." He put his arm around her to walk her back to bed. She forgot to pee. She got up again to use the bathroom. On the way back to bed, her eyes darted back and forth to survey the room.

Chapter 14

THINGS THAT GO bump in the night were long gone from Caterina's mind as she strolled hand in hand with Peter to Starbucks. They picked up their coffees and sauntered down Northern Ave. to Lewis Wharf on a beautiful Sunday morning. They each had an AirPod in an ear, taking turns picking a song on Spotify.

Da de da, Dancin' in September
Da de da, chasing the clouds away.

Peter was singing falsetto to a cover of Earth, Wind & Fire by the band Leonid & Friends. He twirled Caterina with one hand as she balanced her coffee.

"This band is fantastic. I love that the lead singer has your dad's name. The horns are great too."

Peter hugged her when the song was over, and they stopped so she could scroll Spotify on her phone to pick the next song.

"They are very good and are coming to Boston in June. I'll buy us tickets to go. Maybe we can invite Ivan along to thank him for taking us sailing today. The guy needs support right now," said Peter.

Caterina responded, "That's funny. My new case has an 'Ivan' in it." She hit play and picked another Leonid & Friends cover song called "Vehicle" by The Ides of March.

"Us Ruskies are everywhere," Peter laughed as they turned up the volume on her song choice and continued walking toward the Boston Sailing Center a mile away.

When they arrived at Lewis Wharf, many slips were empty as club members tried to get a sail in before the weather turned to showers in the afternoon. A tall, blond woman was standing by one of the boats, staring at them, and she walked toward them when they arrived.

"Petrov?"

"Yes," said Peter.

She stuck out her hand. "Hi, I'm Tatiana. Nice to meet you." She turned toward Caterina. Caterina was struck by how elegant this woman appeared in regular jeans, sneakers, and a thin sweatshirt. She had the grace of a ballerina with every gesture. She looked to be in her mid to late thirties but was aging in a way that made her more exquisite.

Tatiana waited for Peter to introduce his friend. It appeared she did not know Caterina's name.

"This is my friend, Caterina. Where's Ivan?"

Caterina would have preferred the "girlfriend" description but did not get too bristled. Jealousy wasn't her look, right? Maybe. She felt inadequate beside this woman and wished she had put on some colored lip gloss.

"He's in the boathouse filling out the paperwork. He's upset he has to settle for a thirty-foot sailboat, which made me laugh because it seems quite large enough." Tatiana smiled with perfectly straight teeth. She had a very classy New York accent that didn't sound harsh. She glanced toward the water. "I'm excited to go sailing. Ivan will take good care of us."

They waited a few more minutes on the pier talking to Tatiana. She told them her grandmother came over from Odessa in the early seventies, as many Jewish families did, to settle in Brighton Beach, New York. So many families moved to Brooklyn that the borough became known as "Little Odessa." She explained in the Soviet Union, Jews were discriminated against at universities, and her grandfather wanted better opportunities. Her grandmother was a talented ballerina but was not chosen to dance at the Odessa Opera House because she was Jewish. Tatiana explained that her grandmother was an outstanding ballerina and that she had taught her daughter and kids in the Brighton Beach neighborhood how to dance in her living room. Tatiana's mother went on to open the School of Russian Ballet, and Tatiana worked there too.

Peter was intrigued, and he smiled when Tatiana lightly touched his arm and said "Petrov" with her upscale New York accent. Caterina never called him "Petrov."

"Petrov!" a loud call came from the direction of the boathouse as a man walked along the dock waving enthusiastically. He wore a backpack, and his stride looked familiar. As he came closer, he stopped before them, completing their circle of four.

"Ivan," Caterina blurted out in complete shock. The man she surveilled at Boston University and St. Paul Street was now standing in front of her, smiling. Her brain couldn't do the calculations fast enough. His wife, Justine, what did she say when she introduced herself? A "friend of a friend" gave her Caterina's number. Would Peter have given Justine her number? Did he want to expose Ivan's friend's infidelity to his wife, Justine? Who is Tatiana? Is she *really* Ivan's cousin, or was that a front to tell Peter so Peter wouldn't be suspicious Ivan was cheating on his wife?

She instinctively stepped out of the circle, avoiding Ivan's gaze to concentrate on her inner thoughts. Peter wouldn't have given Justine her number because he didn't even know she was a private investigator until the day after she met Justine. He seemed genuinely surprised when he found out. Or did he? Could she trust any of her emotions the last few weeks?

Peter was a bit taken aback by her response and tried to explain her rudeness politely. "Sorry, Ivan. This is Caterina's first time sailing. She's a bit nervous."

Ivan nodded his head as if this were a reasonable excuse. "Completely understandable, but I have sailed Boston Harbor many times. This will be an easy excursion."

Caterina feigned a meek smile and did not say a word. She liked to be in control of situations, and she felt vulnerable. Between beautiful Tatiana, Petrov smitten with her, a rocky sailboat, and now, her target, Ivan, taking the helm, she no longer was looking forward to sailing.

"You've never been to Brooklyn, Petrov?" asked Tatiana incredulously as the sailboat skimmed the waters of Boston Harbor. "Oh my God, you have to come down and visit. There's this little restaurant near my ballet school that makes the best Verenaki. It's right down by the boardwalk in Little Odessa. Right, Ivan?"

She continued. "I moved out to Fairlawn, New Jersey, but my parents still live in Brooklyn. It's like you're in Russia or Ukraine when you visit. Brighton Beach has the highest concentration of Russian-speaking immigrants in the Western Hemisphere. Ukrainians and Russians live side by side and have been neighbors for decades. Since the war started, there's been a lot of pressure to hide your Russian-speaking identity, even if you lived your whole life in either Ukraine or America. We had to change the name of our school from 'School of Russian Ballet' to 'School of Ukrainian Ballet.' It was insane. We had angry parents canceling dance lessons because we were 'the enemy.' I'm like, 'Lady, do you realize Russia is bombing my family in Ukraine?' but they don't care. Everyone just virtue signals and has no clue about this war. We put up Ukraine flags, and now every parent wants to sign their kid up to support the war. The guy in the next store had to change his supermarket from 'A Taste of Russia' to 'International Food.' They still have the best Khachapuri, though. Have you ever had Georgian pizza? It's like a white pizza with cheeses that taste like feta and mozzarella. It's so tangy and salty and delicious."

Tatiana realized her troubles with the war were insignificant compared to Peter's. She apologized with her eyes, but it didn't seem to bother him. He liked to hear her talk about his culture and foods.

"You have to have those Russian dumplings with sour cream. Without it is a crime," Peter answered.

Pearl by the Sea

Caterina could not concentrate on the conversation. She studied Ivan's body language. She was convinced he was cheating on Justine with this Tatiana. Was Ivan jealous that Tatiana was being so friendly to Peter? Caterina corrected her inner thoughts. "Petrov," she said to herself sarcastically with a pang of jealousy.

Tatiana was sensitive to Ivan and Peter's closer connections to the war in Ukraine. Ivan told her a little bit about what Peter went through in 2014. Ivan had been obsessed with the events around that time, although she had to admit it was hard to keep track of the story. She was born and raised in America and had never visited Ukraine or any former Soviet Union country. Tatiana got a glimpse of their heartbreak with the boycotting of her dance studio, but that was the extent of her personal experience. She touched Peter's shoulder lightly. "Ukraine, forever a pawn" was a saying everyone could agree on without getting into politics or sowing seeds of division. It was an easy way to say they bore the brunt of bigger countries' decisions.

Ivan studied Caterina as Peter and Tatiana conversed. He could not decipher Caterina's demeanor. It felt more than just jitters about sailing. It felt more than just feelings of jealousy observing Peter's conversations with Tatiana.

"How did you and Petrov, I mean Peter, meet, Caterina?" It seemed like an innocent question. Was he being sarcastic with his slip of the tongue, not using his Americanized name? Caterina felt too jumpy even to answer the question. She just wanted to get off the boat. The sea changed its personality, and the boat began rocking more. Speedboats would disrupt their flow with choppy waves sent in their direction. The clouds were darkening, and threats of rain seemed imminent. "We better turn around," said Ivan as he turned the rutter and shouted, "Watch for the boom."

Peter turned his attention to Caterina. He repeated, 'Do you know what that means, Caterina? 'Watch for the boom' is to duck your head when the sail switches sides. I'll make sure you're safe."

He stayed close as they lowered their heads, allowing the sail to pass over. A light rain started as they sailed toward the dock. Caterina didn't prepare for rain. Everyone else zipped up their jackets and threw their hoods over their heads. Why didn't Peter remind her it was going to rain? She felt childish to rely on him as if she didn't have a weather app and could check the forecast herself.

They moored the boat before the sky opened up and hovered under the awning to avoid the rain. "I didn't think it was going to start raining for several more hours," said Ivan apologetically to his guests. Everyone thanked him for a fun outing on the water.

"I don't know if I want to drive back to New Jersey tonight," said Tatiana. "I might just get a hotel. I hate driving in the rain."

"You can stay with me, Tatiana," said Ivan nonchalantly.

Caterina let out a nervous laugh. "What? With Justine, your wife, at home?" she said to herself. She decided to snap a picture of Ivan and Tatiana to send to Justine. She didn't know what to make of the coincidence. She needed time alone to process the day.

"How are you doing, Ivan?" Peter asked his friend sincerely when they could finally stand eye to eye. There was gravity to his question, and Ivan responded with equal gravity. "I'm certain I'm doing the right thing, Petrov. The world deserves the truth about the war, even if all sides want a certain narrative. War is messy, and we can't be cowards to the pressure to hide the truth for their narrative."

"The narrative is their truth, though, Ivan. We are insignificant. You saw how Dmitry got carried out of the courtroom surrounded by his thugs waving their flags. Dmitry got away with his crimes ten years ago. Why do you think he won't again?"

It was a fair question that Ivan had asked himself countless times. He had crossed the Rubicon, and he felt no regrets. "I could not live with myself if I didn't expose Dmitry. I made my decision."

Peter hugged him and gave Tatiana two kisses on her cheeks. "Nice to meet you, Tatiana. I will try to make it to Brooklyn this summer. Maybe you could come back in June. We want to go to a Leonid & Friends concert. We'd love to see you again." Peter and Tatiana continued speaking, and Ivan was standing next to Caterina.

She felt uncomfortable, but his eyes seemed filled with kindness and sadness.

Finally, Ivan spoke. "Peter told me he told you about his brother, Alexsei. They were very close, and I'm glad he feels safe with you to open up. He's a good boy, Caterina. A good boy," he repeated, gazing over at Peter. "Take care of him."

His sincerity threw her off balance. Her head was spinning with contradictions and facts.

"Do you want to share an Uber?" asked Peter, and it took her a while to realize he was talking to her and referencing Ivan.

She didn't want to be near Ivan, Tatiana, or even Peter at this moment. She just wanted to escape. "No, it's just a mile and a half. I like to walk in the rain." She said her goodbyes quickly and walked away from the boathouse. She didn't give Peter a chance to weigh in on the decision and didn't care if he followed her, but he did, walking briskly to catch up to her after he said goodbye to Ivan.

"Why don't you want to get an Uber? You'll be soaking wet," he walked quickly to match her stride.

She walked along Lewis Wharf with her head held high, trying to process the day.

"What's wrong, Caterina? Are you mad at me?"

She was silent, and he was genuinely confused, but this was their first fight, and he didn't know how to navigate. He was probably going to mess it up by guessing her thoughts.

"Are you mad about Tatiana? I don't like her, you know. It was just fun to talk to someone who knows my culture. I'm sure you would do the same thing about Italian food."

Caterina stopped suddenly at the absurdity of his theory. "It's not Tatiana." She pointed a finger at Peter. "How do you even know that's his cousin? What do you know about her?"

"What?" This accusation was out of left field, and he could not counter it. "I . . . I don't know, I guess. What do you mean? He said she was his cousin. Why would he lie?"

Pearl by the Sea

Caterina knew their argument would be futile. She would try hard to keep her new case and her personal interests separate. She had been injecting herself into her clients' lives too much, but she and Peter had to be on the same page communicating.

"What about Justine? What about Ivan's wife?" shouted Caterina.

Peter looked confused at her response. "What, what are you talking about? I never told you about some Justine. Who's Justine?"

"His wife," shouted Caterina as the skies opened up and the rain poured down. Peter grabbed her by the arm, and they ran for shelter under the huge underpass of the Boston Harbor Hotel. The enormous American flag hanging from the ceiling bellowed slightly in the wind.

"His wife? Are you googling my friend? Where did you come up with that name?"

Caterina had to tell him. She knew she was breaking Justine's trust, but this felt too coincidental not to explain to Peter. Of all the private investigators, why would Justine pick Caterina?

"Last Saturday, the day before we went to my brothers', I got a new client who wanted me to follow her husband to see if he was cheating on her. She gave me their address, his work address, his car make and model—everything. She wanted a woman PI to follow him around. I staked out his house and work and sent her some photos. I didn't have any leads until today."

Peter's confusion turned into more worry. He was desperate for her to finish the story. "Who? Who was the target? Ivan? Some woman paid you to spy on Ivan?"

"Yes, Justine, his *wife*," answered Caterina.

The wind gusted through the archway, waving the flag. Peter took Caterina by both shoulders and made sure he had her attention.

"Caterina, Ivan is *not* married. I don't know who Justine is, but she is not his wife. Someone is lying to you." Now, it was Peter's turn to fill in some pieces for Caterina. Some pieces of the puzzle he didn't know, but it was clear that this had to be related to his research on Dmitry Panchenko. He didn't want to be drawn into the war. He didn't want to draw her into the war, but that was the thing about this conflict: it would find you.

Caterina's hands were shaking. She wasn't sure if she was nervous, cold, or a combination of both. Her raw fingers typed Justine Kanovsky, and nothing showed up on google. She texted Justine's phone that they should meet. No response. *Ivan is not married*, she repeated Peter's words in her mind. What was going on?

"Let's get you an Uber to go home, Caterina."

"What?" She said, bewildered. "Where are you going?"

"I need to go see Ivan. I need to warn him that someone is following him. Someone who might not want his paper to be published. Think about it. Why would someone pay you to spy on Ivan?"

"I don't understand," pleaded Caterina. "Can I go with you?"

"It's okay, Caterina. I don't want you involved. I don't know what is happening, but whoever is spying on Ivan should not have dragged you into this. It's my fault. I was not supposed to be happy. I knew this was all too good to be true. The war has found me."

Pearl by the Sea

Chapter 15

THE RAIN BECAME heavier as Ivan drove home from Shaw's. He switched his windshield wipers to high as he struggled with the glaring headlights of other cars affecting his vision. He hated to drive at night in the rain. Years of sitting in front of a computer screen made his vision poor. He adjusted his glasses and posture to try to see better. He turned on to St. Paul Street and pulled his Rav4 into the driveway. He instinctively looked into his rearview mirror and turned his head side to side to scan the street. The neighborhood appeared quiet for a Sunday. But he felt unsettled and would have preferred people around. It felt eerily quiet.

He opened his trunk and carried his two grocery bags into the house. He didn't buy much food when he went shopping. He made simple meals, and most nights, he cooked and ate alone. That isn't what he preferred, but it was inevitable he'd be a bachelor when his work and home life blended into one. He had been obsessed with the Ukrainian uprising in 2014 and had spent every waking minute pouring over data about the war. Ivan spent countless hours analyzing home videos, eyewitness testimonies, and CCTV footage. His expertise in data forensics and big data analysis as an engineer gave him an advantage over most researchers. Tomorrow, he will send his paper to independent media, which will be willing to publish his findings. It was mainly about the Ukrainian soldier Dmitry Panchenko, who committed war crimes since the beginning of the upheaval in 2014. Dmitry was the one who beat up Petrov when he was on the ground, helpless with burning flesh and two broken heels. Dmitry was the one who tossed a grenade into a checkpoint, injuring nine people. That was just the beginning. What Ivan uncovered would shake him to the core. He knew the Ukrainian government and the United States government knew about Panchenko's war crimes in Bucha, Ukraine. He knew they knew because he sent his paper to every congressman, including the Senate Intelligence Committee.

Dmitry Panchenko, a Pro-Unity extremist to the core, had been allowed to fail up again and again. In fact, he was protected at the highest levels. His crimes in Bucha were covered up, and he was whisked far away from the battlefield and transferred to a desk job in Washington, D.C., working for the State Department on behalf of the Ukrainian government. Ivan also knew he frequented Dubai in the United Arab Emirates, staying in his multimillion-dollar condominium. The amount of embezzlement from military contracts to Ukraine by those who were supposed to disperse the money was staggering. His financial crimes fit right in with others at the top, which wasn't why he stood out. It was his ruthless hatred toward Russian Ukrainians who were sympathetic to Russia that caused him to cross the line of human rights abuse beyond his direct orders.

Ivan felt the house was just as quiet as the street outside, and he went to grab his phone to put on some music. Then he realized he left his phone in the car, which he often did as an absentminded professor. He had no desire to go back out into the rain and decided to leave it there to retrieve in the morning. He walked over to his computer to play Spotify but sat down to write an email instead. He wanted to tell someone about his paper coming out tomorrow before he would hit "send" to the world. It was the least he could do after all Peter had gone through.

A chill suddenly ran through Ivan. He needed to get out of his wet clothes. He entered his bedroom and watched a flash of light from car headlights scan across the wall. He closed his curtains and held his breath. He felt more spooked by shutting out the light from the outside world than he did from the silence. His Victorian home always made old house sounds, but tonight, the start of the furnace felt as loud as a jet engine and made his heart pound.

Ivan had a history of arrhythmias and hoped he wasn't going into afib. He walked into the bathroom. His stocking feet hit a creaky floorboard. He stopped in his tracks, listening intently to see if the creak came from him or someone else. He stood as still as a statue, concentrating on the sounds around him. The upstairs unit was active, and he could hear muffled sounds of clatter in their kitchen. He exhaled, not realizing he was holding his breath. He opened his mirrored medicine cabinet to take his heart medication with a bottle of water. When he closed the cabinet, he saw movement behind his reflection. He jerked his body around and drew in a quick breath.

There was nothing behind him visually, but he knew it was there. He had no gun in the house. He had no weapons. His phone was in the car, and he had no landline. He felt exposed and vulnerable. He never felt the need to defend himself before, but survival instincts drew him into the kitchen to get a weapon, maybe a knife or a frying pan. He tiptoed to the kitchen doorway and saw a shadow on the other side of the room. He sidestepped toward the knife block to find protection. The shadow walked closer and stared at Ivan with his demonic eyes.

"You," were the last words Ivan spoke. The last object he saw was a flash of steel from a large knife. The warm, sticky blood from his jugular vein was the last thing he felt as his hand reached for his cut throat. And "*Die, Colorado, die*" whispered into his ear were the last words he heard on this earth.

Caterina sat at her kitchen island wearing her cozy pajamas, sipping some hot green tea, waiting to hear from Peter. She had taken a hot shower when she got home from their sailing adventure but still felt a chill after putting on her warm socks. She raised the heat to seventy even though she usually liked it cooler. She had not heard back from Justine, and her only contact with her was the cell number and an email. She plugged the cell phone number into a people finder's website she subscribed to. She had so many subscriptions to look up personal information, including criminal records. The cellphone number didn't turn up to any individual. She looked up Justine Kanovsky again, and no name came up. Did Justine even give her a last name? She assumed it was Ivan's last name but never asked Justine for her license or any other documentation. Caterina felt like an idiot. She was given cash by some stranger in Starbucks to stalk Ivan, and she showed no skepticism. Geico jobs were easy and verified by the insurance company. She had never had a contract outside of the system, and she was sloppy. If she was going to have a career in investigation, she needed to hone her skills.

Her phone buzzed, indicating Peter was in the lobby. She buzzed him in with the apartment's app on her phone. He tapped lightly on the door, and she jumped off her stool quickly to open the door. He looked disheveled in his soaking wet clothes, and his expression was full of worry. She quickly pulled him into the apartment, hugged him, and kissed him. She didn't care she was getting wet and felt warmer in his embrace than she had in the comfort of her apartment by herself.

"Do you see Ivan? Did you tell him about Justine?"

Peter shook his head no. "His car wasn't in the driveway, and I waited an hour on his street. He's not returning my calls or texts. I'm worried about him. Who the hell sent Justine to you?"

"Maybe we should call the police?"

"That's a good idea. They can swing by his place and do a well check on him. Can you call? I'm a bit nervous about my English, and I feel you will get a better response. I'm sorry, does that make sense?"

"Sure, of course." Caterina dialed the main number. Dialing 911 felt like an overreaction. She explained she could not get in touch with her friend and was concerned. The police officer asked when she last saw Ivan, and she stated that it was about four hours ago. The dispatch explained they did not go out until twenty-four hours of noncontact and to call back then.

"I'm sure he's fine," Peter tried to convince himself. "He strikes me as the kind of guy not attached to his phone. I'm sure he will text me later. I don't know all the circumstances surrounding his research, but I think he was protecting me by not telling me the whole story. He wrote many articles about Dmitry Panchenko, the guy who assaulted me the day my brother died. He has been my biggest advocate over the years to share what really happened that day at the Trade Unions Building. When I visited him at his office the other day, he told me he was publishing a big paper with new information. He knew the international community ignored his previous research. People labeled him a Putin sympathizer because he dared tell the truth about May 2, 2014. No one ever wanted to hear a narrative that goes against the Pro-Unity crowd. Any bad press about Zelensky's army was quickly dismissed because nuance is dead."

Peter sadly smiled at Caterina. "Have you ever heard the term 'bifurcation fallacy'? It means if something is bad, then the other thing must be good. With the United States sanctioning Russia and financially supporting Ukraine, all news from Russia has to be bad, and all news from the Ukrainian government must be good. There is no room for any nuance. Ivan is trying to inject nuance into a story, which is not allowed."

Caterina listened, but she did not understand. She's unsure

she could find Ukraine on a map, and terms like Pro-Unity meant little to her. She understood that Peter and Alexsei were caught up in a kind of civil war in their city of Odessa on May 2nd, and there was a fire, and his brother died, but she only cared about Peter's happiness and rarely thought about the war.

She made Peter a cup of tea and squeezed in some honey. He held his tea in his hands, feeling the steam on his face and enjoying her kindness. He placed it on the counter with his fingers still touching the mug. His lip quivered, and his eyes welled with tears that did not fall. "Do you want to hear something crazy? My mom and dad go over to the Trade Unions Building every May 2nd to place a bouquet where my brother and forty-two other Ukrainians died that day. Other families do the same thing. They say a prayer, light memorial candles, or place an item that belonged to their loved one there. Within hours, the Odessa police will confiscate their makeshift memorial. One year, a man was so distraught about his deceased wife, who died in the fire, that he camped out next to his flowers. The police arrested him when he tried to prevent them from removing his memorial. That's a bifurcation fallacy in a nutshell. No one cares for Russian Ukrainians who voted for President Yanukovych and died in a fire protesting a coup. You aren't even allowed to call 2014 a 'coup,' or else you are called a Putin puppet. No one cares about my brother, and they want his death to be ignored. He's an inconvenience, and so am I."

"Who wants it ignored?" asked Caterina.

"Everyone," answered Peter.

They both sat in silence, drinking their tea. Peter checked

his phone from time to time. Caterina checked her email. She had an email from Geico asking her to take on a new investigation. She replied no to the offer, the first time she's ever turned down a job.

Peter sighed with relief when he clicked on his email. "Ivan's safe. He sent me an email an hour ago. Thank God."

Peter read through the email, and Caterina read it over his shoulder. It was in the form of a letter with an attachment.

Petrov,

I want to again extend my sympathy and condolences to you and your parents over the death of your dear brother, Alexsei. I never had the privilege to teach him at the university, but my colleagues told me he was a bright student with great potential. That is what this war has done: cut down so many young men and women in the prime of their lives. America thinks this war started in February 2022, when Putin crossed the border, but you know the majority of us in Eastern Ukraine know the war started long before. Ten thousand died in Donbass from 2014 to 2022, and the world was silent. Civilians were bombed by their own countrymen who were caught in the crossfire. War criminals like Dmitry Panchenko were carried out of courtrooms as heroes even though they inflicted cruelty on their own people. We are all Ukrainians, and we bleed the same and mourn our dead with the same sadness. I don't know how my life will change after tomorrow when I expose Panchenko's embezzlement and war crimes in Bucha, but my research is irrefutable. It may be ignored like my May 2nd research, but I have no regrets about exposing the truth.

God bless you, Peter. Ukraine will forever be a pawn. The angels' tears have created many pearls in Odessa. May the Lord Have Mercy on Us All.

Respect,
Ivan

They read his email several times. Caterina again did not understand Dmitry's research, but he was clearly affected by the death of Peter's brother. "What does he mean about angels' tears creating pearls?" asked Caterina.

"When I went to his office several weeks ago, he showed me an oyster in his office and explained to me the tears of angels created the pearl inside. It's an old myth to describe why something so pure as a pearl could be found in the Black Sea. As I told you, Odessa's nickname is Pearl of the Black Sea."

A tear spilled from Peter's gray eyes, and Caterina kissed his wet cheek, wishing she could kiss his pain away. Her love for him was not enough to fill the hole in his heart, but he was grateful for her compassion. He had hoped that Ivan's research would close the chapter on Alexsei's death, but he never felt closure. He didn't think revealing more evidence would ease his sorrow but could understand Ivan's desire to expose the truth. Whatever he read from Ivan's report, he was prepared to read in full. He would not turn away from the horrors of the war. His classmates have given their lives to fight the Russians, so the least he could do was read a paper a fellow Ukrainian wrote.

With trepidation, Peter clicked on the link to open Ivan Kanovsky's paper titled *Ukraine, Forever a Pawn*, on the attachment. His phone screen displayed a "404 error—the website cannot be found." He refreshed his email and tried several more times to open it.

"Maybe he changed his mind and didn't want to send it to you early, Peter. We will read it tomorrow when he sends it to the world. Let's go to sleep, Peter. It's been a very long day."

Caterina held his hand and led him into the bedroom. She helped undress him out of his wet clothes and held him tight beneath the covers. She had never felt such heat or passion before and was spent afterward. He lay fast asleep in the safety of her love. She tiptoed out of bed to lower the room temperature and then snuggled up against his warm, beautiful body and closed her eyes.

Chapter 16

CATERINA OPENED HER eyes when her alarm went off. She immediately checked her phone for any news of Ivan Kanovsky but saw nothing recent. She rolled over and hugged Peter quickly, then hopped out of bed to meet with her 7:00 a.m. client.

Peter opened his eyes when his alarm went off. He immediately checked his phone for any messages or news about Ivan and saw nothing. He rolled over, rubbing her side of the bed, smiling, remembering the hug this morning and their night last night. He hopped out of bed to teach his class at UMASS.

"I bumped into McDreamy making coffee in the kitchen this morning," Kimmie texted Cat around noon. "I'm making my arugula salad for dinner, and I want to hear all about your sailing adventure. See you tonite." She finished the text with emojis that made Cat laugh.

Caterina's phone buzzed as soon as she put it down. It was Peter wanting to FaceTime. She clicked accept and smiled when she saw his face. "Hello, my love," were his first words, and she thought her heart would melt. "I'm on lunch break between classes and thought I'd check in."

"Same. My lunch was yogurt and granola, which I ate in two seconds, and now I'm still hungry," complained Caterina lightheartedly.

"Well, we did burn a lot of calories last night. That was quite a night," Peter responded playfully.

Caterina turned red with the discussion of her late-night passion being talked about in the daytime. She switched topics quickly. "Any word from Ivan? I've been refreshing my phone all day. I would have thought some news outlets would carry his story."

Peter sighed, "No, nothing, which is a bit worrisome. The only communication with him was the email with the broken link. He hasn't texted me back. I have checked every reporter and news outlet I can think of, but I have not seen his paper. He will be very disappointed if his research is ignored again. Poor Ivan. I will ride my bike over there after work to check on him, and honestly, if I don't hear from him, I want to call the police when it's been twenty-four hours."

Caterina nodded and agreed with him. "I'll drive you over when I get out of work. After all, I do know where his house is after stalking him." She tried to make a joke, but it just brought to the surface the unknown of who hired her to spy on Ivan.

"No," said Peter firmly. "I don't want to draw you into this anymore. I'm trying to figure out how to tell Ivan about my girlfriend spying on him after being hired by his fake wife. It's probably better if I explain it alone. I will stop by your apartment after."

They said their goodbyes and hung up. "He said 'girlfriend,'"

Caterina smiled to herself.

After work, she sauntered to the Starbucks where she met with the fake wife, Justine, last Saturday. She ordered a venti and sat in the same seat. She remembered Justine wore sunglasses and sat with her back to the cash register. Caterina checked the cameras and wondered how sophisticated the CCTV was and from how many angles. When there was a lull in customers, she walked back up to the register and asked to speak to the manager. A man in his thirties approached her and put on his insincere, caring face when a customer complained.

"Hi, hi, my name is Caterina. Um, I was in here last Saturday, and, well, this is a weird question, but I sat right there, and my friend sat in that chair. Is there a way to see your CCTV of that day? I have the exact time we were here from my texts." Caterina turned her phone around to show some texts.

The manager changed expressions to a more natural one since this wasn't someone bitching about putting soy milk in instead of oat milk. "I don't know anything about that stuff. That's not part of my job description. I think these stores have some private security company that manages that stuff." He went in the back and pulled out a four-inch binder. "It's some global cybersecurity company owned by this guy Manish Gupta. I don't know, but I guess you should call his company. I just report to my boss, who takes care of any issues. I mean, I'm not going to waste his time asking about this shit. I guess you could get a subpoena or something."

The manager was getting into the conversation as it was something he never thought of before. He started talking about other branches that have been robbed or people doing drugs in bathrooms. "We don't allow bathroom access here, which really cuts down on crazy shit. Why do you want to see the video? Is your friend a sketch or something?"

His inquiries were getting to her line of thought, and she just raised her eyebrows with a smirk. "Okay, thanks for your help. Great service, by the way." She threw in the compliment for no particular reason.

"Okay, see you tomorrow, Caterina. Let me know how you make out."

She stopped in her tracks when he said her name. Then she realized he had written it hundreds of times on her iced coffee. She now felt embarrassed she didn't know his name. She'd make it a point to read his name tag tomorrow. "Okay, see you tomorrow."

She sat on a bench halfway between Starbucks and the condo and pulled out her phone to check the news again. She first checked her email and saw the subject line of the *Boston Patch* email that always got her to click the story. "*BU professor murdered by . . .*" was the subject that she felt was a crazy coincidence, and she clicked on the story. It continued from the clickbait. "*BU professor murdered by stabbing in his residence Sunday night after what may have been a robbery. Engineering Professor Ivan Kanovsky was found by police this afternoon after neighbors complained his car had not moved so they could get to work this morning. Police found the victim with multiple stab wounds in his apartment, and an investigation is underway.*"

Caterina dropped her ice coffee on the sidewalk, and it

splattered on her pants and on a passerby who swore at her and kept walking. She didn't bother picking up the plastic cup. She had to walk to change position to see if the words she just read would scramble into a new reality. She stopped abruptly on the sidewalk and reread the story, but it read exactly the same. Ivan was dead. Ivan was murdered. She never met anyone who was murdered. She felt like she was living in some crime show.

She tried to call Peter, but he was still in class. *Oh, poor Peter*, was her first thought that he would be sad for his friend. *Oh, poor Ivan being murdered* was her second thought. Then a flood of thoughts and questions invaded her mind. Did *she* lead the murderer to Ivan? Was someone spying on her while she spied on Ivan? She looked around to see if she was being watched. Then she walked quickly back to her condo to get to the safety of her home.

She opened the door and found Kimmie in the kitchen. "Oh my God, what's wrong, Cat? What happened?" asked Kimmie when she saw how distraught Cat looked.

Caterina paced back and forth, moving her hands frantically with the same motion. "He's dead. Ivan is dead."

"Who's Ivan?" asked Kimmie.

"Peter's friend, the guy who took us sailing."

"Oh my God! Did he drown or something? Did you guys crash? Are you okay?"

Caterina violently shook her head. "He was murdered. Killed. He was alive yesterday. I met him, and now he's dead. I'm freaking out." Caterina handed Kimmie her phone to read the *Boston Patch* article.

"Oh my God, that's horrible. Crime is so bad in this city. That's not a bad part of town, either. Thank God we have good security around here. I don't think I'd want a unit at street level. Freaks me out a bit."

Caterina shook her head again. She could never explain this story to Kimmie to have her make sense of it. She couldn't even make sense of it now. What was she going to tell her? Ivan was probably murdered because he was exposing a skinhead war criminal who had a Nazi tattoo that also happened to be the guy who beat the shit out of Peter when he jumped out of a burning building with his now-dead brother? How would she tell her beautiful, innocent Kimmie that story? Tears started to flow from Caterina's eyes. She hugged Kimmie tight, slobbering on her shoulder. She pulled away to get some paper towels to blow her nose. Her eyes were bloodshot from crying.

A firm, quick three knocks were heard at their front door, making both Kimmie and Caterina jump. No one ever knocked on their door since they had the lobby buzz system. Kimmie walked over to the peephole and saw two men and a woman in matching jackets standing closely together. "What the fuck?" She motioned for Cat to look through the small, round opening. The people knocked again, which made them both jump again.

"FBI, please open up."

"What do we do?" whispered Cat to Kimmie. She opened the door with the latch still on. "Hello?" said Cat through the crack of the door.

The woman leaned close to the crack. "Good afternoon.

We're so sorry to barge in without notice. We just wanted to speak with Ms. Antonucci about an incident involving Ivan Kanovsky." She had a friendly tone, and Cat answered, "One second," and closed the door to undo the latch and let them in.

The three entered in an almost comical way to not be unobtrusive, but it was still very jarring for the two roommates. The three agents pulled out their badges, and Cat spotted the gun on the woman's holster under her dark blue FBI jacket emblazoned with the word FBI in yellow.

"Hello, I'm Agent Kevin Auten of the Boston Field Office," said the taller man. "I have some sad news about Ivan Kanovsky." The agent hesitated a bit, and Kimmie jumped in.

"We just read about it on *Boston Patch*. Did you guys catch whoever stabbed the guy?"

The agent looked at Kimmie but ignored her and returned to speaking gently with Caterina. "Yes, I'm afraid there has been a stabbing. We want to ask you a few questions, Ms. Antonucci, if you don't mind. We would like you to come to our office for a quick conversation about yesterday's events. As you can imagine, time is always a factor in these cases."

Kimmie's eyes went wide as if she were watching a TV show play out. Caterina glanced over at Kimmie nervously. She wished she had time to explain about Justine and Ivan and the Ukraine war, but there was no time. "How do I know you guys aren't imposters?"

The FBI agent Kevin sighed, slightly irritated, and quickly tried to cover his response with a grimaced smile. "Pull up the FBI Boston headquarters website on your phone. Dial the main number, press 7 when prompted, and tell the operator my name and your name."

It sounded like she wasn't the first person to ask this question. These guys probably played out this same scene all the time. She did as they said, and the woman on the phone confirmed the agents' arrival.

"Do I have to go?" was Caterina's second question, and again, Kevin smiled and gave his rehearsed response.

"You are under no obligation to go with us. You are certainly not a suspect; you are just one of dozens of people we question to gather information about any particular case. We appreciate any cooperation that may help us in our investigation. It is purely voluntary."

Caterina nodded and understood. Why wouldn't she cooperate? She wanted to help Peter and his friend Ivan. She asked her final question. "Can I call my friend before I go?" Agent Auten gave his partner a quick glance and then once again plastered his insincere smile on his face. "We ask if you wouldn't mind handing us your phone now for the journey." He pulled out a plastic bag. "We will give it back to you when we are through. We won't be together for more than a couple of hours. Do you understand?"

She didn't understand. This was all new to her. She never met an FBI person before or knew someone who was murdered and desperately wanted to speak to the man she loved. She sheepishly dropped the phone in the bag and said goodbye to Kimmie, whose eyes were still as wide as saucers.

They drove up Route 1 North to 201 Maple St., Chelsea,

and pulled into the parking lot of a modern-looking, eight-story building that was FBI headquarters. It was positioned between the Hilton Logan Hotel and Chelsea Middle School and seemed very inviting, with a large green landscaped grass area lined with maple trees. "Our building is one of the leading buildings in Boston for a zero carbon footprint," the female FBI agent bragged as if this meant anything to Caterina. They walked her through the metal detector in front, which they were allowed to circumvent, and chatted in a friendly manner with the officer positioned in the lobby. Then they took the elevator to the fourth floor and entered a small room with a few chairs.

Agent Kevin was clearly in charge of the questioning, and the others jotted down notes and listened to the exchange.

"So, for the record, could you give us your full name and date of birth?"

"Caterina Antonucci, date of birth June 2, 1995."

"Ms. Antonucci, how well did you know Ivan Kanovsky?"

"I didn't know him. I mean, I only met him once, yesterday. That's it. I don't know him."

"How do you know Petrov Leonidovich?"

"Who?" Then she realized they were talking about Peter. "Peter? I met him at my gym, Life Time gym in Seaport. I'm a personal trainer there, and he was my client."

"I see. You were assigned to him?"

"Assigned? Well, not really. He came to my office and asked for sessions."

"I see, and he asked for you personally?"

The memory was so flirty and fun. She could remember it like yesterday. He made her blush when she looked into his sexy gray eyes and said, "I want you."

"Well, I guess he did. I mean, I was the first trainer to do his questionnaire," she answered, omitting the color of his eyes and his sandalwood smell.

"When did you start having a romantic relationship with Petrov Leonidovich?"

She hadn't. She started having a romantic relationship with sexy Peter Geller, who had great legs, not some guy named Leonidovich. "Um, I guess after his first session, he asked me out, and, you know, we've kind of been dating since."

The two agents were scribbling away in their notebooks. She felt uneasy with how many details they knew about her life so quickly. Was Peter in the next room answering questions? Did he mention anything about her beautiful eyes and falling in love with her? Did he call her his girlfriend to the agents?

"Is Peter here?" she asked, but they ignored her question.

"Was there any time of day yesterday you could not account for the whereabouts of Mr. Leonidovich?"

She wished he'd stop calling him by that name. She didn't know the person they were referring to. She replayed the timeline of events from their walk over to the Boston Sailing Center to their night of lovemaking. It seemed like weeks ago. "Um," her voice started to quiver. "We were worried because we hadn't heard from Ivan, so Peter went by his place to check on him. He saw his car was not in the driveway and then returned to my place."

Pearl by the Sea

"I see. What was the time frame you were apart from him?"

"I don't know. Maybe four hours? From 4:00 p.m. to 8:00 p.m., perhaps. Roughly something like that."

The FBI agents scribbled. Caterina rubbed her hands together firmly.

"You said you didn't know Ivan Kanovsky. Why were you stalking him in front of his house and at his workplace?"

The question threw her off. She started to feel light-headed and dizzy. The female officer pushed her water bottle closer to encourage her to drink. Caterina unscrewed the plastic cap with a shaky hand and took a sip.

"Um, this is a bit of a long story." She rubbed her hands together again. "Should I have a lawyer or something?" She hardly expected to feel so unsettled. She didn't know what to expect when she volunteered to come down to FBI headquarters.

"That is certainly your right. You are not a suspect; this is simply gathering as much information as possible about an investigation. We can stop today's questions, but then we must reschedule and coordinate with you and a lawyer. We want to get started on the case as quickly as possible. Does that make sense?"

It made sense to her. She had nothing to hide. She wanted to help them solve the murder, so why did she feel she was betraying Peter? Was her story believable? Some stranger pretended to be Ivan's wife and paid Caterina to stalk Ivan. She realized the FBI could easily subpoena the CCTV footage at Starbucks. Her skepticism turned to optimism that they could get to the bottom of who set her up to spy on Ivan. She explained to them about the woman who contacted her, what she wore, and what she looked like, and she even offered to hand over the hundred-dollar bills Justine gave Caterina. She would now definitely file that money in her taxes next year. She made a mental note to remind herself to jot that down. If the FBI knew, the IRS would find out too.

They thanked her for her time and drove her back to the condo, giving her the iPhone when she got out of the car.

It was well after 9:00 p.m. when she got home, and she was starving. Kimmie gave her the leftover salad and some bread. She gulped it down and handed her a beer.

"Peter came by while you were gone about an hour ago. He looked super worried you hadn't called him."

"I know. I saw his texts. I'm going to call him right after I eat. What a crazy day. I feel so bad for Peter. He's had so many deaths in his life. I don't think he can handle another one. War sucks."

Caterina took a sip of her Sam Adams, and Kimmie was confused about what war she was talking about and what it had to do with a robbery.

"Okay, sweetheart, I have to get to work soon. Are you going to be okay? Do you want me to have Jack come over to keep you company? He would, y'know."

"No, that's all right. I'm so tired. I'd feel like I'd have to hang out and tell the whole story again. I just want to go to bed."

"Okay, Peter was really sweet. He was very worried about you."

Worried about her or worried about what she told the

police? She shook the thought out of her head. The FBI was just being thorough, asking so many questions.

She said good night to Kimmie and changed into her cozies. Then she dialed Peter on FaceTime, and he answered right away. He was in a black T-shirt and sweatpants and looked freshly showered. She could imagine his sandalwood scent through the phone. He ran his hand through his dark hair, which was still a bit damp. He had the beginnings of stubble from the end of the day that made him look even more handsome.

"Hey," said Caterina.

"Kimmie told me the FBI came by. I talked to them briefly at the apartment. Poor Ivan. I'm in shock. I should've waited for him to come home. I should have gone back last night."

Caterina reassured him he had done nothing wrong. "We called the police. You went by to check on him. How the hell were we supposed to know he'd be killed? We were only going to tell him about Justine, not warn him he was going to be . . ." She couldn't even utter the word *murdered*.

"I know, I know, you're right. Poor Ivan. All he cared about was his research. Maybe he was threatened, and that's why the link didn't work. Maybe that's why it wasn't in the papers. He might've resisted demands from one of Dmitry Panchenko's thugs. Panchenko must've heard that he was releasing evidence against him. I have no idea how he would have known, but he must've found out."

Peter rubbed his hand through his hair again. He looked so distressed about his friend's death. "I am so sorry to bring you into my pain, Caterina. You didn't sign up for this when we went on that first date. If I had any idea I was putting you in harm's way, I would have never walked into your office. I'm sorry."

Caterina's eyes started to well. A tear trickled down her cheek. Peter wanted to jump through the phone to hold her. It was the same feeling he had after their first date at Oysters on the Bay in Seaport. He wanted to pick her up in his arms and carry her away to a faraway place, in a time long ago. Tahiti or the Nile, a few kisses ago. He wanted her to know he had loved her for many lifetimes. The beautiful woman on the phone was someone who he had always loved.

"I remember you," he whispered in a husky voice, referencing the Nat King Cole song he sang to her. "I remember you," he whispered again, touching the screen with his hand.

She placed her hand on the screen to touch his. "I love you too, Peter. I always have."

Suddenly, a large boom shook their world. Peter dropped the phone that landed facedown. All Caterina could see was darkness, but she could hear the shouts.

"Put your hands up! Put your hands up! Don't move! Put your hands up!"

She screamed into the phone, but no one answered. "Peter! What's going on? What's happening?"

It was eerily quiet as she heard shuffling, and she finally heard Peter shout in desperation. "I love you, Caterina. I love you with all my heart, my perla."

The darkness turned to light as she saw Agent Kevin Auten's face on her phone and his hand getting closer to the screen to turn it off.

Pearl by the Sea

Chapter 17

CATERINA COULD NOT get out of bed. She texted Kenneth she was not coming to work and threw the covers over her head. Kimmie checked on her every couple of hours, but Caterina ignored her offers of coffee or food. When Cat still had not left her bed in the afternoon, Kimmie called Caterina's parents, who drove over to take her home.

Caterina did not resist. She stumbled into the car and stared out the window like a zombie. The ride took twenty minutes to her childhood home in Medford. There, she resumed the same position, curled up in her bed, not speaking to anyone. She texted in sick the next day. She started the day the same as yesterday, comatose from the shock of the arrest of Peter. She guessed it was an arrest. He hadn't called her and probably used his one call to contact a lawyer. Caterina's dad called to inquire about his whereabouts, but local police were at a loss, and federal police would not disclose any information.

Caterina's mom, Arlene, cautiously approached her daughter with offers to make her soup or a sandwich, but Caterina shook her head, whispering, "No, thank you." She was numb to the situation. Usually, when she was stressed, she could revert to her lists. She would run through her lists of presidents or metacarpal bones, but her body had no desire to combat her pain. Pain actually would've been welcomed. This was worse than pain, as it felt like she no longer existed.

Arlene and Caterina's dad, Aldo, whispered outside her room, debating how to help her. Caterina could hear the concern in their voices, but she made no attempt to assuage their worry.

On Thursday morning, Caterina forced herself out of bed to go to work. She slept-walked, getting dressed in her uniform her mom washed. Her dad drove her to Seaport for work.

"I'll pick you up after work, sweetie," said her dad when he shifted the car into park. "Uncle Jimmy is going to come over tonight to talk to you and me about Peter and see if we can figure out what is happening."

Jimmy was Caterina's uncle, her mom's brother. He was the family member who got her interested in doing private investigator work, and she always thought he was a bit lazy with his research.

Caterina gave her dad a sad smile. "Thanks, Dad, for everything, but I'm just going to stay at my place tonight. I will be all right. Tell Uncle Jimmy thank you."

Aldo gave her hand a quick squeeze. "I'm sorry," he said vaguely, not sure what he meant with the comment.

Caterina managed to avoid conversations at work. She was aware of the whispered talk around her from clients and staff. She let her clients run through their routines without giving much input. Kenneth didn't assign her any new gym members. Even Kenneth was reserved in his interactions with Caterina.

"Do you think he killed his friend?"

"I heard they arrested him."

"I was swimming in the lane right next to him last week. He seemed like such a nice guy. I heard she was dating him. Poor girl."

Caterina walked the mile home from the gym to her condo. All she wanted to do was curl up in her bed again. She opened the door to her place and saw Jack and Kimmie sitting on the couch side by side as if they were waiting for her to come home. They both stood up and gave her quick hugs, but Caterina could feel Kimmie was holding back. Kimmie sat down quickly, pulled her oversized sweatshirt over her hands, and curled her feet up to make herself smaller. Jack leaned forward with his elbows on his thighs, furrowing his brow in a concerned look.

Caterina thought they might've heard from Peter. A flash of panic that he was dead crossed her mind. She collapsed into the chair next to the couch. "What?" she pleaded, "What?"

Jack spoke for both of them while Kimmie stayed quiet. "Cat, you know we love you. You know that, right?"

It wasn't Peter. This was something else.

"Cat, I'm sorry what happened to Peter. This royally sucks. I liked the guy. We both did. People can be like that."

What was Jack implying? People can be like what?

"It's just," Jack clenched his hands together, "Kimmie hasn't been sleeping since Sunday. She's scared, and it's putting her in a very bad situation."

Caterina looked at Kimmie, who avoided eye contact. Kimmie kept her eyes on Jack and dug her feet under him on the couch to draw them closer together. She pulled the sleeves of the sweatshirt farther over her hands.

"Right now," Jack continued, "we think it's probably better that you stay at your house where your mom and dad can care for you."

"What?" Caterina used her actual voice for the first time in two days, and it snapped her back to reality. "What are you saying, Kimmie?"

Jack got defensive that Caterina was trying to drag Kimmie into the conversation. "It's not Kimmie's fault, Caterina. I'm her fiancé and don't want her to be scared. I'm moving in today." Jack stared at Caterina. "You have to understand. She doesn't know Peter. Neither do you, really, and they just arrested the guy for killing someone. I mean, we're just as worried about you, Cat. I mean, thank God nothing happened to you, and you're safe. We just don't know the dude."

"I don't know Peter? You actually think Peter could *kill* someone?" Caterina's voice started to rise and shake. "I know him better than anyone on this planet. He's the kindest, smartest, most sensitive man I have ever known. I love him. He loves me. He did *not* fuckin' kill Ivan." Her voice faded a little, and tears flowed. "He didn't," she repeated in a whisper.

Jack was not going to be persuaded by tears. He was getting irritated when Caterina did not take Kimmie into consideration. "Jesus, Cat, Monday, you left Kimmie alone with the guy when you went to work. Do you know how irresponsible

Pearl by the Sea

that was? Do you?"

Caterina just gritted her teeth. She could not believe how quickly they turned on Peter. No one knows if he was arrested. No one knows anything. She felt alone in her concern and love for Peter. She felt everyone around her had dismissed him as a stranger and was ready to move on with their lives. How could anyone think Peter could kill someone? How could they believe he was guilty so quickly?

"Fine, I'll get my stuff." Caterina stood up to walk to her bedroom.

"Cat, there's no rush," Jack tried to be kind after his victory. "You can leave all your stuff here; no rush to move it out. Just take your time."

Caterina ignored his consolation and grabbed a suitcase to pack her toiletries and a few outfits to stay with her parents. It took her twenty minutes. She sat on her bed, staring at the wall. Her bedroom didn't have a view of the harbor. The room suddenly felt impersonal, not the home she had felt for the last few years. She rubbed her hand over the spot where she and Peter made love just a few days ago. She had never known such happiness and joy. He made her feel like she was truly loved. She tried to imagine what he was thinking and where he was. She felt his arms around her, hugging her close. Caterina's mind started a list. Facts about the case, people involved, evidence to be pursued. She wanted to know what happened to Ivan on Sunday night after the sailboat ride. She wanted to know what happened to the release of Ivan's paper and why the link did not work. She wanted to prove Peter's innocence.

Nothing else in her life felt more important than this moment in time. She needed to find out the truth.

Caterina pulled into the driveway of her house in Medford. She sat her parents down and told them everything she could about the situation. Her dad was a retired cop who could absorb the story's twists and turns. Arlene just got up midway through her story to go into the kitchen.

Later that night, Caterina moved her mom's Peloton bike out of the pathway from her bed to the bathroom so she wouldn't trip on it like she did last night. She supposed her mom planned to convert her bedroom into a workout room and didn't consider her daughter's preference for aesthetics in the decor. Caterina placed her laptop on the desk and began to research.

She googled "School of Ukrainian Ballet" in Brooklyn, New York, and called the number, asking for Tatiana. She left a message with her name and cellphone. She researched Tatiana, which was very easy as she heavily promoted her school on Instagram, TikTok, and Facebook.

She checked PACER, the federal courts' electronic record database, for any news on Peter. Nothing was there.

She searched for Ivan *Kanovsky + Petrov Leonidovich Geller*. She searched for Ivan *Kanovsky + Alexsei Leonidovich Geller*. She found Ivan's 2014 paper about the Trade Unions Building fire and researched the forty-two victims who died that day. She read in Ivan's paper that Dmitry Panchenko was arrested for beating up Peter, but his Pro-Unity comrades rushed the courtroom and carried him away from the trial. No judge would sit for the case because of death threats. She read how Ivan was criticized for his evidence showing Dmitry Panchenko was caught on camera throwing the grenade from a car at the Odessa checkpoint. The grenade injured nine people. She studied Dmitry Panchenko's face from the multiple photos that Ivan added to the paper. There was one with Dmitry and his Azov Battalion friends waving their red and black flags and wearing their Azov patch of the same black sun tattoo Dmitry had on his chest. There was a picture of Dmitry Panchenko shirtless, with his bald head shining from sweat. An AK-47 was across his chest under his black sun tattoo.

Caterina studied his face. Did this man send some thugs to kill Ivan? Caterina read Ivan's forty-seven-page paper that was very damning to Dmitry and then googled *Dmitry Panchenko + Odessa*. All the articles were very positive about Colonel Panchenko. She found no negative article outside of Ivan Kanovsky's 2014 paper. There was a picture of Panchenko standing in his camouflage outfit next to President Zelensky, receiving an award. There was another picture of him receiving the Stepan Bandera award from a Ukrainian general for his service in the SBU. Caterina researched the SBU, which was Ukraine's security service. She researched the name Stepan Bandera, who was a far-right leader in Ukraine during World War II who sided with Hitler at one point. His OUN-B group were radical militants who were controversial during the war. Pictures of Panchenko changed from army uniforms to suits, and it appeared he suffered an injury in the Bucha massacre in March 2022.

Bucha, Ukraine, was one of dozens of cities fought over since the start of the Russian invasion in February 2022. Panchenko appeared to transition to a more civilian job after these battles. Caterina read about his career over the last two years and scrolled to his most recent picture. Her hands started to shake as she hovered over the keyboard. She read the paragraphs under the picture. Dmitry Panchenko was working with the United States State Department in Washington, D.C., on behalf of the Ukrainian government. His vague role was facilitating a working partnership in both countries' efforts to defeat the Russians. Dmitry stood in an ill-fitting suit next to Secretary of State Antoinne Bucklin and the senator from Massachusetts, leader of the Senate Intelligence Committee, Eric Mason. Dmitry smiled with a crooked smile, clearly pleased to be taking a picture with these two men. Caterina zoomed onto his face. His black sun tattoo was covered up with his suit and tie, but he could not cover up his eyes. They stared back at Caterina, and she felt a chill run down her spine. He looked psychotic to her.

"Dinner," Arlene shouted up the stairs, and Caterina quickly slammed the laptop shut. She gripped her right hand with her left to steady the shaking. Dmitry Panchenko was in the United States.

Chapter 18

CATERINA PLANNED ON going by Peter's apartment after work to ask questions. She remembered she had paid for the Uber on the way home from their first date, so she found his address on the app. She Uber'd down so she wouldn't have to worry about a parking spot. She also felt a bit paranoid that someone might have tagged her car with a tracer.

She thought how easy her job would be surveilling people if she put a tagger on someone's car, but she tried to stay within the law with her tracking.

The Uber driver dropped her off in front of a triple-decker on Dorchester Ave. It was a bit run-down but appeared in better shape than many of the triple-decker homes on the street. Gentrification hadn't entirely made its way to the neighborhood, and she definitely would not want to roam these streets alone at night. She was near the infamous "Mass Cass" area, the intersection of Massachusetts Ave. and Melnea Cass Boulevard, known for its homeless shelters and methadone clinics.

She wasn't even sure what floor Peter lived on. She just knew he rented a room at this address. She knew his room was small. When they FaceTimed, it seemed a bit sparse. She wished she had screenshot one of their FaceTime chats so she could have his picture. She realized the only photo she had was of his selfie with his Starbucks coffee near her house. She pulled his photo up on her phone and knocked on the front door. She tried it, but it was locked. She tapped on the window on the first floor and saw a curtain move inside. She went over to the area of movement, heard the door open, and hustled back to the front door.

An older Asian woman wearing jeans and a T-shirt stood in front of her. She waited for Caterina to speak, looking skeptical at this solicitor.

"Hi, I'm Caterina Antonucci. My friend, Peter, Petrov, Peter Geller lives here."

Caterina turned the picture around and showed the woman.

"You police? So many police Monday. Broke my door. Five hundred dollars!"

Caterina was confused about what five hundred dollars meant. "Can I see his place? I-I left something there." Caterina showed her the picture again and the Uber ride information from a few weeks ago. "Friend, I'm Peter's friend," Caterina tapped her heart instinctively.

The woman waved her in and gestured for her to follow her up the stairs. They climbed two flights to the third floor. At the end of the hallway was a brand-new door next to chipped paint walls.

"Five hundred dollars for new door," the woman was clearly more annoyed with the broken door and not the fact her tenant was abducted in the middle of the night by a group of federal law enforcement officers.

Caterina pulled out three hundred-dollar bills for the woman. "For the door. Sorry about the door," even though she had nothing to do with breaking it down. "Can I go inside quickly and get my stuff?"

The landlord seemed happy about the cash and thanked her with a grateful smile. She took out her set of keys and used the shiniest key on the ring to unlock the new lock. "Go," she waved inside. "Come down and knock when done."

Caterina thanked the woman, who hesitated to wait for some more cash but then gave up and went downstairs. Caterina stood inside Peter's room and was flooded with emotion. She wanted to throw herself on his neatly made twin bed in the corner of the room but didn't want to waste time if the landlord decided to change her mind and kick her out. Worse, she may be calling the police with a card they gave her for such situations. Caterina didn't know what she was looking for, but she wandered, lifting objects and putting them down. There were no electronics in the apartment. The FBI must've confiscated all of them. She found a recent card on his nightstand with the return address Odessa, Ukraine. She pulled out her phone and took a picture of the return address. The card was cute dogs, and the inside script was in Cyrillic, so she could not read it. She took a picture of the inside. She found his bike lock key on a lanyard. She threw the key in her pocket. She went into his closet and buried her nose in the clothes. They were all freshly laundered and had no smell of him. She wanted to smell him. She found a black T-shirt on the top of the laundry. She picked it up, and the scent of sandalwood immediately flooded her senses. She desperately wanted to have his body fill the shirt, but all she got was remnants of him.

She flung the shirt over her shoulder and looked around the room again. It mostly was books and papers about the former Soviet Union, some in English, some written in Cyrillic, which she assumed was Russian since he said he didn't know Ukrainian. She wanted to find a big poster on the wall that said, "I'm innocent. Dmitry killed Ivan, not me!" but all she got were books and clothes. She took the shirt and the bike key and shut the door behind her.

She knocked on the woman's door to thank her, said goodbye, and left her number, but she looked like she just wanted to throw it out.

"Two weeks and call the trash man. Two weeks," she emphasized that she would throw out Peter's stuff if he weren't back.

Her response shook Caterina in its brevity and lack of empathy for Peter's situation, but who could blame her? She probably dealt with crazy situations as a landlord renting out rooms. Certainly, a door busted by the FBI would be one of the crazier situations, but you never know. This was, after all, near the Mass Cass area.

Caterina went around the side of the house at the end of the driveway and saw Peter's bike locked to the metal gate. She undid the lock, rode his bike back to Life Time gym, and locked it up at the enormous bike rack for gym members who

Pearl by the Sea

often biked to the gym from the neighborhood. She got in her tan Honda Accord and drove back to Medford, picking Peter's T-shirt off the passenger seat and drawing in the beautiful memories with each breath.

Caterina walked into the kitchen to the smell of lasagna. Her parents and Uncle Jimmy were finishing dinner, and her dad was loading the dishwasher, which was his nightly job after her mom cooked. "Cat!" Uncle Jimmy bellowed out, getting up a bit stiffly from the table and leaning heavily on the chair with his right arm. His protruding belly appeared to have had several portions of lasagna over the years.

"Uncle Jimmy." Cat hugged him tightly.

"Do you want some lasagna, honey?" asked Arlene. "It's still warm." Cat realized for the first time in days she was hungry. She sat down with her uncle at the table and ate as he started on coffee and dessert.

After her dad pressed start on the dishwasher, he sat with Jimmy and Caterina. Arlene hovered cleaning the kitchen but left to do laundry when they started to talk about Peter. Her coping mechanism was avoidance when it came to her daughter's problems. Both mom and daughter felt they always disappointed the other.

"Sweetheart, I want to show you something," said Aldo, Caterina's father.

He opened a manila envelope with an uncreased paper inside. He turned it around in the direction she could read. "Me and Uncle Jimmy took your time stamp at Starbucks and pulled some strings to get the CCTV of that day. They got a good shot of 'Justine' when she took her sunglasses off. We ran her face on Google Photos, and it turns out Justine is Joan Barry of Brockton, Mass. She's an actress, among other jobs. Uncle Jimmy tracked her down and talked to her."

"What, Uncle Jimmy?" shouted Caterina. She was shocked that these two were able to figure out her identity.

Aldo leaned in. "Listen, don't tell your brothers we're looking into stuff. Me, I'm a retired cop, and I don't give a shit, but your brothers are still in the game and need to be kept out of inquiries. You know what I mean?" Aldo looked over at his brother-in-law. "Jimmy don't give a shit anymore, either. He's been checked out for years at this stuff." Caterina blushed as she knew Jimmy had a reputation for doing his car insurance investigations half-assed.

"I'm so impressed that you guys figured this out," said Caterina, very curious about their methods, but it seemed they were happy to be obtuse on the strings pulled.

"Cat, the Boston cops are saying they are completely constrained on this murder case. The feds want complete jurisdiction over the details. My cop friend says he's done a lot of homicides and has never seen so many Boston Field Office guys swarming a place. Makes you wonder what it's all about."

Aldo glanced up the stairs to where Arlene retreated and whispered in a softer tone so as not to upset his wife. "Me and Jimmy are just worried about you, Cat. I mean, you know I really liked Peter. Hell, he made my mom cry with his karaoke crooning, but you have to forget about him. If he's involved with hiring actresses and murderers that bring in the Feds, you

Pearl by the Sea

better just run for the hills and be happy you didn't get hurt, baby. This is stuff that's none of our business."

"God, Dad, you sound like Peter's dead. He's not. He got arrested and set up for the murder of his friend. That is *my* business because I really like him. I love him." Caterina wrapped her hands around her coffee mug. She took a sip, trying to warm up her body. Sitting here with her private investigator uncle and her dad felt at least these two showed *some* interest in the case. She felt like she was with her people who liked the nitty-gritty of lists and speculation and hashing out theories.

"Don't you guys see what is happening? Someone hired an actress to get my location at Ivan's location. They wanted it to look like I was having a relationship with Ivan. They want it to look like a classic love triangle case. Peter finds out I'm having an affair with Ivan and, in a rage, murders his friend. *Boom*. They have a suspect in the murder, the guy who knows Ivan's secret, and they silence two men in one swoop. This was a premeditated murder. This was a premeditated framing of Peter. Whatever Ivan was going to expose about Panchenko's life must've rattled a few people, and we need to find out why to prove Peter's innocence."

"Wait," Jimmy paused, "you were sleeping with Ivan too?"

Aldo told Jimmy to shut up, being more upset Jimmy wasn't following Caterina's line of thought than talking about his baby sleeping with someone. "Jimmy, she's saying whoever hired Joan Barry did it to set Cat up in a pretend love triangle, not a real one. The Feds see Cat is at Ivan's place, at his workplace, and they think she knows Ivan."

"Exactly," said Caterina. "We talk to Justine, I mean, Joan Barry, and ask her who hired her, and we have found the killer."

"Jesus, why didn't you explain this better, Aldo?" said Jimmy irritated, "I don't want to figure this damn thing out now if Cat's in danger."

Aldo reached out his hand to his daughter and tapped her hand. "She's gonna do it either way, with our help or not. Might as well go along for the ride."

Chapter 19

"Justine" was surprised when she received the phone call from Caterina. She agreed to meet her at a Dunkin' Donuts in Brockton. Caterina arrived early, her modus operandi, and was surprised Justine, or she should say, Joan Barry, was already there.

Caterina asked Joan if she wanted anything before walking to the register to get herself a coffee. She got a DunKings, which was the iced coffee Ben Affleck advertised at the Super Bowl a few months ago. Cat was a Starbucks girl but wanted to try it.

"The DunKings," Joan chuckled, using her Ben Affleck voice when she saw the large toothpick of three munchkins on her iced coffee. "I loved that commercial. You know, I was an extra in *Good Will Hunting*? Yup, I walked across the MIT campus when they filmed Matt Damon's scenes. I've done a ton of movies in Boston."

"So, tell me, what happened to me? How did you get to Seaport?"

"Well, my agent called and gave me some guy's number.

Sometimes, I go through my agent, and sometimes, my agent lets me do things independently when he wants nothing to do with it. He just said some Indy guy was filming, and I met the description for the character's age—no big deal. I would get paid for a whole day for what sounded like an hour's work. The guy texted me my part, saying I was playing a wife who hired a private investigator to see if her husband was cheating on her. The guy said the movie was called *A Delicate Marriage*, and all the people in Starbucks were actors like me. He said it was his unique filming style. I didn't know where the cameras were. I stayed in character and answered the other actors' lines that I didn't know beforehand. He said it was to make the encounters more natural. I just answered how I thought my character would answer based on the scenario. They said, 'Give the private investigator five hundred dollars,' which he gave me to give you."

Joan Barry continued. "Then a few days later, some other guy called me and asked me about the acting gig, and I confirmed it was me. I thought he wanted me to do more scenes, but he just hung up."

"The second guy was my uncle. He tracked you down from the CCTV in Starbucks."

"Why? Wait, are you an actress?"

"No, I gave you my real name. In real life, I'm a private investigator, so I thought you were actually Ivan's wife who wanted me to track down your husband. I still have the five hundred dollars you handed me. You emailed me and said you wanted to hire me, and that's why we met."

"I didn't email you. I thought we were acting out a scene from a movie. I thought the concept of not knowing where the camera was, and kind of ad-libbing lines was cool. I must've been pretty good if you thought I was Ivan's wife."

Caterina realized that Justine knew nothing about the case. She debated telling her about the murder of Ivan Kanovsky but held back so as not to upset the woman. She seemed like a nice lady. "So, this director you met, how often did you talk to him?"

"Well, it was all through email and texting. I didn't meet him until the day of filming. We met near Legal Seafood and walked down to Starbucks, where he gave me five hundred dollars. My instructions were to walk to the woman in the red coat. I was to wear my sunglasses. That's it. I said my lines, ad-libbed to your questions, and he told me 'Good job' and that he'd call me soon. I thought it was weird that I didn't get to meet the other actors, but you know directors. They are all a bit different."

Caterina realized this woman had probably met Ivan's killer face-to-face. She took out her phone and opened it to see screenshots of Peter and Dmitry. The one of Dmitry was in the suit next to the secretary of state. She pulled the phone close to her chest. Then she cleared her throat. "Can you describe him?"

"Well, he had an Eastern European accent, like Russian or Slavic."

Caterina drew in a breath and showed her both pictures, switching back and forth between the two men.

"That's him. I know because of his eyes," said Joan emphatically.

Caterina's heart sank. Peter's eyes. His beautiful, gray, caring eyes.

Caterina turned the phone to Joan with the photo of Peter's face. "Him?" she said tentatively.

Joan swiped the phone to Dmitry's face. "Him," she pointed at Panchenko. "Those eyes. They're just . . . I don't know. Just wicked creepy, don't you think?"

Caterina covered her face with her hands and let out a sigh. She pointed her skewer of munchkins at Joan, who declined one, then popped one into her mouth. She took a swig of her iced coffee. She was relieved that she finally had confirmation it was Dmitry Panchenko behind this scheme and more relieved that Peter had been vindicated. Peter was not the killer.

"Yes, very creepy," agreed Caterina, popping another munchkin into her mouth.

The drive to Boston University took longer than Caterina had imagined, with rush-hour traffic. She arrived on campus, paid the meter with her Boston Parking App for a couple of hours, and followed a student into the engineering school. Caterina googled the floor of the professor's office and pressed the elevator to the third floor. Then she walked down the hall, casually glancing at room numbers until she came to Professor Ivan Kanovsky's office, room 317. She tried the door, but it was locked. The hallway was quiet, and she saw no other professors or students on the floor. She walked down the hall until she saw a housekeeper emptying a barrel in an office.

Pearl by the Sea

She cleared her throat so as not to startle the person. "Excuse me." She looked at the name tag that said Nyima and would not try to pronounce the name. "I was wondering if you could unlock an office for me for a second. I need to retrieve something in Professor Kanovsky's office."

The housekeeper stepped into the hallway, pointing to the professor's door. He wasn't sure if this student knew of Ivan's murder. It was a bit of an awkward moment.

"You see, I'm taking Professor Kanovsky's computational data analysis class Tuesdays and Thursdays, and, well, I left a really important book in his office. I'm going to get in big trouble if I don't return it to the library. It's like this size." Caterina made the gesture with her hands. "Kind of reddish brown. It says Computational Data Points for Digital Forensics. Oh, I think third edition. I really need to get it, and, well, I heard about his, you know, death." Caterina shook her head, wearing a frown to confirm she knew what happened to the professor.

The housekeeper felt relieved that he didn't have to break the news about the professor's murder. Her story seemed reasonable. He unlocked the door.

Caterina spoke innocently. "I'll wait out here if you can get it for me. I think I saw him put it on his table when I was here for office hours last week."

Caterina smiled an innocent smile and pushed her thick black reading glasses back up on her nose. She usually only wore them for heavy reading, but she felt she looked more like an engineering student with them on.

"Go check," said the housekeeper, and he went down the

hall to finish cleaning the office he was in.

Caterina took off her glasses as they made things a bit blurry. She scanned the room. Like Peter's room, the professor's office had no signs of electronics in it. She tried drawers in his office for any papers or folders that said "Ukraine; Forever a Pawn," which was the title of the broken link that Ivan sent Peter. She could not find anything that fit the description. She sat in his office chair and looked at the desk's surface. That's when she saw it. The oyster paperweight Peter described that Ivan had brought from Odessa. She remembered Peter referring to the pearl formed by the angels' tears. She picked up the oyster and undid the tiny latch. Inside was a thumb drive. She threw it into her pocket, closed the oyster, and placed it back on the pile of papers.

"Thanks," she shouted down the hall as Nyima proceeded to lock the door to the professor's office.

Caterina's heart raced as she pressed the lobby button and then pushed open the doors onto Commonwealth Avenue. The streets were busy with students and Red Sox fans leaving Fenway Park. She saw a man in a Red Sox T-shirt leering at her until his friends shoved him along. She felt exposed and vulnerable. She needed to act fast to determine if this was Ivan's paper on the USB.

She walked briskly to the Boston University Book Store and bought four USBs, two with her credit card and two with cash. She shoved two into her jeans pocket and two into the store bag. She walked up the staircase to the rows of computers and sat down next to a student. She pretended she was logging in, but she didn't have a password since she was no longer a student at BU. "Shit, shit," she said, holding her head with one hand. "Oh my God, I'm such an idiot. Oh my God, I'm so dead. Shit." She hit the keyboard on the PC.

The boy beside her stopped typing and took an AirPod from his ear. "You okay?"

"Oh my God, sorry; I didn't realize I was so loud." She pretended to recognize him. "Hey, are you in my kinesiology class with Dr. Powers?"

The kid looked surprised she was engaging more with him. "No, not me."

Caterina laughed and touched his arm slightly. "Well, your handsome doppelgänger is really nice." She looked back at the computer. "I'm such an idiot. I typed my password wrong three times, and now I'm locked out, and I need to submit my paper by nine. Shit, it's almost nine. I'm so screwed."

"I have like forty-five minutes left on my log-in if you want to use mine, but I don't know how that'd work if you're not signed in."

"Oh my God, that would be awesome. I'll get my password and explain it to my professor when I get home. Hopefully, he won't fail me."

Caterina could hardly wait for the kid to switch places when she started uploading the thumb drive into the PC. She ripped open the packet USBs and made copies. The kid tried to talk to her, but she couldn't concentrate on the conversation, so he just gave up and played on his iPhone. The upload speed was fast, and she made four copies in minutes.

After she finished, she put two USBs back in the bag and two in her jeans. "I'm not all here today. I didn't even label my thumb drives to figure out which was my paper."

"Who the hell uses thumb drives anymore?" the kid asked. Caterina logged off and thanked him, leaving him disappointed that his good deed of the day didn't result in anything further.

She exited the bookstore and walked toward her car. A man in sunglasses with a COVID mask and a black baseball hat started to follow her. She crossed the street and turned around to see him crossing the street. She walked briskly, and he matched her stride, keeping about ten feet back on the sidewalk. She pulled the straps of her backpack tighter with her BU bag still in one hand. She decided to run, an action she had done all her life but never before in fear. She hit a pedestrian's shoulder as she ran past and did not apologize. She was too afraid to form words. She willed herself to look over one shoulder and saw him pick up his stride. It was clear he was chasing her. She ran faster across the street and shoved herself into the aboveground subway train that ran along Commonwealth Ave. She watched him try to run diagonally across the street, avoiding the cars to get on the train. He disappeared from view, but she was unsure if he made it on. She concentrated on his style of running. It appeared he ran with a limp. She remembered reading that Dmitry Panchenko was injured in Bucha, Ukraine. She wondered if it was he chasing her.

Caterina switched trains at Park Street and got off at Broadway. She was too afraid to exit the train station, so she switched back to the northbound side to ride the red line to South Station. She did what she had done her whole life. She ran. She ran and checked over her shoulder. There was no one following her. She tried to catch her breath, holding her arms above her head, breathing in through her nose and out through her mouth. She walked along the sidewalk, watching the action at Cisco Brewery, which recently opened up for the season. She felt safer with the crowd. Should she enter Cisco's? Should she go to Kimmie's condo? She laughed a nervous laugh if Dmitry were to follow her, and she led him to Kimmie. Jack wouldn't be too happy about that. It was a stupid thought, and she wondered if she might be a bit mad to ponder such a thing at a time when some skinhead was chasing her. She had to keep her head in the game.

She walked some more. She checked her watch. Life Time closed half an hour ago, but she had her key pass. She was often the first one there in the morning and had twenty-four-hour gym access. She could gather her thoughts there and call her dad or uncle to pick her up. She walked away from the crowds of the restaurants and the brewery. She crossed the street and stopped halfway across to look over her shoulder, but nothing was there. She breathed heavily with relief, scanned her key, opened the door, and tried to close it. The door was resisting. She looked down and saw a foot blocking its closure. The door was ripped open by someone, and she ran.

Dmitry Panchenko closed the door slowly until he heard the click of it locking. She was trapped. The area was dark except for illuminated Exit signs and intermittent floor lighting.

She dug the two thumb drives out of her pocket and threw them into a cup holder on a treadmill. She needed to get her phone out of her backpack to call 911. She crouched between two stationary bikes and retrieved her phone from her backpack. Her phone needed facial identity, so she had to look at the screen to unlock it. The brightness of her phone gave her location away. Panchenko ran toward her and knocked the phone out of her hand, kicking it across the room.

Caterina got up from her crouched position and ran, darting between the equipment, stopping temporarily behind the leg press Nautilus machine, trying to figure out her next move. There was a phone in the yoga studio across the hall. She would run to that room.

She could not sense where he was. She saw no shadows or movement, so no time felt like the right moment to move. She just needed to fight her paralytic fear. She wanted to whisper, "Three, two, one," but instead, she held her breath and made her move. He was right behind her and quickly followed her to the studio. The motion sensors lit up the room, and the bright lights threw them both off a bit. He watched her eyes scan to the corner where the phone was located, and he effortlessly walked over and ripped the cord from the wall.

"Give me the thumb drives," he demanded calmly. He had removed his COVID mask and sunglasses earlier so she could now look into the eyes Joan had described as creepy. They were more than creepy. They were sadistic. His accent sounded similar to Peter's, but his voice was deeper and rougher in tone.

She slid down the mirrored wall, still gripping the BU

bookstore bag. The two USBs were in the bag, and so was the receipt for the two. She slid the bag across the room, but it only moved a few feet. She was too afraid to attempt a second launch. He walked closer to her, and she observed his limp close up. He bent down and picked up the bag, inspecting the receipt and the USBs. He shoved them into his jacket pocket.

He studied Caterina. She had her hands wrapped around her legs, shaking. He seemed to enjoy her distress. Both were assessing the other. Caterina was plotting her escape, and he was enjoying her fear. The stillness of their bodies caused the motion lights to go out, and she thought to crawl to the door, but the moment she moved, the lights went back on, and he was blocking her way. He laughed a sickening laugh, and she did not want to look back into those eyes again, so she crouched down again with her head slightly bowed, her hands clasped tighter to stop her shaking.

"What do you think you are possibly accomplishing by getting involved in this matter? What is it with you? Do you have a thing for men who are traitors to their countries? Does that get you off?" He spit out the words with contempt.

"Stop, please," she begged.

"You were such an easy target. Some amateur sleuth who thinks she can stick her nose into this war. That's what this is, you know. War, and, by the way, your country is on *my* side, *not* Russia's." He stepped back a bit and studied his image in the wall of mirrors, rubbing his hand on his right leg where the bullet had entered years ago.

"All I had to do was put two targets together, and then any

narrative can be formed. Ivan left his phone in the house and came out to your car to kiss you. Then you drove to his work, left your phone in your car, and made love to him in his office. Your DNA is in his office. Thank you for that. Then you, Peter, and your lover, Ivan, went sailing, and Peter found out you were sleeping with Ivan. He went to his apartment to kill him and was arrested—a classic love triangle. Peter's DNA is on Ivan's water bottle and backpack. My threats are all eliminated, and I can continue to help my country defeat the enemy."

"Stop," she whispered. "You know that's a lie."

"The truth is whatever I want it to be. I'm a lowly narrative janitor in this event, and you are even lower than me. I can spin it that Peter was in on it the whole time. He was told to spy on his friend and bring you into the story as the lover. He is now laughing at you and drinking champagne with his comrades."

Caterina looked in horror at Dmitry with this scenario, and he laughed again. "See? Look how easy it is to play with your emotions. You are such a novice that I pity you."

Panchenko shoved her foot to make her look up. "I do want to make one thing very clear, though. Today is the day you forget about all this. I am giving you a way out of this. Return to your TikTok and Instagram posts, ignoring the war surrounding you. Go back to your ignorance, whistling by the dead bodies of soldiers who have died for freedom. We don't need stupid whores like you meddling in this war. Give me the thumb drive now, and I'll leave."

She placed the backpack in front of her and proceeded to open it.

"No," he grabbed the backpack and dumped the contents on the floor in case she had any weapon in there. He found the USB from Ivan's oyster and shoved it into his pocket.

"You shag some Russian vermin for a few weeks and think you can play detective in this war? You disgust me. Go away, Colorado filth; just go away."

Panchenko left her lying on the floor, and she curled up into a ball until the lights turned off again from no motion. In the dark, she strained to hear him but was met with silence. She finally dared to stand up, and the lights came on in the room. She plugged the phone back into the wall and called her dad.

"Sweetheart, it's past midnight. I've been worried about you. How did it go with the actress in Brockton? Was she able to tell you anything about who hired you?"

Caterina forgot she hadn't caught her dad up to speed since she met with Joan Barry at Dunkin' Donuts. Her day felt like a week.

"I have a lot to explain. I'm okay, but I need you to pick me up at Life Time, and we also need to call the police. I was robbed, so if you see a Boston cruiser when you get here, don't be alarmed. I can't wait to see the CCTV of the Yoga studio. I'll explain everything later."

Caterina slowly walked over to her backpack, picking up her strewn items on the floor. She searched the floor for her iPhone, discovering it near the free weights. The last thing she did was pick up the thumb drives she placed in the treadmill cup holder on her way in and put them in her pocket. "Amateur, my ass," she muttered to herself, throwing her backpack around her shoulders.

Chapter 20

KENNETH ASKED CATERINA to take the week off until things settled down. Dimitry Panchenko robbing her in the Life Time gym was serious. No one wanted to be involved in whatever matters were going on surrounding the murder of Ivan Kanovsky, especially if she brought the trouble to her place of work. Caterina totally got it but had no regrets about getting Panchenko in full view of the cameras in a brightly lit Yoga studio. The police were given copies of the CCTV, and she asked them to send it along to the Boston FBI field office.

Caterina tried to contact the FBI herself, but no one would take her phone calls. She even drove over and tried to leave her card, but the security officer at the door said he was a cop, not a secretary.

Caterina emailed a copy of Ivan's paper to FBI Agent Kevin Auten along with time stamps of when she was with Panchenko. She gave Auten the name of an eyewitness to his murder plot, Joan Barry of Brockton, Massachusetts. The evidence was undoubtedly enough to arrest Panchenko if they would arrest Peter on the more flimsy love triangle nonsense.

She checked PACER again for any information on the federal crimes database, but Peter's name was nowhere to be found. She tried every combination she could think of, inputting his name into the national registry. She became obsessed with the case and picked apart Ivan's paper with notes, highlights, and thousands of Google searches to hyperlinks. The story was daunting for someone with little knowledge of the area, but she wanted to be an expert on Ivan Kanovsky's research.

She made several paper copies of his research, all 345 pages, half of which were footnotes to video testimonies and other papers. She did not mince words with her parents about her intent to expose a war crime that the United States State Department and the Senate Intelligence Committee were covering up. Her mother busied herself with grandchildren and ignored Caterina's antics. Her father indulged her to a point, but even he was grateful everyone was ghosting her on her pursuits. He hoped the more she was ignored, the more the events of the last month would just fizzle away. Who would want their daughter caught up in such danger?

No one read Ivan's paper. No one understood the seriousness of his research. There is a reason Dmitry Panchenko murdered Ivan and framed the one man who was motivated to expose Panchenko after his brother died. Peter would be in the way, and silencing him buried the scandal.

Not only had Caterina read everything there was to know about the day of Alexsei Leonidovich Geller's death on May 2, 2014, but she was now learning about Panchenko's crimes since the Russian invasion of February 2022. At the beginning of the

Russian incursion into Ukraine in early 2022, the fog of war and the fight to win the hearts of Americans was fierce. There were so many far-fetched stories on both sides of atrocities. The Ghost of Kyiv and the Snake Island soldiers were two early myths that dominated social media days after Russia invaded.

On February 24, 2022, just two days after the war started, brave Ukrainian soldiers refused to surrender, responding with expletives instead of surrender. This led to their deaths, and was caught on audio. President Zelensky personally announced their heroic deaths defending the Black Sea outpost of Snake Island in an emotional video. He promised each guard would be awarded the title Hero of Ukraine. The problem was that they did not die defending the island but rather were caught alive as prisoners of war.

The *New York Times* would quote people spreading the known lie, and they would justify it by saying, "If the Russians believe it, it brings fear. If the Ukrainians believe it, it gives them hope."

Just days later, on February 27, 2022, the Ghost of Kyiv appeared all over social media with a video of his air battles with Russian pilots. The Ghost of Kyiv was a mythical MiG-29 pilot who shot down six Russian planes. Congressman Adam Kinsinger shared a tweet by the Ukrainian government saying, "People call him the Ghost of Kyiv. And rightly so. This UAF ace dominates the skies over the capital and country and has already become a nightmare for invading Russian aircraft." Again, the problem was this herculean pilot did not exist. It was simply a flight simulator video. Thousands of Facebook groups shared fake videos, reaching 717 million Facebook followers.

The former head of security for Facebook and the director of the Stanford Internet Observatory told the *New York Times* that social media companies have decided to "pick a side." Alex Stamos acknowledged the bias in the propaganda war.

Ukraine continuously violated the Geneva Convention's rules by sharing war prisoner videos. They were widely circulated online. Ukrainians would say, "But didn't Russia violate the international rule of law by invading in the first place?" This was the rationale of social media censors.

Caterina read how the first few weeks in February 2022 drew a line in the sand for many and how neighbors became enemies. The Russian language was forbidden to be spoken in public in many Ukrainian neighborhoods, especially those that housed ultra-nationalists, such as the Pro-Unity crowd that had formed the Azov Battalion back in 2014. Pictures of Ukrainian Russian-speaking men, women, and children tied to telephone poles with clear plastic wrap were widely circulated online. The victims' pants were pulled down, their faces painted blue, and each had a cloth in their mouth. It sent a signal to anyone who dared speak Russian or say anything against Zelensky and the Kyiv government.

It was hard for Caterina to look at the humiliating pictures of innocent children, some as young as seven, tied up in this manner. It reminded her of how much hatred Panchenko spewed toward Peter and other Russian-speaking Ukrainians. Children caught in the crossfire were taught to hate the neighbors they played soccer with just the day before.

Caterina willed herself to keep reading. Her motivation for learning was as strong as her love for Peter. Her passion for Peter drove her to be passionate about Ivan's story. The more she learned about some of the actions of Dmitry Panchenko and other Azov members, the more she wanted to prove Peter's innocence in the murder of Ivan Kanovsky.

Ivan also did not sugarcoat Russian atrocities. This was not a one-sided paper, as he clearly was for a united Ukraine. He acknowledged that the war started in 2014 after the Maidan coup and the ousting of Ukrainian President Yanukovych. After that, the province of Crimea voted in a referendum to break away from Ukraine. Also, the two biggest provinces in the Donbass region, Donetsk and Luhansk, refused to acknowledge the new Ukrainian leader installed, Yatsenyuk. For eight years, Kyiv and the Donbass skirmished at their border, resulting in twelve thousand dead. All were Ukrainians, mainly on the Donbass side. No shots were fired in Crimea, and no one was killed in their referendum.

Caterina had no idea about this eight-year civil war that began before Americans started putting yellow and blue flags on their Facebook profiles and on their lawns.

Dmitry Panchenko's career since 2014 carried him up the chain of command after the private military was blended into the national army. Dmitry was in Bucha during those weeks in late February and early March when they were defending the city from the Russian soldiers. The Ukrainians won the battle, with Russian soldiers retreating on April 1st. Hundreds on both sides died from the conflict. The mayor of Bucha accused the Russians of genocide, of executing and raping civilians and lining the street with their bodies, spaced about twenty-five yards apart. Russia accused the Ukrainians of a "false flag operation" with Ukrainian soldiers executing its citizens who helped Russian soldiers during their time of occupation. White bands were tied around the dead people's arms, signifying traitors to Ukraine. Russia asked for a United Nations Security Council Meeting to investigate the deaths and the unusual staging of the bodies on the main road in Bucha.

Russia accused Dmitry Panchenko of executing his fellow Ukrainian citizens with gunshots to the head, and Ivan Kanovsky linked eyewitness testimony and even one video of a murder. The footage was difficult to watch, but it was clear in Caterina's mind the man was Dmitry Panchenko.

There is even a video of him shirtless with his black sun tattoo, which matches the black sun symbol of his Azov Battalion flag. The flag waved over the city after the Russians fled on April 1, 2022. Panchenko appeared to be leaning on one leg with his crutches off to the side—a war hero wounded in the infamous Bucha short-lived victory.

After his awards and commendations as a wounded hero, he shifted to desk jobs in the war department. Here is where he was accused by some in the Ukrainian military of embezzling funds intended for the war. Corruption was rampant in the Ukrainian government, but Panchenko's greed was so extreme that even his superiors could not look the other way. After he purchased a luxury condo in Dubai and a luxury car to match, the department reshuffled him away from purchases and sales and over to the State Department. Here, he was away from guns and away from piles of money to squander, and he could just pose for pictures with dignitaries who praised him for his battlefield heroics.

Ivan Kanovsky's exposure of Dmitry Panchenko's crimes was thorough and exhaustive. Ivan quoted an unnamed American official who compared his exposure of the war crimes to Wikileaks releasing the footage of a US helicopter strike over Baghdad on July 12, 2007, that killed seven people, including a journalist working for the Reuters News Agency. Bradley Manning was sentenced to thirty-five years in prison for giving Julian Assange the footage. The killing of the journalist caused a partisan uproar, with Democrats cheering Julian Assange's bravery in exposing the mistake. Support for George Bush's Iraq War was abysmal. President Barack Obama later commuted Bradley Manning's sentence, now referring to the soldier as Chelsea, his chosen name he switched to while incarcerated.

It was true that a viral video of "our side" doing something terrible could be enough to sway an already war-fatigued country. The latest sixty-one billion-dollar Ukraine package was facing controversy in the House of Representatives from congressmen capitalizing on the antiwar sentiment from their constituents. Cries of "securing our border first" and turning off the spigot in the treasury were loud. The Senate passed the bill with no problem, but things were getting messy in the Republican-controlled Congress.

"Dinner," Arlene shouted up the stairs, and it brought Caterina back to reality and away from war. Then Caterina sat for a long time thinking about this concept. Did she actually live in reality when she was unaware of the horrors of a civil war in Ukraine for eight years and now a full-fledged nation-fighting-nation war? Is anyone willing to look past the Ukrainian flags in their windows that are now fading and look at nuance? Was any political will or media interested in looking into Peter's innocence? Everyone around wanted Peter to go away and did not care about him or the story. Sure, they cared about Caterina, but not enough to move an inch out of their comfort zone to learn his story and hear his side.

"Did you hear me?" Arlene repeated, having not moved from the bottom of the stairs until Caterina responded.

"Okay, Mom, coming," shouted Caterina. She closed her laptop and picked up her phone. She had not heard from many friends or family and had no new messages. She opened up her photos to see the one picture she had of Peter, the selfie he had taken in front of Starbucks. He looked handsome, bright, and carefree. She kissed the photo gently, closing her eyes. She understood why this intelligent man switched his major to philosophy to understand human nature. He wanted to explore how evil men could execute their neighbors without remorse. He wanted to learn about the Dmitry Panchenkos of the world, who survived and thrived in division and friction. She thought about the term Panchenko used when he was beating Peter while he lay on the gravel with two broken heels and his flesh still burning from the fire. Caterina looked into the same eyes when Dmitry called her a "Colorado whore." She learned Colorado was a beetle with the same colors of the St.

George flag many Russians used. It was an ethnic slur that the racist rolled off his tongue with such hate. Did Caterina want to learn more about this hate or merely whistle by the graves of dead soldiers? She now understood why Peter did not want to involve her in Ivan's work and did not let her go to his apartment. He tried to protect her from the horror.

She kissed his photo again. Peter taught her real love, and Panchenko taught her real hate. She was not going to let the haters win. She loved Peter with all her heart and soul. She would fight for the man she loved, even if she had to do it alone.

Chapter 21

CATERINA'S WEEKS OF research were now closing in on week six. Arlene and Aldo were starting to worry about her mental health. She barely left the house, spending all day on her laptop emailing anyone interested in the story. She had not heard back from any media company, politician, or friend who wanted to check in on what happened to Peter. It was as if he just disappeared and vanished from this earth.

The newspapers also were not that curious about Ivan Kanovsky's murder. This felt unusual to Caterina as Boston loved a good murder mystery. All inquiries to the police resulted in a runaround. The Boston police said it was out of their jurisdiction since it was being handled at the federal level. The federal level said they would not comment on an ongoing investigation. Caterina's frustration increased, but it only made her want to break through the stalemate even more.

Every day, she checked PACER, and it wasn't until a week after her twenty-fifth birthday that Petrov Leonidovich Geller finally was posted on the website. There it was in black font, including his case number, court location, and the date the indictment was uploaded to the court electronic records. Caterina was well versed in researching court documents with all the car accident cases she investigated. She clicked on the indictment and saw that it was sealed. There was no way to know why it was sealed. This would be at the court's discretion. Sometimes, it was done for national security reasons, which may be the case in this scenario. She had so many mixed emotions. She was excited to have proof of life that Peter still existed finally, but it did not bring her any closer to understanding the severity of the charges and how to prove his innocence.

She ran downstairs with her laptop open and placed it on the kitchen table where her parents had coffee.

"He's been indicted. It's for real. Look, right there."

Arlene sighed and looked out the window, sipping her coffee. Aldo nodded his head solemnly, not knowing what to say.

"This is ridiculous. He did not kill Ivan. Dmitry did," Caterina adamantly stated.

Arlene got up to load the breakfast dishes into the dishwasher.

"What, Mom? Say something—anything," Caterina pleaded.

Arlene started to cry, and Aldo got up to hug his wife. "Caterina, you know this subject upsets your mother. Just don't bring it up around her. I mean, 'Petrov,' 'Ivan,' 'Dmitry,' . . . These names are a bit, well, you know, scary and Russian, and we're just not ready for your intensity, Caterina. Your mother just worries about you."

Caterina was annoyed that her dad rushed to defend her mother when his baby girl was clearly having difficulties in her life.

Pearl by the Sea

"Well, gee, Dad, I'm so sorry my existential crisis doesn't fit into your perfect lives. I'm sorry I finally found a guy I love, and he happened to get framed for murder. How inconvenient for the two of you. Do you want to kick me out like Kimmie did? I have no problem with that because I won't give up helping Peter."

Aldo walked over to his daughter now, trying to bridge his wife and daughter together. He gave Caterina a hug, which made Arlene cry harder. Her tears welled up in her eyes.

"We just love you, honey," Arlene whispered with her voice cracking. "Kimmie loves you too. She has been asking about you."

"She calls you and doesn't even talk to me?"

"She's worried about you like we all are, honey. Just let it go. Let it go. People who are in charge will figure this out. They know what they're doing."

Caterina couldn't believe her mom and best friend were talking about her behind her back. She closed the laptop and silently went upstairs. She threw herself on her bed like a petulant child and played her Spotify playlist of love songs Peter shared with her. Her pillow became wet with tears, so she flipped the pillow over. She was crying for Peter. She was crying for his brother Alexsei, for Ivan, and for all those harmed by this stupid war. She could now find cities like Bucha, Odessa, Kyiv, and Mariupol on the map when, two months ago, she could not even locate Ukraine.

She finished her playlist and played it a second time, flipping her pillow over once again.

Suddenly, her phone buzzed. She wiped her eyes and read the text.

"**Want to get lunch?**"—**Kimmie**.

Did her mom tell her to call? She didn't care. She needed Kimmie and her friendship at this low point. She needed to hug her best friend.

"**Sure**," replied Caterina with a heart emoji.

"**How about that Mexican restaurant you visited with that cat killer Hinge date?**"

Then another text: "**Too soon?**"

Her texts made Caterina smile. Kimmie could always make her laugh.

"**Lol. Okay. See you at one o'clock?**"

She ignored that she didn't offer to have her stop by the apartment first. Maybe she wasn't even telling Jack she was meeting her. Caterina parked at Life Time. One of the perks of her job was having a parking space there, but she was wondering if her privileges had been revoked after not having worked in six weeks. She chanced it, and, thankfully, her key pass still worked.

"Hey, you," said Kimmie when she arrived ten minutes after Caterina. They hugged tightly and slid into the booth. It was busy on a Saturday, even with it being a rainy day. "Should we darty? It's five o'clock somewhere, right?"

Caterina smiled, and they both ordered margaritas. It felt good to catch up and talk about *Love Island*, Kimmie's job, friends having milestones, gossip, and, of course, Kimmie's wedding plans. The only subject Kimmie wanted to avoid was

Pearl by the Sea

talking about Caterina and Peter. If Kimmie had her druthers, she wanted Caterina to move on.

After they finished their fish tacos, they debated to get a second drink each. They indulged and ordered two more margaritas, perhaps to lower their inhibitions so they could talk of taboo subjects. Kimmie licked the salt off her peach margarita on the rocks. "I should not have this much salt or calories so close to the wedding. I'm in the hundred-day countdown."

To Caterina, it felt like it was an eternity talking about the wedding, and she couldn't believe they had months to go. "Nonsense. If anything, you have lost some weight, and I've put on ten pounds."

Kimmie appreciated the compliment. "You needed a few more pounds. Me, on the other hand, I have to be careful. Have you been running? Your mom tells me you haven't gone to work and spend all day in your room." Kimmie placed her hand over Caterina's. "I'm worried about you, Cat."

"Are you? Or did my mom text you to reach out to me? You seem to talk to her more than me lately. I didn't know you two were so chummy."

"C'mon, Cat. You know your mom can't handle any of your drama. She never could."

"True," said Caterina. "I feel like this is just a pattern with us. She'd rather be talking to you about the wedding than she would about my jailed lover being framed for murder by a psychopathic killer. I don't understand why."

Kimmie laughed at Caterina finally cracking a joke, even if it was dark humor. "You know this is your own choice, Cat.

No one is asking you to go above and beyond the call of duty in trying to figure out a murder. Jack won't even let me bring up your name because he doesn't take your career seriously. I hope you understand about the maid of honor thing. It doesn't mean you're not my best friend in all the world. It's just that Jack doesn't want the drama dragged into the wedding plans. I know you don't want to be in charge of showers and bachelorette parties at this time." Kimmie always rambled when she was drunk. "I think it's best for you as well. You can enjoy the wedding as a guest and not have to be paired with the best man, Jason, all night. By the way, I'm done trying to throw the two of you together." Kimmie continued. "Don't be mad at Jack with this decision. He just doesn't get it."

"Do you?" Caterina asked seriously and hopefully.

Kimmie licked the rim and took another sip. Her eyes looked a bit glazed, and she smiled a bit. "I mean, of course, kind of. I think women, by nature, are more into these murder mystery thingies. Look at how many women do serial killer podcasts. It's a huge market for women." Kimmie played with the rim of her glass. "I mean, look at all the publicity around the Karen Read murder trial. I know more women who know every detail of her murder case, and guys are like, 'Karen who?'"

"Who is Karen Read?" Caterina asked.

"Are you serious?" said Kimmie. "You never heard of the Free Karen Read campaign? She has tons of groupies that wave signs on the overpass of the highway that say she is being framed for murder. She even has some fanboy blogger called 'TurtleBoy,' who makes up conspiracies of other people killing

Pearl by the Sea

her boyfriend. He says the cops are trying to cover up who really murdered her boyfriend. I can't believe you don't know about this case."

Caterina googled TurtleBoy, and the very first thing that came up was hundreds of stories about Karen Read. "Hmm," said Caterina, reading an article.

"That's what you need, Cat. A podcast and a TurtleBoy." Kimmie laughed, not knowing how much her advice was being taken to heart.

Caterina walked around Seaport to sober up before driving home after their two-margarita luncheon. She walked down to the Massachusetts District Courthouse. She read the sign, John Joseph Moakley US Courthouse, First Circuit. She had walked by this courthouse hundreds of times along the Seaport boardwalk. It felt like the restaurants and condos were all built around this building as it was one of the older landmarks along the harbor walk in that area.

Caterina sat on the stone wall outside the courthouse, looking out on Boston Harbor, recalling her first date with Peter at the oyster bar and taking the water taxi to East Boston and Charlestown. She recalled their sailing adventure on this very water with Ivan and Tatiana. It felt like a lifetime ago, feeling so carefree in Peter's arms. She remembered his sad response to Ivan's disappearance, saying that he was not supposed to be happy. She wanted to hug away all his pain. She wanted nothing more than to save this man from a possible lifetime in prison. She studied the courthouse. Did it have jail cells? Where was Peter? Why hasn't he tried to contact her? She wrote to the address on the envelope she found in his room. She wrote a short, vague letter of introduction of who she was and her contact information. She mailed it last week, but if Caterina's mom was this upset, she could not imagine the pain of Peter's mother.

The salt air sobered her up. She studied the courthouse again, then drove home to hatch her plan. If no one but her were going to fight for Peter, she would need to find a TurtleBoy.

Caterina opened her social media. She wasn't much of an influencer, but she had accumulated many followers on Instagram and TikTok. She had Facebook, but mostly her mom's friends were on there. She would post on all three. She posted the one picture she had of Peter and placed the hashtag *#FreePeterGeller* next to the photo with his gray eyes smiling and his raised Starbucks coffee. He looked no more like a killer than Bambi. Friends and family could undoubtedly see his innocence, she hoped. She then posted again, saying she would be in front of the Moakley Courthouse on Saturday, June 22, 2024, at 10:00 a.m. She knew it was a busy time for graduations, showers, and weddings, but she felt there was no time to lose. She wanted Boston to know her boyfriend was being framed for murder, and the government was covering it up.

Chapter 22

CATERINA CHECKED HER phone again after jumping out of the shower. Her social media posts about Peter had two or three likes each and zero comments. It was early Saturday morning. People were probably still sleeping. She packed her four protest signs into her Honda and drove from Medford to Life Time gym, then walked over to the Moakley Courthouse, arriving at 9:30 a.m. Her daylong vigil was to start at 10:00 a.m., but she wanted to beat anyone that might show up.

It was a beautiful June day, and Boston would be crowded with people. She was glad there wasn't much wind to blow her signs away. She placed them flat on the grass with her backpack on top of them to weigh them down. Her four signs were various sayings she wanted to convey to her audience. One was a picture of Peter with the hashtag *#FreePeterGeller*. He looked handsome in his Starbucks selfie with his crooked-toothed smile. The second sign was Ivan Kanovsky looking more serious from his BU faculty photo. Above the picture, Caterina wrote in bright red letters, "*Who killed BU Professor Ivan Kanovsky?*" A third poster was all words in a huge font asking a question to the head of the Senate Intelligence Committee, "*Why won't you talk to me, Senator Eric Mason?*" Her final poster was a picture of herself with the hashtag *#DuckGirl* and a website for her new blog. Caterina figured, why not? If TurtleBoy could generate publicity for the Karen Read trial, she should try to draw attention to the false arrest of Peter Geller. It was worth a shot.

She could only hold one sign at a time, so she picked up the one of Peter Geller. She stood facing Boston Inner Harbor with the Moakley Courthouse behind her. It was an impressive building and was the place maker for the redevelopment of the Seaport District. So many buildings sprang up around the courthouse after it was built. The Before and After photos of the area since it was created were startling. The large, expansive lawn extended out from the semicircular side of the building, which had all windows. Thirty passages of quotes are carved into the stone of the building. Caterina had walked by the courthouse often, reading the inscriptions. She never thought in a million years she'd be out here today trying to draw attention to her cause.

She stood with her sign for about an hour, and then at ten thirty, she decided to livestream the speech she wrote. She was hoping someone would show up to hold her phone to stream, but she, instead, used the selfie stick she brought to record. She was glad she wrote it on paper, not on her phone since her phone was needed for the stream. She looked around her for any friends or family and resigned herself to no one showing up. Finally, she pressed the record button and began.

"Hi, everyone. I'm out here in front of the Moakley Federal Courthouse today to draw attention to the unlawful arrest of my friend Peter Geller, who was falsely accused of murdering BU Professor Ivan Kanovsky. If you want to learn more about this case, visit my blog #DuckGirl, and I will post updates." She looked down at her words. *"I have always appreciated this architectural marvel that is the cornerstone of Seaport. I have jogged by the Moakley Courthouse so many times in my years working and living in Seaport, but now, it holds a very personal meaning for me since Peter Geller was framed for murder.*

This past week, the inscriptions on the building have made me pause and appreciate our justice system. Words carved into stone have adorned public buildings of democracy since ancient Athens. Justice Oliver Wendell Holmes and Justice Louis D. Brandeis were the two justices who the ancient defenders of civic ideals inspired. Holmes's words of wisdom are located in the Jury Assembly Hall. He wrote a dissenting opinion in the Abrams vs. United States case in 1919 when the Supreme Court ruled in favor of harsh punishments for those who opposed President Woodrow Wilson's sending troops to Russia after the Bolshevik Revolution. At the time, anyone who opposed Wilson's policies risked arrest. The court upheld a twenty-year prison sentence for New Yorkers who dropped pamphlets from the roofs of buildings objecting to the use of American troops. Justice Brandeis pointed out it was 'perfectly logical to persecute people for their opinions if you do not doubt your ideas and power.' Human nature would naturally want to sweep away all opposition. Holmes understood that those in power tended to silence wrong thinking, so he thought we should be 'eternally vigilant against attempts to check the expression of opinions that we loathe and believe to be fraught with death.'

"*Justice Holmes would prove prescient in his dissenting opinions and delivered one of the most influential speeches in the history of the law, 'The path of Law,' at BU law school, the very university where Professor Kanovsky taught his eager students.*

"*Another justice, Felix Frankfurter, also observed that 'the validity and moral authority of a conclusion largely depended on the mode by which it was reached.' Felix warned a fair process is especially critical 'at times of agitation and anxiety when fear and suspicion impregnate the air we breathe.' He thought, 'Appearances in the dark are apt to look different in the light of day because secrecy is not congenial to truth seeking.'*

"*That is what is happening now as I speak. Peter Geller's indictment is sealed. There is no transparency in his arrest, and we are constrained in our ability to help him. This building,*" Caterina pointed to the building, "*this building was made with repurposed bricks of warehouses that lined Boston Harbor. American workers spilled their blood, sweat, and tears to promote our democracy. We should demand that our Justice Department uphold that tradition by not engaging in a kangaroo court system that mocks our ideals. Justice Brandeis drew inspiration from Pericles' oration to the Athenians in the fifth century, who, even back fifteen hundred years ago, knew 'the greatest menace to freedom is an inert people and that public discussion is a political duty.' I will not be deterred in my fight for Peter Geller. Just because we support Ukraine in the war against Russia doesn't mean we should suspend the moral clarity of our Constitution. It's times like this when we send hundreds of billions of dollars to a country across the globe, and we should expect transparency and not secrecy in the fight for democracy. It's times like this—"*

A young woman interrupted Caterina. "Excuse me, hi. Can you help us?" Caterina stopped her livestream, which went a bit off-script. She put down her selfie stick.

"Okay, sure. What do you need?" asked Caterina.

"Could you take our picture?" The woman handed Caterina her phone and positioned herself with her husband by the water with Inner Harbor in the background.

Caterina let out a sigh. She held up the camera. "Sure," she said and took the photo.

"Oh, could you turn the camera the other way? I like landscape photos for the background. That's why we came to Boston, right?"

Caterina turned the phone, took a few more photos, and returned the phone to the woman.

"Thanks, have a great day," said the woman. "Oh, and free Peter Geller," she added, reading Caterina's sign.

Caterina sighed heavily and picked up her phone to see how many views she had on her Facebook livestream. Thirty-four, and no likes or comments. She clicked it off, walked over to her signs, and picked up one. Another half hour passed, and she had a couple of passersby stop and read the sign but asked no questions. Finally, she saw familiar faces when her brother, his wife, and kids approached her spot.

"Hey, sis, thought I'd stop by and say hi."

Caterina was thrilled to see her brother. "Gio, hi." She

hugged him tightly and gave kisses and hugs to her two nieces and sister-in-law.

"Hi, Auntie," the older niece greeted her. "Is this about your boyfriend, the guy that came to Uncle Tony's house?"

"Yes, yes, it is. He's a good guy," answered Caterina so proudly.

"Didn't he kill a cat or something?" The precocious eight-year-old turned toward her dad. "Did he, Daddy?"

Giovanni hugged his daughter awkwardly. "Um, sorry, Caterina. She's confusing the stories. She probably hears grownups talking and gets mixed up." He turns to his daughter. "No, sweetie, he definitely did not hurt a cat or any animals."

There was some silence for a moment that Caterina broke. "Well, thanks for coming out here. Do you want a sign to hold?"

Gio shyly responded and looked over at his wife. "Well, we are actually on our way to the Children's Museum, so we don't have time. We just wanted to say hi."

"Oh," Caterina tried to hide her disappointment. "Oh, cool." She turned toward her nieces and gave them both hugs. "Have fun. That's a great museum."

"Okay, bye. See you on the Fourth of July at Tony's," her sister-in-law hugged her quickly and held the girls' hands to move along.

"Okay, bye," Caterina repeated as they all walked away.

She checked her phone again. Silence. Her arms were tired, and she decided to sit on the stone bench between the boardwalk and the courthouse. She drank some water from her

Stanley mug and munched on an apple. After her snack, she picked up the Ivan Kanovsky sign and tried maneuvering into a shady spot on the sidewalk. She had on an old BU T-shirt and black athletic shorts. Even while wearing her Hoka sneakers, her feet started hurting, and she shifted her weight. An enthusiastic family of three stopped to read her sign. It was a mom and dad and their son, who looked about eighteen. The father started talking to Caterina.

"Who murdered Ivan Kanovsky?" the father read the sign. He turned to his son, hitting his shoulder gently. "See? This is why I love Boston. When I went to college here, it had the energy of free thinkers and brave souls ready to fight the system. Great, just great." The dad wore a Polo shirt with a Boston College insignia on it. "My son is touring schools up here for college."

"Nice," said Caterina, grateful for the friendly conversation. "Do you want me to take your picture?" Caterina had already helped half a dozen people take a picture with the Inner Harbor in the background. She snapped the photo for them and handed the phone back to the son. "Where are you thinking?"

"Well, we've seen a ton, but I really like Boston University. I'm hoping to run track."

"Nice, that's my alma mater," Caterina said, pulling at her BU T-shirt.

"Who is Ivan Kanovsky?" asked the boy.

"So," Caterina hadn't used her elevator pitch on many people since no one had shown interest in the story. "He is, well, he was, a professor in the Engineering Department at Boston University who was murdered several months ago, and my boyfriend was arrested and framed for his murder."

The boy's father decided he had enough of free thinkers and brave souls and put his arm on his son to hurry him along, but the boy expressed an interest.

"Whoa, that's nuts. What happened? I'm looking at the Engineering School. No one mentioned this guy on the tour."

"Well, he was a brilliant professor in large data analysis and was about to launch an exposé about a Ukrainian war criminal who embezzled millions from the money we donate to Ukraine. I believe they," she pointed to Moakley Courthouse, "I believe they framed my boyfriend as the fall guy because it was convenient. They also dragged me into the story by hiring me to follow Ivan. I'm writing a blog as DuckGirl if you want to hear more about it."

"We went on the duck boats yesterday," the boy politely replied, not knowing how to respond to the elevator pitch, which Caterina thought went pretty well.

"Enough, Zack. Don't engage with crazy. Let's go. The Boston Tea Party tour starts soon."

Caterina was getting cranky. The heat and fatigue of standing alone without anyone caring about the disappearance of her boyfriend was causing her to reach a boiling point. Here was this guy bragging about Boston and its "good trouble" energy, and he called her crazy. She wasn't crazy. She was trying to shout it from the rooftop like those dropping the antiwar leaflets in 1919. She was history. He was watching dissent live,

Pearl by the Sea

and he called her crazy. She had enough and took her anger out on the unsuspecting family.

"I'm not crazy," she shouted, which made her sound more crazy. The family was a few feet away, and the father hustled his family along. She didn't know why she screamed it . . . maybe out of sheer frustration. Maybe for shock value, but for whatever reason, she shouted it. "Well, if you go to Boston University, I hope your professor doesn't get hacked to death!"

The mother stopped and turned around in horror, and then they all walked briskly away. Caterina literally covered her mouth after she shouted the words. It wasn't this family's fault Peter was arrested. She needed to focus her energy on people like Senator Eric Mason, who could do something about it. She put down her Ivan sign and picked up her "*Why won't you return any of my calls, Senator Eric Mason?*" sign and held it for a while. After two more hours of sign holding, she sat down again to eat a banana and a granola bar. She stared up at the windowed facade of the empty Moakley Courthouse on a Saturday. She closed her eyes when a welcomed light breeze came by to provide slight relief from the heat. She resigned herself to one more hour, and then she would quit. She stood again to take up her cause and smiled silently at all those who passed by, trying not to accost young families again.

She checked her watch. Half an hour had passed. She was ready to quit. A group of pedestrians stopped in front of her, pointing to their left down the sidewalk. "Oh, wow, check these guys out." Caterina overheard the comment and turned to where they were pointing. She saw a group of about a dozen muscular males and females in various athletic outfits walking down Fan Pier. They were the fittest group of people Caterina had ever seen together in public. As they walked closer, she recognized one of the women. It was Alda, her bodybuilding friend. She could say *friend* now since Alda asked for a Facebook friend request. Alda stopped in front of Caterina and gave her a big smile.

"Hey, Caterina, I thought I'd bring some friends to help you today." Alda extended her arm to her group of friends, about five men and women, all deeply tanned and muscular. She introduced each one, and they shook Caterina's hand.

Caterina was so surprised and happy for the support. "Oh my God, Alda, wow! This means so much to me. I can't tell how much."

"Well, I saw your pathetic livestream this morning, which stopped abruptly with someone shouting if you could help them. I wanted to come down and see this for myself. We had a competition last night, so many of us are in the area and still rockin' our bronze look. I thought it would be fun to show you some love."

At Alda's direction, Alda's friends all proceeded to strip themselves out of their shirts, shorts, socks, and sneakers. Someone passed around the oil, and they liberally applied it around their bikinis and thongs. They lined up with all of Caterina's signs and her in the middle. Those not holding signs did the competition poses, showing off their physique, and a crowd appeared, taking photos and videoing the dozen bodybuilders. After the photoshoot, they broke off into individual photoshoots with one another. It was an excellent backdrop for pictures.

Alda and Caterina stood together to talk.

"This is an incredible show of support. I can't thank you enough. Honestly, I was surprised to get your Facebook request a couple of weeks ago. I thought you hated me."

"I did hate you," laughed Alda. "I was angry about everything: the car accident, losing my case and not getting a settlement, and then losing my disability claim. I was angry at the world, and you were an easy target. Sometimes, innocent people are the focus of all your anger."

Caterina laughed, thinking about telling that poor high schooler to be careful his professor doesn't get hacked to death. She directed her anger at the innocent as well.

"No, I totally get it," said Caterina. "Sometimes, I get too involved in my surveillance target's life."

"You mean you show empathy and treat them as human beings instead of a dollar sign on an invoice? That's not a bad thing, Caterina." Alda placed her hand on Cat's shoulder. "I really appreciate you taking the time to drive all the way to my competition just to tell me I was a good nurse. I know what you were trying to do, and, well, it worked. After I lost my disability claim, I went back to nursing, and I really like it a lot. I'm on the labor and delivery floor at Melrose Wakefield Hospital. It's a fantastic job, and I still have time to work out and compete. My back has never felt better." Alda smiled a big smile. "Last night, I placed in the 'Best Physique' category. It felt really good to see the benefits of my hard work. I felt proud."

"Well, you look fantastic, Alda. You also did the night I saw you compete."

Caterina and Alda were going to hug, but Alda was still slicked up with oil. She took out her towel to dry off, and the other bodybuilders all donned their athletic clothing to say goodbye to Caterina. It was the support she needed at the right time. It gave her the confidence and the motivation to continue her fight for justice for Peter. She packed up her signs and drove home to write about the day on the DuckGirl Blog.

Chapter 23

"'*WHO KILLED IVAN Kanovsky?' That is the question Caterina Antonucci, a local native of Medford, Massachusetts, is asking today in front of the Moakley Federal Courthouse. Ivan Kanovsky, a professor at Boston University, was found stabbed to death in his Boston apartment this past April. Local police thought it was a possible robbery until the federal government swooped in to take over the murder investigation. Our sources have told us that UMASS Professor Peter Geller has been arrested and charged with the gruesome stabbing of Professor Kanovsky. Both men are Ukrainian citizens, and the motive may possibly have been a personal dispute.*

"Ms. Antonucci spent the day holding signs claiming Geller's innocence and is asking our own Massachusetts Senator Eric Mason for help with the sealed indictment. Her fellow personal trainer friends came out to support her and made quite a splash down on Fan Pier. Here is a photo of the bodybuilding group posing with signs to support Ms. Antonucci, also known as Duck Girl, to draw attention to Geller's arrest."

The TV news showed the dozen bodybuilders posing with Caterina's signs. "*Well, she sure has her work cut out for her, but it appears her friends will help with the 'heavy lifting.'"* The anchorman puts air quotes around the words "heavy lifting."

"*Oh, Chet,*" the anchorwoman groaned at his bodybuilder joke. "*So, Brad, how did the Red Sox make out today at Fenway?*" she said, turning to the sportscaster.

Caterina closed her ABCNews App after she watched the excerpt from last night's broadcast. She couldn't believe she made the news. Alda knew her stunt would draw attention, and she was right.

The bodybuilding photoshoot was not the only event from yesterday that was making its way around the internet. Someone filmed Caterina yelling at the teen and turned it into a TikTok. The packaging was perfect: a five-second clip of Caterina yelling, followed by freezing the video on the mother's horrified face.

People were mimicking the clip with their own variations.

"How was your day at school?" a teen dressed up as mom asked her friend playing the student. "Great day! My teacher didn't get hacked to death!" Then the mother made the same horrified face of the teen's mom. It made Caterina cringe. If she didn't know the person murdered, she might stifle a giggle in polite company at the dark humor, but to her, it was deeply offensive.

Wasn't it Woody Allen who said, "Time plus tragedy equals comedy"? Well, for Caterina, she couldn't imagine any time in the future when she would think the circumstances would be funny, but now, it seemed like people felt they could talk about her cause. Her friends and family liked it and shared the photo

Alda tagged her in on Facebook. She had ABC and other news outlets calling to ask her about her blog and to get quotes.

Caterina clicked on her blog *#DuckGirl* and saw how many views she had. She was surprised to see thirteen hundred people had visited the site since it launched yesterday. She tried to rationalize that being a TikTok fad was a positive response and helped get more people interested in Peter's case. She wondered if Peter was aware of any of her efforts. Did his lawyers tell him, or did he have access to the internet? She was so frustrated at the silence. It felt worse than death because she knew he was still alive but could not touch him or speak to him. She missed him so much. Her grief was as deep and powerful as her love for him. She had never connected with another person as she did with Peter. She truly felt they had known each other for lifetimes. No one listened to her and understood her as he did right from the start. He loved her idiosyncrasies that other people found off-putting and weird.

"Peter, I miss you," she said out loud in her empty bedroom. "I love you," she said in a quieter voice.

The following week was a whirlwind of her posting to her blog and responding to strangers' and friends' comments. She wondered if this is how TurtleBoy felt about his blog. She started reading his articles and became interested in the Karen Read case. She researched the prosecution's evidence, and it seemed completely obvious that Karen hit her boyfriend, Boston police Officer John O'Keefe, with her car. She was fascinated with the number of strangers that weighed in on her guilt or innocence. TurtleBoy played a significant role in the Karen Read defender's crowd.

"Are you coming with us?" Arlene's mom yelled up the stairs to Caterina's room. Caterina closed her laptop and ran down the stairs to talk to her mom in the kitchen. "I'll drive over myself in case I want to stay later," Caterina responded to her mom's offer for a ride to her brother's Fourth of July cookout. "I'm going to leave soon too."

"Okay, you can bring over the fruit salad. It's in the downstairs fridge. See you over there."

Caterina cherished the rare moments when she was alone in the house. Her parents were retired and loved to be at home together or watch any combination of grandchildren. They'd offer sleepovers and movie nights with the grandkids, and her brothers would take them up on the offer. Her whole immediate family would be at her brother Tony's house, and she felt melancholic thinking about what a great day it was when Peter came to the last party. Her eyes started to well, and she fought the urge to cry.

Her heart jumped when she suddenly heard a flash bang outside, causing her to cling to the kitchen island. Some kids in the neighborhood were setting off firecrackers. She had no idea she was wound so tight until she analyzed her reaction to something so innocent. After the loud bang, it was eerily quiet. She heard a noise next to her, which made her jump again. It was the air-conditioner starting up.

She had a right to be nervous. Dmitry Panchenko was still out there somewhere. The police did not follow up with any of the evidence she sent their way about Panchenko robbing her in the Life Time gym. She wanted to reach out to Joan Barry to have her identify Panchenko as the one who hired Caterina, but she was hesitant to get the innocent woman involved if the police weren't tracking her down. She gave the police her name, and it was their job to pursue a robbery, right? The air-conditioner kicked off, and the house was quiet again. She now hated to be alone in the house. She grabbed her keys to leave, then remembered the fruit salad in the basement. She suddenly became terrified to go downstairs. "This is ridiculous," she said to herself. Why would this guy be hiding in her basement? She had put Ivan's academic paper on her blog. People could read the link from there. Her paying cash for the two extra USBs spoiled his attempt at stealing the thumb drive. He only took the original thumb drive and the two in the bag with the receipt.

Her basement wasn't finished like some of her friends, with wall-to-wall carpeting and a leather sectional sofa. Her basement only had a concrete floor, and the fridge was between Christmas decorations and outdoor furniture. She opened the door to her basement to descend. The stair beneath her foot creaked loudly, causing her to stand as still as a statue, willing there to be nothing down there. "Think logically, Caterina. The chances that Panchenko is hiding in your basement, ready to strike now because he knows your mom would ask you to bring the fruit salad, are infinitesimal. Be reasonable." The gap between rational thinking and her fight-or-flight instincts was very wide at the moment. Her heart was about to burst out of her chest, it was beating so loudly. She took another step on another creaky stair, took a deep breath, ran down the last five stairs, opened the fridge to grab the salad, and ran back upstairs. She shut the door loudly behind her and leaned against the door, waiting for her heart to slow down.

Victory.

Chapter 24

TONY'S STREET WAS lined with cars, and Caterina dropped off the fruit salad on the front steps while she hunted for a space. Wakefield was always busy on the 4th of July with children's events in the morning, a big parade in the afternoon, and a concert and fireworks along Lake Quannapowitt at night. Going to her brother's house each year was a family tradition, and everyone could view the fireworks from his front porch.

"Hey, here's DuckGirl," her brother Dom yelled as he saw her open the screen door to the backyard.

"Oh, shut up, Dom," replied Caterina.

Dom laughed, and his brother joined in. "Seriously, DuckGirl? You went with DuckGirl? I mean, you do realize your name is Cat and you could've gone with CatGirl, right?"

"Yeah, I think that's already taken with DC comics, y'know? I didn't want any copyright issues."

"Well, you had no problem ripping off TurtleBoy," her brother Gio laughed. "And, Jesus, that outburst, Cat. You're all over the internet screaming at that kid. I'm sorry, but that clip is a riot. That mom's face when you yelled is priceless." The two brothers started laughing.

"Leave her alone," a sister-in-law joined them to defend Caterina. She gave her a hug and a peck on the cheek. "They're just jealous you're famous now, and they're not." No one believed what she said, but it helped to defuse their taunting. She turned toward Caterina with her back to her husband and brother-in-law, and they wandered away. "Seriously, Cat, are you doing okay? Mom says you spend all day up in your room on your computer typing and muttering to yourself." Her sister-in-law took a sip of her White Claw. "It's just, well, I mean, maybe you're getting too caught up in your own version of events that you want to be true. You don't see the bigger picture. I mean, that guy TurtleBoy has some crazy conspiracies about who murdered that cop. Maybe those in charge know more about stuff than you bloggers."

Caterina didn't know what to say. She was more than a blogger to Peter. She was his girlfriend, his lover, his confidante. She knew Peter better than she knew her sister-in-law, whom she had known half her life. How could she explain in an elevator pitch that the government was framing her boyfriend to muddy the waters on the real killer, an actual war criminal who murdered his own countrymen execution style? Should she just do a TikTok of the video she witnessed of Dmitry Panchenko holding his pistol to a man's head and pulling the trigger? That video was what Ivan Kanovsky wanted to show the world, but the world can't handle anything negative about Ukraine. Everything has to be black and white, with Russia always bad and Ukraine always good. There was no room for nuance in the propaganda war. Ivan was murdered to hide any negative press about the Ukrainian military.

"Yeah, you're right. I'm just some stupid blogger," Caterina answered and walked away.

Everyone was laughing and joking at the cookout. She had moments of fun with her family, but then someone would say something to set her off. Everyone was oblivious to her grief, and she just wanted to leave before she had another bitchy response that the family would not understand. She was another meme ready to happen.

The night sky was getting darker, and everyone gathered at the front of the house to watch the fireworks. Coolers and blankets were dragged to the lawn. Caterina stayed in the backyard and settled into an Adirondack chair by the fire pit with her hands wrapped around a hot tea. She stared into the fire, trying not to think about Peter's burn from the Trade Unions Building fire ten years ago. She brushed her fingers on her arm, remembering touching his scarred elbow. Her mind drifted from burning buildings to her burning passion for the man she loved.

"Do you mind if I join you, honey?"

Caterina returned her focus to the present and saw her grandmother being escorted to her by her dad.

"Grammy, you're still awake? Of course. Are you warm enough? Here." Caterina rose out of the low chair and pulled two sturdy chairs side by side so they were snuggled in close together, watching the fire.

"You don't want to watch the fireworks?" Grammy asked Caterina.

Caterina stared into the fire. "Nah, just not feeling it."

They sat for a while in silence, both content in each other's company.

"You know what's weird?" Caterina broke the silence. "America celebrates rebels that turned against the British government. Then we celebrate our government, which crushed the rebels in the Civil War. You had these guys that all went to West Point together and were friends, and then a few years later, they were killing each other on the battlefield. Just weird how you never know someone is your enemy until someone tells you they are your enemy."

Grammy listened, "That's interesting."

"Like, what would possess a man to kill his neighbor because one day they woke up and someone told them they were enemies? War is so scary."

Grammy listened some more and knew they were not talking about America but Ukraine.

"I'm sorry about what happened to Peter. I'm sure you miss him. I don't pretend to understand the story. It seems very complicated, but I know you are hurting, and I'm sorry, sweetheart."

Caterina pulled her grandmother in closer with their arms interlocked. "Thank you, Grammy. That means the world to me for you to say that. I wish I had sisters. My brothers just tease me."

"That is what has made you so strong in this world, Caterina. It must also be in the name."

Caterina laughed as her grandmother shared the same name. "Thanks, Caterina," Caterina said to her grandmother.

Pearl by the Sea

"Do you know who I was named after?" asked Grammy.

"Actually, no, I never really thought about it. I know I'm named after you, but I never really thought about who you were named after. Was it a family member?"

"No, my parents grew up in Italy, and my father was very progressive for women's rights. He loved Italian history. He was a brilliant physicist nominated for the Nobel Prize in Physics. He left Italy during the rise of Mussolini because he was ostracized at the university for his outspoken views on the Italian leadership. He came to America for a better life and found it."

"He reminds me of Ivan Kanovsky, who was brave enough to speak out, too," remarked Caterina.

"Yes, when I was born, he named me Caterina. My mother always said I was named after this beautiful opera singer, but my dad would whimsically tell me I was named after Caterina Sforza, a brilliant scholar and warrior in her own right. She was born in Milan and died in Florence. She outlived three husbands. The first two were assassinated due to power struggles. She once rode her horse when she was seven months pregnant to help one of her imprisoned husbands. She tricked her way inside the castle and refused to leave, even with threats of them killing her children. She told the guards that 'The Sforza family would avenge the dead children, and killing them would just make the resistance stronger.'"

"Oh my God, that's crazy. Did they kill them?"

"No, they did not harm her or her children. They knew constraining her just made her look stronger, so they set her free."

"Interesting," Caterina said obtusely, staring into the fire. She thought about her grandmother in a whole different way. She had never spoken to her before about adult subjects. Her own mother would run from any controversial talk, but here was her grandmother saying she was named after some Italian badass woman.

Grammy continued, "You know, Americans are so detached from war now. They don't understand its tragedy at a visceral level. My dad fought for America during World War Two, and your grandfather fought in Vietnam. These men knew war and, I think, had a deeper appreciation of the Fourth of July beyond cookouts and fireworks. They knew they were the lucky ones that made it back alive."

Grammy paused again as if she was thinking of her lost love. "I'm sorry for what happened to Peter's friend, and, of course, I'm sorry about Peter's arrest. War is hell." Grammy rubbed Caterina's arm. "I really liked him. He has an old soul for such a young man."

"Thanks, Grammy, I agree. I think it's because his brother died when he was so young, and then he knew no one cared about the tragedy because it made the Pro-Unity guys look bad. His parents weren't allowed to put flowers at the Trade Unions Building where the fire was. The same thing is happening with the propaganda now. That guy Dmitry Panchenko was protected back then and is being protected now."

The fireworks were going off, but the trees blocked their view. They could hear muffled laughter and chatter during the pauses. Grammy snuggled up close to Caterina and began to sing sweetly. She sang the Nat King Cole song her husband would sing to her in their twilight years, and then Caterina sang the Nat King Cole song that Peter sent her on their first date. The lyrics were beautiful, and when the angels asked what thrilled him the most, he would answer, "You." "I Remember You" was a song Caterina must have played several times a day since Peter shared it with her after their date at the oyster bar. Caterina's grandmother joined in, and Caterina stopped to listen to the woman's sweet singing voice.

When Grammy was through singing, she sighed and smiled. "I miss Grampy. When your Peter sang, it reminded me so much of my husband. He had a good voice too."

Caterina never thought about her grandparents as anything but their roles in her life, not their marriage or their love.

"Did he sing those love songs to you when you guys were dating?" asked Caterina.

Grammy laughed, "Heavens no. We were so young and awkward around each other back then. We had your father so quickly, and your grandfather got shipped off to Vietnam. I think we fought our first decade of marriage and barely said a kind word to each other. No, it was during his last year when he was frail and knew he was not long for this earth. He wanted me to know how much he loved me, although neither of us went as far as apologizing for our mistakes in those early years of marriage. We both knew we had forgiven each other long ago. He was such a good man."

"He sounds it, Grammy. I wish I had gotten to know him as an adult like I'm getting to know you now. I love you, Grammy."

"I love you too, sweetheart. If you ever need someone to talk to, please call me at Sunrise or stop by."

"Absolutely, Grammy."

Suddenly, her grandmother yawned and looked very tired. Caterina asked, "Is Dad going to drive you back, or do you need a ride? I can bring you home."

"I would love a ride. Your father is drunk and seems in no hurry to leave. Why do you think I came down here to butter you up? He'd have me sleeping on Tony's couch."

They both laughed, knowing that was not why her grandmother had come to talk to her. They shared a bond of both knowing the loss of the one they loved; for Caterina, a brief affair, and for her grandmother, a lifetime of marriage.

Tony returned to check on the fire to ensure it was supervised. "What are you two giggling about back here?"

"Oh, just girl talk between the two Caterinas, that's all. Ready, Caterina?" said Grammy.

"Ready, Caterina," said Caterina as she helped her grandmother out of the chair to drive her back to the assisted living facility, both singing the Nat King Cole song softly, "I Remember You."

Chapter 25

CATERINA IMMERSED HERSELF in the blog and communicated with news outlets ready to listen to her story. She had tried dozens of elevator pitches to explain Peter's innocence in just a few sentences. It was a daunting task, but she thought delivery was as important as the message. Some journalists took time to try to understand the story, but more often than not, they muddled the storyline so much that it argued the opposite of her intent.

She couldn't keep up with new friend requests on Facebook, and her followers on TikTok continued to grow. Many were women who loved a handsome man they could support in his time of trouble. Caterina would get jealous when she read some comments from women who obviously noticed the same things she did about his looks. She brushed the juvenile thoughts from her mind and tried to build a community of support. There had to be someone out there who could turn this case around.

She walked out of a CVS on High Street in Medford and headed toward her car. A man was standing next to her Honda she did not recognize. She slowed her walk to size him up before reaching the stranger. He was wearing a business suit, nothing too flashy, but he certainly stood out among the shorts and T-shirts on a hot day. He reached out his hand to shake hers, and it was still cool from probably just jumping out of an air-conditioned car. She spotted a black Lincoln Navigator idling a couple of spots over that was clearly his.

"Hi, Ms. Antonucci?" he asked, "I'm Robert. Nice to meet you. I was wondering if I could have a moment of your time to talk about the case you're working on."

Caterina had no outstanding private eye cases she was investigating. She had taken no new clients, so she assumed he was speaking about the Kanovsky murder.

To clarify, he continued, "I'm referring to your friend, Peter Geller." The stranger made no hints of positive or negative news. He was polished and gave off the vibe of some amorphous government person.

"Who are you?" Caterina asked.

"Robert Fisher." He pulled out his wallet and showed her a laminated identification card. "I'm part of NAFO, an organization which counters Russian propaganda and disinformation across social media. There's my member number." He points to the number #78452. To strengthen his credibility, he added, "We have members all over the world."

Caterina took the identification card out of his hand and read it. NAFO stood for North Atlantic Fella Organization; his picture was of a cartoon dog wearing a hat. The card didn't even have his name on it. Caterina laughed at the card.

Pearl by the Sea

"Did you seriously give me a card with a cartoon dog on it? Do you *really* want me to think your name is Bobby Fisher? *Really*? I know what NAFO is. I've been immersed in Ukrainian and Russian shit posters for a month now. I know you guys think Dmitry Panchenko is a great guy, so I have nothing more to say to you."

"Hold on, Caterina." He made a point not to touch her but just raised his hand. "It really is important you speak with me now. Here is the address I would like to bring you to for our chat." He handed her a Boston address on a yellow sticky note.

Caterina read the paper and replied, "Senator Eric Mason has his Boston headquarters at this address. I know because I've tried to get into his office several times to speak to him. Do you work for Senator Mason?"

"I can't comment on that."

Caterina thought about his offer. It was really her only lead, so she could not refuse it. "I will go, but I'm taking my own car."

"Fair enough, Ms. Antonucci. I will meet you out in front of the building." He adjusted his sunglasses and walked to his car to get in.

Caterina realized this was not a kidnapping since he gave up so quickly driving her. She knew that parking was a pain in the neck around the government center and decided to hitch a ride with him instead.

"Hold up," she shouted as he moved slowly out of his space. "I'll go with you."

He put the car in park and gestured for her to get in. She

opened the door to the Navigator. It was cool inside, with the radio blaring. She buckled her seat belt and put her CVS bag on the ground, realizing she still had it in her hand.

"Do you like JayZ?" Robert shouted over the music while turning the volume down a bit.

"Not really," shrugged Caterina, "but I like this song a bit."

They drove from Medford to the JFK Federal Building, mostly in silence, listening to JayZ. Caterina still could not figure out if he worked for the senator from Massachusetts. Robert gave no hint of his intentions. The Lincoln pulled up to the curb, and the valet was handed the key to park the car. Robert held open the door to the Federal Building and flashed his NAFO badge to the guard at the elevator.

"Did you just . . .?" she asked the stranger.

"Did he just flash you a cartoon dog ID?" asked Caterina as the doors of the elevator door closed with the guard not changing his expression. She turned to Robert, who was still wearing his sunglasses. "Are we going to see Senator Mason?"

He remained silent, and when the elevator doors opened, he led her through a nondescript door into a nondescript room with a table, a few chairs, and shelves filled with nonpersonal items like plastic plants and books. Robert gestured to her to sit down and offered her some coffee or tea. He asked her to put her phone on the table, and he inspected it to make sure it was not in use and kept it close to him.

"Water is fine," said Caterina, getting impatient with the secrecy. "Senator Mason's office is on the fifth floor. We're on the eighth. Whose office is this? Can you arrange a meeting

Pearl by the Sea

with Mason for me? Do you know anything about Peter? Do you know where he is jailed?"

Robert removed his sunglasses and sat in a leather swivel chair across from Caterina. He folded his hands on the table and studied her. He finally spoke. "I don't get it. I don't understand why you are pursuing this case. Yes, I have spoken to Senator Mason, and off the record, I want to tell you he is not happy. That little stunt you did in front of the courthouse and this DuckGirl publicity scheme motivate nutjobs to call his office asking him about Peter Geller. Mason is extremely busy and has more pressing matters to tend to. Your antics are complicating things."

Robert opened the bottled water in front of him and took a sip. "Mason just got a $61 billion aid package to Ukraine passed in the Senate last week. Now, some yahoos in the House are repeating your insane conspiracy theories and trying to get some momentum to vote 'no' on the bill. Do you understand how not supporting Ukraine at this time is going to hurt Ukraine's efforts in defending their country against Russia's invasion? Do you understand how important our support is for the sake of democracy?"

Caterina crossed and rubbed her arms briskly. She didn't know if the accusations or the air-conditioning were making her shiver, but she was freezing. "I-I don't know anything about that stuff. I just want to help my friend Peter. His lawyers told me I couldn't even talk to him. Do you understand I have not heard from him since April?"

"Well, if you don't know anything about this stuff, then

maybe you don't realize you are in over your head," Robert said, leaning in more on the table. "Do you know what a useful idiot is? Do you know Russians love to use simps like you to spread lies to sway people? Support for Ukraine needs to happen at all levels. If some dumbass thinks voting 'no' on the money to Ukraine is going to get him reelected in November, then he is going to vote 'no.' We can't let that happen. If you don't understand this stuff, then kindly shut the fuck up. Excuse my French," said Robert, eliminating any pretense that this was a friendly conversation.

Caterina was disappointed he was giving no details about Peter but slightly excited that her newfound fame was getting enough attention to warrant this meeting. It had to make them somewhat nervous if they sent a grunt like this to talk to her.

"Listen, fella," said Caterina, a tongue-in-cheek reference to his North Atlantic Fella Organization title, "I'm not trying to influence foreign policy. This is a personal matter to me, that's all. I know Panchenko killed Kanovsky. I know Peter is innocent. I know why Panchenko killed him, and I'm not going to be intimidated by some guy with a cartoon dog badge swearing at me."

Robert smiled a little, clearly getting pleasure at her retort. He struck a nerve with her, and she did not cower.

"Well, my badge comes with every government agency behind me to combat Russian disinformation. I have DOD, DHS, CIA, DARPA, FBI, ODNI, right down to the Department of Transportation behind me to make sure traitors like Ivan Kanovsky and you don't spread lies about our

Pearl by the Sea

country. Just to make myself clear, the Department of Defense may have changed its name from the Department of War, but it is unequivocally involved in the Ukraine/Russia War. If you think for one second your little blog is going to win against a trillion-dollar propaganda machine made up of every letter agency in the American government, then I have a bridge to sell you in Brooklyn."

He was quite pleased with his little rant. He seemed to like to play tough guy, and she was trying not to be intimidated, but she was. "I thought our government was not allowed to use propaganda on its own people. Don't we have a Bill of Rights or something? Isn't that illegal?"

He laughed at her rebuttal. "That ship sailed long ago. Our outreach is now overt. Voices of America is broadcast in every language spoken in the United States. All those Somalians freezing their asses off in Minnesota should know how great America is and not get all their news from Al Jazeera. Controlling minds is more important than bullets in a war. It is not enough to try to influence other countries. The threats come from within our country now."

Caterina thought about her speech in front of the Moakley Courthouse, referencing the antiwar New Yorkers who went to jail for dropping pamphlets. She guessed not much had changed since then. If anything, budgets and technology have made it easier for the government to control the narrative.

"How can you defend the government in this situation? You know Peter didn't stab Kanovsky. You know that Nazi Panchenko murdered him. I've seen his Nazi tattoo and a video of his war crimes in Bucha, Ukraine. How can you say that Ivan's research is Russian propaganda? How can you defend someone as heinous as Dmitry Panchenko? Shouldn't Americans know the truth?"

"Oh, you're so naive, sweetheart. What you are dabbling in is misinformation, obfuscation, and, like I said, idiocy, for Russia. You think Panchenko is the only person who did something bad in Bucha? Why promote this one Ukrainian and not say anything about all the atrocities the Russian army did in Bucha? By highlighting Panchenko, you ignore all of the Wagner Group killings. You think one black sun tattoo on Panchenko's chest makes him the bad guy? Do you know how heroically he fought against an invading army? Do you even know why the Russian unit is named Wagner? Do you? Because Wagner was Hitler's favorite musician. That's why. Is your blog going to talk about that? Americans don't need idiots like you and Ivan Kanovsky gaslighting Americans who know nothing about this war. You want to whitewash a shitload of Russian atrocities to emphasize one far-right Ukrainian? Do you see how this hurts America?"

Now, she was getting more intimidated. Was he somehow implying Kanovsky was a US-sanctioned murder? Was her own government involved in framing Peter? She was picturing all the photos of Dmitry Panchenko with senators and the secretary of state. Did Panchenko have full approval to silence Ivan's exposure of Panchenko's war crimes and embezzlement? She suddenly felt defeated. How could she help Peter against her own government?

She rubbed her arms again, and her voice quivered, "I just wanted to help my friend."

"Well, you didn't. I don't have to tell you shit. I'm giving you a courtesy call here to keep you updated. Geller's lawyers think you are their golden ticket. They think putting you on the stand in his murder trial would sway a jury. Gorgeous girlfriend with a sweet Boston accent defending her handsome boyfriend. They're probably right, and frankly, the DOJ doesn't have time for this nonsense, especially if you keep stirring the pot."

Robert pulled on the lapels of his suit jacket and looked closely at Caterina to ensure she was listening. "It's over. Now. Today. Your link to Kanovsky's paper doesn't work anymore. The United States government has coordinated with social media to scrub his paper. We did it before when Geller's link to Ivan's paper didn't work. You are essentially silenced. In matters of national security, social media companies take suggestions from the government seriously, and they oblige. Peter's case is closed. He was deported a week ago and is now in Ukraine. The United States government is no longer indicting him for the murder of Ivan Kanovsky, and you can confirm this yourself on PACER in a couple of hours." Robert checked his watch.

"Go home, Caterina. It's over. I know you had a good time fooling around with that trash Russian, but he is not welcome in America anymore. I suggest you stick with your own kind and stay out of trouble."

Caterina was shocked. Peter was gone. She hoped he was in Boston somewhere in jail, but now she learned he was thousands of miles away. Her eyes started to well, and tears streamed down. She tried to pull on her short sleeves to wipe her face but ended up just wiping her cheeks with her hands and drying them on her shorts.

Robert got up and brought over some tissues that were on the shelf. "This is what I don't understand," he said obtusely. "You're getting all worked up for some nobody. He must be really good in bed or something."

His rudeness cut her like a knife. She couldn't believe her own government was treating Peter and her so abhorrently. She wanted to slap Robert hard across the face. She had never felt the urge to hurt someone, not even Panchenko when he insulted her and stole the thumb drives. She couldn't believe how abruptly her story with Peter ended. It felt surreal; her head started spinning that he was only an illusion and the last few months weren't her real life. All that time and effort to help Peter were futile after a half-hour office chat with some anonymous man from the government.

"Why can't I just tell on you? Tell the world what you are doing to an innocent man. What about Kanovsky's murder? It just goes unsolved, and Boston is supposed to accept this and move on?"

He realized she didn't get it. That was okay. She was new to this. He took another sip of his water. "Have you ever heard of the Gerasimov doctrine?"

Caterina shook her head.

"Valery Gerasimov was defense minister and chief of the Russian Federation Army. He was credited with the new warfare strategy of combining military, technology, culture, and

Pearl by the Sea

other tactics to win the sympathy of a local population. This new warfare strategy Russia used against America during the 2016 campaign to elect Donald Trump and used it again in 2020 to spread lies about Joe Biden. America was caught exposed in 2016, but we have improved our strategic geopolitical information technology in the last eight years. Our budget has increased exponentially to develop a better doctrine than Russia's. Two-bit bloggers sympathetic to Russia cannot compete with our nonlinear warfare. In other words, Caterina, we won before you even knew the game."

There was a knock on the door, and a woman in a suit handed Robert an item. It was Caterina's CVS bag. Robert placed it on the table and pushed it over to Caterina. "It was nice to meet you, Caterina. There's a car downstairs waiting to take you back to Medford. Senator Mason knows nothing about this meeting. No one in the building will admit that a meeting has ever taken place. I am the Ghost of Kyiv, and my goal is to stop disinformation like a good fella," Robert said, tugging on his suit lapels again.

He stood up. "Don't give up your day job, Ms. Antonucci. Stick with lunges and jumping jacks, and stay out of the spy business. You're not that good at it. Elevators are on your right. You will get your phone once you're outside."

With that, he opened the door and walked away.

Chapter 26

CATERINA DIDN'T KNOW what to do. She sat behind the wheel of her car, crying with the news that Peter was deported. For what? Being a kind person? Getting caught in the crossfire of war when he and his brother wandered into the Trade Unions Building after a soccer game? It was an innocent action that killed his brother and now ruined Peter's life.

Caterina checked her blog, and sure enough, all links to Ivan's paper reported a "404 error" of not being found. She checked PACER and saw *that the United States of America vs. Petrov Leonidovich Geller* case was dismissed. The last submitted documents were sealed, just like the indictment.

She didn't know who to call or who would care. She imagined every conversation with her mom or Kimmie would be platitudes of "Maybe this is for the best," wanting her to forget about her love for Peter and "move on." She thought maybe her grammy would understand, but she didn't want to stress her grandmother with stories of strange government men picking her up in their black vehicles. Why did everyone diminish her love? Didn't everyone cry their eyes out when that old lady from the *Titanic* movie was still pining away for Leonardo DiCaprio eighty years later? Why should love be measured in length and not depth? Her love for Peter was the strongest bond she had ever felt in her life. She thought she could now relate to the older woman in *Titanic*.

Caterina threw her Honda into drive and blared "Empire State of Mind" exiting the CVS parking lot in Medford. She headed toward the Mass Pike, rapping the JayZ lyrics and singing the Alicia Keys chorus at the top of her lungs.

She switched to her Peter playlist and sang along to all the songs she and Peter shared, like "I Remember You," "September," "Vehicle," and a dozen more. After the playlist was over, she played it again as if the repetition would bring him back, and he'd be sitting next to her in the passenger seat singing along. She sang along to one of his favorite Frank Sinatra songs, "Summer Wind." It felt so apropos now. It made her heart skip a beat. Did he sense their relationship would end abruptly?

The song faded out, and she put on her blinker to merge from the Mass Pike to Route 84 toward New York City. Her eyes were getting heavy, and she decided to pull over at a Hampton Inn off the highway and finish her destination to Brooklyn in the morning. Tatiana's dance studio would be open for business tomorrow, and she wanted to talk to her. Tatiana had ignored all Caterina's attempts to communicate, but Caterina had the urge to see her again, face-to-face.

Caterina woke up the next day feeling drugged. She wandered down to the continental breakfast, but her stomach was doing too many flips, so she walked past all the selections. She stopped at a Starbucks a few buildings from the hotel and ordered a large, iced coffee. She then typed in the address for the School of Ukrainian Ballet, Brighton Beach, Brooklyn, and hit the road. She arrived in "Little Odessa," which Brighton Beach was fondly nicknamed for the area's dense population of Russian speakers. After parking, she wandered the boardwalk of this seacoast town and listened to the mixture of languages from tourists and locals. Most sounded Russian, but it was very common to hear Uzbek, Georgian, and Ukrainian along the shore. Elderly couples of Babushkas and Dedushkas strolled the boardwalk enjoying a cool morning before the sun rose too high in the sky. Caterina checked her watch. It was nine a.m., and the studio would be open.

The dance school was located between a food market that changed its name from "A Taste of Russia" to "International Food" and an insurance company with English under Cyrillic letters. She followed moms and little girls into the building. The girls were led into a studio while the moms sat along wooden benches across from one another and chatted, mostly in English with rich Slavic accents. It reminded Caterina of Peter's pronunciation of words and flooded her with memories. Caterina walked up to the teacher greeting the students in the doorway and asked if she could see Tatiana. The dance teacher said she was in her office and pointed around the corner.

The office door was open, and Tatiana was sitting behind her laptop. She looked surprised when she recognized Caterina standing before her, patiently waiting. Caterina wasn't sure if

Pearl by the Sea

Tatiana was good with faces, but Tatiana immediately recognized her. She didn't greet Caterina but jumped up to close her office door and nervously sat back down.

"Caterina, what are you doing?"

Tatiana asking a question was a good start, thought Caterina. It was much better than silence. Just this one sentence was worth her drive. What was she doing? It was an excellent question.

"Tatiana, hi. I just wanted to tell you in person that I'm sorry for your loss. I'm sorry about Ivan," Caterina said softly. "It was so tragic, so awful. I just wanted to tell you in person."

Tatiana absorbed her words and stayed silent for a while. "Thank you. I'm sorry I didn't return your phone calls. I had the police calling me, asking me so many questions. I just wanted to ignore it all. I'm sorry if I blew you off."

Tatiana had a New York accent that had no hint of European origin. Her mother was born in Brooklyn, and Caterina remembered her saying she had never been to Ukraine.

"I understand," sighed Caterina. "It's been hard on everyone, especially Peter, as you know." Caterina was hoping mentioning his name would open Tatiana to talking.

Tatiana's eyes darted around the room to assess if anyone had walked through the walls since she closed the door. When she confirmed they were alone, she spoke again. "I can't, Caterina. I can't get into this. I loved my cousin, but I only got to know him since he started teaching at Boston University. It's not like I know that much about him. I can't have this murder investigation connected to my school. It was bad enough that

I had to change the name of my school from Russian Ballet to Ukrainian Ballet. If those moms out there think I'm related to some traitor, they will march their daughters right out of my school. I can't get involved."

Caterina's heart sank. She was not going to find solidarity and strength with Ivan's cousin. She found another coward writing off Ivan and Peter for the sake of a narrative. People were so afraid to go against acceptable propaganda. Truth be damned.

"You know Ivan isn't a Russian sympathizer and a traitor to Ukraine. C'mon, Tatiana. You know Peter had absolutely nothing to do with his murder." Caterina raised her voice and lowered it when she saw Tatiana getting nervous that someone might overhear the conversation.

"Caterina, I know you love Peter. From what I saw on the sailboat, you two were really cute together. He was worried you were going to get hit by the boom. I could tell he cared about you. I'm sorry about how everything worked out. Really."

Caterina cherished her words. They brought back memories of Peter and her sharing their earbuds, singing and dancing together on their way to the boathouse. Caterina had another memory pop into her head.

"Thank you, Tatiana. It's sad how a day that started so great ended so tragically with Ivan being murdered. I remember it started raining pretty hard, and Ivan offered you a place to stay. What happened?"

"Are you thinking I'm a suspect, Caterina?" Tatiana spat out the accusation in a hushed tone. "This is why I ignored

Pearl by the Sea

your calls. I don't need the drama around here. I didn't ask Ivan to study such controversial subjects. I have absolutely nothing to do with people wanting to kill him. I have thought about his offer every day since he died. If I had slept over instead of getting a hotel, I might have saved his life, or, shall I remind you, I also might have been murdered. Sometimes, we can be in the right place at the right time and the wrong place at the wrong time. I was neither that night, so it's no use rehashing it. We all need just to move on. I care about my students, and I care about my community and business. Odessa is another world to me, and I can't have it ruin my life like it ruined Ivan's."

Tatiana stood up and did something that surprised Caterina. She gave her a big bear hug and held both Caterina's shoulders firmly. "You are a beautiful young woman, Caterina. You need to forget about Peter. We are helpless in this situation. If we thought the American courts were going to give him an unfair trial, then the corrupt courts in Ukraine would be even worse. My family knows that Peter did not kill Ivan, but we will be destroyed if we fight the system, Caterina. Be grateful for the time you two had together. As I told Peter on the sailboat, 'Ukraine will forever be a pawn.' That is a harsh reality we have to live in. We are insignificant in this battle. Peter is not a king, and you are not a queen. You're a pawn. The sooner you accept this reality, the faster you will drop your one-woman crusade. Nothing good will come of it. I hate to be a buzzkill in your investigation, but I can't be dragged into this. I won't be."

Tatiana opened the door to her office and walked out with Caterina looking quite stunned. "I'm sure your daughter will love taking dance lessons here," Tatiana said loudly as she walked past the moms sitting on the benches. Tatiana opened the front door of the building and walked outside with Caterina, closing the door behind them and leading her down the sidewalk until they were in front of the International Food Market. "Goodbye, Caterina. Enjoy life. My grandmother left the Soviet Union years ago for a better life here in America, and I'm proof she succeeded. Don't get sucked into this controversy when no one wants you there. Be grateful you can go on with a good life."

Tatiana turned around to enter the building. Caterina was shocked that Peter's case had been brushed under the rug here in America, only to have it resurface in Ukraine. "Peter wants me there," she said quietly to no one as she started down the boardwalk in Little Odessa.

Chapter 27

"**Shhh, she's here.**" The room went as quiet as a semiprivate room in a restaurant can be. "Surprise!" the group of women cheered as Kimmie walked through the door with several of her bridesmaids. They were all dressed beautifully with loose curls in their hair. Everyone went along with the charade that Kimmie was surprised as hugs were passed around.

Caterina sat with a group of girls from Medford. She was delegated to the nonbridesmaids' table. She didn't care she wasn't a bridesmaid and found relief in being excused from the daunting task of planning events. The open bar of mimosas was a popular drink with tall glass tubular dispensers on the bar. Her friend seated next to her was sipping a lavender-colored liquid from a champagne flute. "Have you guys tried this elderflower mimosa yet? It's so good." She leaned close to Caterina so they could hear each other over the loud volume in the crowded restaurant. The drinks flowing late in the morning certainly helped raise the noise level.

"You have such an interesting life, Cat. Mine's so boring. All I do is go to work and come home to Teddy. You're out there solving murders and gallivanting around with gorgeous European men." Her friend took another sip of her mimosa. "I'm so proud of you for helping that guy get back home. You're a hero."

Caterina answered sarcastically, although the girl was unaware of her tone, "Yeah, a real hero."

"How'd you get into all that private eye stuff anyway?"

Caterina was sipping tea with her fingers wrapped around the mug. "Well, my uncle Jimmy worked for insurance companies investigating auto claims, and he interested me in the work. It seemed like decent money to supplement my personal trainer job. I'm still trying to figure out what to do with my life. I'm thinking about going to physical therapy school."

"That's awesome," said her friend, half-listening. "You were always a fighter, Cat." She turned to the other high school friend in the conversation. "Remember when poor Cat broke her leg and hobbled around the high school with that clunky brace and crutches forever?" They both laughed at the memory, and Caterina was trying to find the humor in the memory.

She didn't know how to react, so she just said matter-of-factly, "Yeah, I tore my ACL and had reconstruction surgery."

The two didn't really listen to her remark and stood up quickly when they saw Kimmie approaching their table. Squeals were shouted as everyone gave Kimmie hugs and air kisses on the cheek and told her how beautiful she looked. She really did look lovely in a simple white summer dress, with her blond hair partly pinned up and loose curls bouncing off her back. Her pink lipstick matched her stiletto pink shoes.

Caterina hadn't dressed up since her dates with Peter, so she wore a floral summer dress to her ankles. Her thin frame was not accentuated with the loose-fitting style. She was back jogging and working at Life Time and quickly lost the few pounds she had gained sitting all day on her laptop. She was still living with her parents but was home less and less, picking up more shifts. Kimmie was standing in front of her, and they both felt tremendous love for each other. They hugged so tight until someone broke them apart to drag Kimmie to her future mother-in-law's table. The guests each took a turn in the brunch buffet line, and the mimosas continued to flow. Most of the shower presents were mailed to Kimmie's address, so there was no endless watching of the presents being opened. A few who still liked tradition brought their gifts along. A big cheer rose as the groom and his best man entered the Salt & Stone restaurant. Jack and Jason both looked handsome in their pastel dress shirts and black pants. Jason and Caterina had always been civil with each other since their breakup years ago. They had little choice since they bumped into each other often enough, coming from the same circle of friends.

She sat at her table while the bridesmaids placed Kimmie and Jack in front of the group to play shower games. Caterina had a couple of empty seats around her, and Jason sat beside her with his desserts. He raised his plate to offer her a treat, but she waved a hand to decline. "No, thanks."

"You've always been disciplined, Caterina. That's why you still look amazing," Jason smiled, popping a bite-size cheesecake into his mouth.

Cat smiled back. It was nice to get attention, and she was glad she and Jason were comfortable with each other, especially after their awkward breakup.

"You got over breaking up with me easy enough," commented Jason, which Caterina thought was absurd. If anything, he broke up with her after she found his secret Facebook Travel Group Page. He freaked out, yelling she was a snoop and didn't trust him. Was his memory false or hers? Maybe they just had different versions of events. However, she was not going to argue about what ended their relationship.

Caterina wanted to clear the air, nonetheless. "You know, I didn't think your travel group Facebook page was weird at all. I thought it was kind of cool you photoshopped yourself all over the world and talked to people about travel. I actually thought it made you an interesting person. Everyone has secret interests that they don't think others will approve of. You like to travel, so what?"

Jason was surprised that she had just blurted out his secret past. "Well, I guess I was embarrassed to be caught lying. I felt exposed, like you found out I was a fraud or something. You found out I was lying when I said I went places I never went. I thought you wanted nothing to do with me."

"Well, I obviously knew you didn't go to Africa or Antarctica. Lots of people have alter personas online. You weren't the first. I didn't expect you to freak out when I discovered your page. It's not like you were hiding it that well."

"Cat, only you would've found it because you love to snoop on people and are good at doing research. Most people could never put two and two together. Smart," he playfully said, touching a finger to the side of her head. "You know, I did end up traveling a bit. I went to Costa Rica last year, and I'm going to Italy next year."

"That's cool, Jason. That's awesome," she smiled at Jason, who smiled back. Caterina took a bite-size cheesecake off his plate and ate it. He laughed. "You must eat those in one bite, not nibble on them like a mouse." He paused a minute, not knowing how to talk about anything serious in Caterina's life. He got bits and pieces from Jack and Kimmie. All he knew was it had to do with some foreign guy Caterina fell for.

"Are you still with that guy?" Jason asked vaguely. Caterina smiled back. "No, he is back in Ukraine. He's not allowed back in the United States. He's on some list."

"A list," Jason repeated. "I remember you with all your lists. You could always do that party trick rattling off the states and presidents and shit. You still do stuff like that?"

Caterina smiled a sad smile. Thinking of her bilateral injury list, she had added Peter to it with his two broken heels. She smiled, thinking of the list of songs that he sent her. "Not really," she said vaguely. "I have a new project. I was thinking maybe you could help me with it. I started this website when I was blogging about Peter. I'm changing it to a kind of restaurant review site, mostly alfresco dining stuff around Boston. Well, I thought it might be fun just to pretend I traveled worldwide reviewing seaside restaurants. It's just for my personal use, a kind of stupid hobby. Would you help me with the pictures?"

Jason started laughing. "You want me to help you photoshop yourself into cities you have never traveled to—like I used to do?"

"Yeah, just for fun," she repeated.

"Sure," Jason shrugged. "What are you doing tonight?"

The shower events were winding down, and Jack and Jason loaded the gifts into Jack's car. Kimmie still stood remarkably well in her high heels, running on adrenaline. She gave Caterina a big hug. "I love you. I can't wait to party with you in five weeks. Can you believe how close the wedding is coming up?"

"Crazy," Caterina repeated. "September will be here before you know it." Kimmie and Jack's wedding was Sunday, September 1st, and Peter's trial date was set for three days later in Odessa, Ukraine. Not that anyone was aware of his trial or the actual date. As she told Jason, sometimes you just had to hide your crazy from the rest of the world. "Time is flying by."

Chapter 28

JASON WAS A big help with redesigning Caterina's website. All *#DuckGirl* links and articles were deleted and replaced with clickbait to posts about "Where to find the best oysters in Boston" and "What to pair with Pacific Northwest oysters." Caterina quickly became quite knowledgeable about the bivalve mollusk and immersed herself in YouTube videos that taught her about harvesting these delicacies. She learned that most oysters in American restaurants come from two regions: the Atlantic Coast, from Maine to Florida, and the Pacific Coast, from British Columbia down to Mexico. The West Coast oysters had more elongated shells with jagged, fluted edges, tasted more creamy, and were medium-bodied. Their flavor had the essence of cucumber and melon based on many variables from the salt water. East Coast oysters were the more common teardrop shape you see in advertisements with the flat top and cup bottom to hold their briny liquor when you scooped one into your mouth.

As with wines, oysters are defined and named by the location of where they were harvested. *Terroir* is French for a "sense of place" and involves all the factors that produce a unique flavor to a wine. *Merroir* describes this same distinct fingerprint for each oyster farm. Algae blooms, climate, the chemical composition of the salt water mixing with freshwater, and speed of water flow are just a few examples of variables that can make your favorite oyster from, say, Duxbury, Massachusetts, taste more buttery and more delicious than any other region.

Oysters are alive and grow. They open their mouths to filter water and can help keep a healthy eco environment for other creatures in the sea. Occasionally, a foreign object can get stuck in an oyster, and its defensive mechanisms will go into overdrive to protect itself from this intruder inside its shell. An oyster will lay down a beautiful, crystallized lattice of special calcium carbonate that envelops the foreign object. Soon, this masterful layering completes its task, and a light, round, sturdy pearl is formed inside the mollusk. The unique layering of the calcium carbonate displays dozens of luminescent rainbows when refracting light. A string of pearls was considered a must-have luxury for women of society in Europe and America back in the day. A pearl represents beauty combined with strength. The glistening necklace was the perfect combination of lightness and durability.

Caterina titled her new website "Pearl by the Sea," referencing when Peter called her "My perla by the sea" when they dined together along Boston harbor. Also, a shout-out to Odessa, Ukraine, known as the "Pearl of the North Sea," a nickname for its beautiful architecture and the strength of its population.

Caterina removed comments on the website so only she could see them. Initially, all the comments were about Peter Geller and DuckGirl. She ignored inquiries into his status by his fan club. People could Google stuff if they were that curious.

Jason helped Caterina add pictures of her visiting oyster restaurants in France. There is a deep history in the country's love for the delicacies. There are over 2,500 oyster farms alone in France, and an oyster could taste uniquely different from another oyster raised just fifty meters away, similar to vineyards' uniqueness. She had pictures of her reviewing oysters in Seattle, Ireland, and even Japan. She believed the website looked interesting and that any oyster enthusiast would enjoy her musings.

Today, after work, she headed over to Row 34, a great new restaurant in Kendall Square in Cambridge, named after the thirty-fourth row of the Island Creek Oyster Farm in Duxbury, MA. Skip Bennet, the owner of Island Creek Oysters, decided to fully grow the thirty-fourth row of oysters in their trays versus submerging them in the ground when they were six months old. They were a hit and, thus, became the name of a trendy restaurant.

"You're going where? With whom?" shouted Kimmie while she was on the elliptical, forgetting to turn down her music while talking to Caterina. She quickly pulled her speakers out of her ears and spoke normally to repeat her question. "Where are you going tonight?"

Caterina had already talked to Kimmie three times while working out at Life Time, and she saw Kenneth giving her the hairy eyeball for stopping to speak with her again. Kenneth had not been too friendly to Caterina since she returned to work. The workplace atmosphere felt awkward, and Caterina was taking more shifts closer to Medford, but when they needed help, they always called her.

"I told you, I'm going to this restaurant, Row 34, in Kendall Square. I'm reviewing it for my Pearl by the Sea website."

"I thought you were doing that stupid blog just as an excuse to go out with Jason. I thought it was ingenious for you to ask for his help. You know, I always thought you guys looked great together." Kimmie slowed down her speed and resistance to continue talking. She seemed to spend more time cooling down than actually working out. "You know, it wasn't cool to lead him on like that."

"I wasn't leading him on, Kimmie. We were just talking. I genuinely wanted his help, and that was it. We got together a couple of times to work on the website. I never pretended it was going to lead to anything."

"C'mon, Cat. You know he still likes you. He was bummed you snubbed him when he went in for a kiss. Do you know he's bringing another girl to the wedding? You completely blew it with him, Cat."

"I didn't blow anything. I'm happy he's seeing someone. He's a good guy, even if he's a little too honest in his play-by-play of our 'date.'" Caterina puts the word *date* in quotations.

"So, who are you going out with tonight? Please don't tell me a Hinge date. My nerves can't take another cat killer. Actually, a cat killer sounds mild compared to what you went through with Peter. Maybe screening your dates like you used to wasn't a bad idea."

"No, it's not a date. I'm going by myself. You can come if you want. I'm pairing the Row 34 oysters with a nice Russian River Chardonnay. I can't wait."

"Please, Cat, no more Russian names. Ivan, Petrov, Dmitry—that was enough of that. How about you open your mind to one of Jack's friends at the wedding next week? You'll be turning heads in the dress you're wearing. You look like Cleopatra in that outfit, no joke."

Caterina smiled. "That's what the cat killer Hinge date said about me. I think Sidar must be Egyptian because of his surname. They like cats over there in Egypt."

"You're killing me, Cat. Forget the Cleopatra nonsense. How about you look like yourself, beautiful."

"I have to get back to work, Kimmie," Caterina said quickly when she saw Kenneth walking toward the cardio room. "If you change your mind about tonight, call me."

"Better yet, if you change your mind about Jason, call *me*," replied Kimmie.

Chapter 29

ALL OF KIMMIE'S hopes and dreams came true on Sunday, September 1st. Not her wish for Caterina and Jason to get together, but her own "happily ever after" of her wedding day. Caterina was beyond thrilled for the lovely couple, but her hopes and dreams for this week differed greatly from their nuptials. Ever since she became aware of Peter's court date, she had planned to go to Odessa and fight for his freedom. No one around her was aware of her goal. They felt comfortable in their analysis that she was trying to move on.

Caterina shared her thoughts with no one, not even her grandmother. She wanted no electronic or verbal communication regarding her plans to travel to Ukraine. She handwrote a letter to Peter's parents telling them to expect her arrival for the trial and to have his lawyers add her as a witness. If what that cartoon dog fella said was true, that the United States government was concerned she'd be a great witness, then it would also be true for the Ukrainian officials. She knew it was a great risk. Dmitry Panchenko robbed her for obtaining Ivan Kanovsky's paper. Her links to his paper were scrubbed on social media at the behest of the federal government. She was told to "fuck off" by someone from the government who dressed in a nice suit and liked JayZ. All her friends and family told her to forget about Peter, but she couldn't. Ever since she was a kid, when someone told her she couldn't, it motivated her more than ever to shout to the world, "I can!"

She looked beautiful in her aqua blue dress with her hair teased up in a loose bun accented with sterling silver earrings dangling from her ears. She did not attend the group hairdressing event that morning, even though Kimmie invited her. She wanted to remain freewheeling today, with no particular person relying on her for a ride or even to show up. When the vows were complete in the area adjoining the reception hall, Caterina made sure she was the first one out the door to find her table number and slipped it into her pocket. She wanted no one to know who was supposed to be in the empty seat at the table when dinner was served.

She removed her cell phone from her silver clutch purse and hid it behind a floor plant, ensuring it was on silent and facedown. If someone was tracking her, she wanted to be traced to the wedding reception for the next few hours. Kimmie and Jack were taking pictures with the wedding party on the lawn while two hundred guests milled around the cocktail hour with hors d'oeuvres and drinks. During some downtime in between bridal party photos, Caterina walked quickly up to Kimmie and whispered closely to her ear.

"I have to leave now, Kimmie. Please don't announce it to anyone, and play dumb if anyone asks. Just say I told you I wasn't feeling good. I love you, Kimmie, so much."

Kimmie didn't know what to think about this sudden departure from her wedding. Caterina had not shared any details about Peter since he was deported. All Caterina talked about this summer was the upcoming wedding and her oyster website. Kimmie had no time to process Caterina's statements as she was summoned for another photo. She just responded, "You are my best friend in all the world, Cat, and you always will be. I love you too, so much."

With that, Caterina returned to the patio, accepting a glass of chardonnay from a waitress. She stood at a high-top table with high school friends, trying to find her best opportunity. She spotted it when a friend, Sharon, rested her iPhone on the high top. Caterina picked up the phone and held it up so the Face ID caught Sharon's face, and Caterina turned it side to side. "Oh, I love your phone case, Sharon." Her friend gave her a quick nod and continued the story she was engrossed in telling. Caterina ordered an Uber to the World Trade Center in Seaport, where the wedding reception was being held, and it was nine minutes away. She left twenty dollars under Sharon's phone.

Caterina walked briskly to the exit, and once outside, she took off her heels and ran fast to her parked car. She paid a premium for her spot but wanted quick access to her Honda. She threw off her loose-fitting dress and threw on jeans, a T-shirt, and the sneakers she had laid out in the backseat. Then she grabbed her backpack and ran to the front of the building, waiting for a silver Highlander with a license number ending in

GC21 to pull up. With a minute to spare, she stood there taking deep breaths, turning her head on a swivel to search for the car. Usually, she could track a vehicle on the Uber app, but the notifications were being sent to Sharon's phone. Right on time, an Uber pulled up, and Caterina waved him down and opened the backseat, "Bruno?" she asked, and he confirmed his name.

"Hi, Sharon. You are going to the airport, right?" replied Bruno. She felt weird answering to a different name but replied, "Yes, thanks."

Bruno talked the whole car ride about how he had only been in Boston for two years from Brazil and how much Seaport had changed since he started working for Uber two years ago. Caterina gave him the obligatory "Uh-huh" once in a while to acknowledge she was listening and check her cheap watch for the time. A direct flight from Boston to Warsaw was leaving at four o'clock, and she checked yesterday on someone else's log-in at work that there were at least twelve seats available. Bruno pulled up curbside. She felt bad that she couldn't add a tip to the app, so she gave him ten dollars in cash and hoped Sharon hadn't noticed her ghost ride to Logan Airport yet.

Caterina approached the United Airlines customer service and asked for a ticket on flight UA1762, leaving at 4:02 p.m. She handed her passport, license, and credit card, and her ticket was processed. She knew she now had an electronic trail, but she couldn't avoid not giving her passport at this stage. She hoped for the best and walked through security, placing her sneakers and backpack on the conveyor belt. She walked through the body scanner and retrieved her backpack on the other side. She unzipped her bag and checked on the two thumb drives she was bringing of Ivan Kanovsky's paper to the trial. She looked around to see if someone was watching or following her, but it appeared people were carrying on with their business. Perhaps she was being overly paranoid that someone would care she was going to Peter's trial. Maybe that fella from the government harassed Americans daily with his big brother attitude, and she was not that special. She had no idea, but it felt better to be careful.

She waited for Group C to be called to board the plane. It was a ten-hour flight to Poland, and she planned to rent a car and drive from Warsaw to Odessa for another fourteen hours. She thought a flight into Ukraine would be more of a red flag that she was on the move and maybe entering via Poland would slip under their radar. She hoped to sleep on the plane so she would be awake enough to drive all Monday and have a couple of days of buffer for any glitches. She scanned the gate area and saw a man reading a newspaper with his face hidden. She found this odd. Who reads a newspaper nowadays and uses this type of disguise to hide their face? She could not take her eyes off the man, waiting to catch his appearance when he pulled the newspaper away from his body.

"Group C can now begin boarding the plane, Group C," said the flight attendant. Caterina swung her backpack over her shoulder, not taking her eyes off "newspaper man" until her ticket was checked and she was walking down the gateway. She turned over her shoulder to see if he boarded after her. She looked for a man with a newspaper folded under his arm but saw nothing.

Pearl by the Sea

There was plenty of legroom on the flight, and after dinner, it was clear that the passengers intended to sleep. She had a window seat, which made inspecting the passengers more difficult. Hours after watching people get up to use the bathroom to determine if they were a threat, she finally succumbed to sleep.

She dreamed of waking up from her sleep and seeing "newspaperman" sitting beside her on the airplane. He looked like Dmitry Panchenko and gave her a wicked smile. It was not "present-day Panchenko," the one who chased her into Life Time gym with his grown-out hair, but skinhead Panchenko, shirtless, with his black sun tattoo emblazoned on his chest. He slapped the folded newspaper into his palm as if he were about to scold a dog for being naughty. He tapped louder and more determined with each strike. "*Who do you think you are? Do you understand I have diplomatic immunity to do whatever the fuck I want? I have carte blanche to buy whatever weapons I think are necessary to defeat Putin. You think two dorky professors and some gym rat from Boston can take me down? Do you?*" He laughed a sinister laugh as he hit the newspaper harder and harder.

Caterina was startled out of her nightmare and inspected her environment. It was quiet except for the noises of the humming of the plane and the snoring of her seatmate. She had to use the bathroom and tried to navigate around the sleeping woman without disturbing her rest. She briefly turned her head side to side, sizing up each person curled up in a ball under a blanket or with a sleep mask on or donning a neck pillow. No one made the hair on her neck rise. Afterward, she returned to her seat, waiting for the flight to land in about an hour. Finally, she breathed a sigh of relief that eased her tension.

She retrieved her backpack from the overhead bin and walked through customs, no longer searching for "newspaperman." When she gave the customs agent her paper describing where she was staying and her intended purposes for visiting Warsaw, she was asked to step aside and be escorted to a private room. Two armed police and a man in a suit were in a cramped room, and the man in the suit was typing into his computer. When they determined she did not speak Polish, another guard was brought in to help interpret.

"He is asking you for your backpack. He says Interpol has flagged you for possibly disseminating Russian propaganda. This, by no means, is an arrest. It is simply a courtesy to ensure the safety of Poland during these uncertain times of war. I'm sure you understand." The man paused, listened to the man in the suit, and interpreted the Polish into English. "He would like to see your phone."

"I don't have it. Um, it broke last week, and I haven't had a chance to get to the Apple store."

The man in the suit listened to her answer and was not satisfied. He dumped all of her stuff on a long table and, with blue-gloved hands, went through her belongings, finding the thumb drives in her makeup bag. After being satisfied they were the only electronics, he placed them to the side and folded her stuff back into the backpack, doing a better job packing than she had done. He spoke, and the guard nodded his head.

"Here is a claim number. We will hold onto the devices,

and on your return trip, you may claim them at customs. If you lose your claim ticket, you can also present this flight ticket or your passport to have your items returned. As I'm sure you know, Warsaw is a popular connecting point into Ukraine, and we have to be vigilant in our fight against Russia. *Slava Ukraini*," he added, handing her the backpack.

She did not return the phrase but just nodded and walked in the direction he pointed toward. Interpol flagged her? What? Was this a joke? Isn't Interpol for terrorists and international bank thieves? She was far from Boston and just headlines of war. Over here, they were one country away from bombs being dropped and soldiers dying. She knew this, though, and her love for Peter outweighed all circumstances. She was determined to see this through. So, with no cellphone, no evidence, and just herself, she marched on to Odessa. She decided not to rent a car and, instead, took the train from Warsaw to Odessa to be amongst people. It felt safer than driving across the border by herself.

She bought her ticket and boarded the train. The ride would take fifteen hours and was not as comfortable as her plane seat. She shifted position often and was not tired enough to sleep, so she just stared out the window at the countryside.

Her window was dirty, and there wasn't much to see outside. She shifted again in her seat, trying not to bump the two other passengers in their small compartment. It was a sleep train, so they each had a seat and a bed to stretch out in. She chose the top bunk since the couple she traveled with did not seem to care for the height. The train stopped at the station when they reached the border between Poland and Ukraine. The train attendant came by each compartment, gathering everyone's passports, and they waited. Was there going to be another interrogation and inspection of her belongings? She had no idea, and her fellow passengers spoke little English to ask them questions.

The wait turned from one hour to four hours. She panicked that the delay was all her fault, and she was waiting for armed guards to come bursting through the door to arrest her. The train was becoming stifling hot, and cigarette smoke from the hallway made its way through the cracks. She tried to open the window, but it would only open an inch from the top and did little to relieve her comfort level. After almost five hours, someone knocked on the door, and a Ukrainian border official in camouflage fatigues opened the latch. He sized Caterina up and down and took extra time handing back her passport, openly staring at her. She felt uncomfortable and took the passport back with downcast eyes. The couple did not seem concerned about the long delay and chatted as the train started up again and chugged into Ukraine.

She quietly thanked God she gave herself extra time for the trip. She was not much of a world traveler, and the logistics of traveling in a foreign country by herself were not in her skill set. Finally, after what she thought would be a fifteen-hour ride that turned into a twenty-four-hour ride, she arrived in Odessa. She ended up sleeping most of the trip in the top bunk, and the heat facilitated a deeper sleep than she thought would be possible under the circumstances. She had no more nightmares, which was also a relief. She tried to avoid the bathroom train and found a bathroom in the train station.

The Odessa train station was beautifully adorned with marbled columns and massive chandeliers hanging from lofty ceilings. Fresco paintings lined the walls of other Odessa sites that were part of the city in the second half of the nineteenth century when the train station was built. One hundred years earlier, Catherine the Great gathered brilliant architects to develop her newly named city. She could never have imagined how much the population would grow.

Architects Franz Frapolli and Alexander Bernardazzi, among other skilled artisans, built a mixture of Art Nouveau, Renaissance, and Classical-designed buildings. Caterina observed the Odessites milling about the area. There were occasionally soldiers in random spots inside the train station, but it appeared to be primarily people going about their daily business. One thing she observed was the lack of young men in the crowds, a sad indicator that many were conscripted into the war, or worse, having made the ultimate sacrifice of dying for their country. Of course, many wealthy families sent their young men out of the country for the remainder of the war to avoid the draft.

Caterina washed up in the train station bathroom and changed into a fresh outfit from her backpack. She fluffed her hair and applied some colored lip gloss, then headed out to her first destination. She had plenty of hryvnias, the Ukrainian bank notes. She mostly had them in one-hundred, two-hundred, and five-hundred notes. Forty hryvnias were equal to one dollar, and giving someone a hundred-note hryvnia was about two dollars and fifty cents.

Outside the train station, she caught a cab to her first destination in Odessa, the oceanside restaurant of Di Mare. She heard they had delicious oysters.

Chapter 30

CATERINA WAS EXHAUSTED from her nonstop forty-eight hours of travel. She wanted a shower desperately but needed to obtain the package she sent weeks ago to the Di Mare Seafood restaurant. The place was a welcomed oasis after cramped airplanes and trains. It was located on a seaside boulevard along the Black Sea. The open space and sea breeze evoked nostalgia for her first date with Peter at the Oyster Bar in Boston. She swung her backpack over her shoulder with a sudden burst of energy and walked toward the summer terrace. A young hostess was standing at the entrance, and Caterina smiled at her.

"Hello, this is beautiful," Caterina pointed toward the outdoor patio set with soft blue tablecloths and crisp white napkins, evoking freshness and a Mediterranean vibe.

The hostess smiled. Her English was not strong, but she knew some phrases and understood more than she could speak. "Just one?" She picked up a menu and escorted Caterina to a table along the water's terrace.

The place was empty at two o'clock on a Tuesday, which felt sad to Caterina, but she welcomed the solitude. Before she sat down, she spoke again to the hostess. "My name is Caterina Antonucci. I'm from Boston in America." The young hostess smiled, and Caterina was unsure how much she understood, but she continued. "I write a food blog called 'Pearl by the Sea.' I wrote a letter to the owner telling him I would be here today. Is he here? Matteo?"

"Matteo?" the girl repeated. "Yes, soon." She pointed to the street, mimicked driving, and smiled.

"Water?" another younger woman asked as the hostess walked away. Caterina answered yes, and then she reintroduced herself and asked for the owner. She wished she had her phone to pull up her blog, but she only had her passport.

"Do you need time, or ready to order?" asked the waitress.

The menu was, thankfully, in Ukrainian and English. "Yes, I'll have a dozen oysters and a glass of Chardonnay, thank you."

The waitress brought over some delicious warm bread that was crisp on the outside and soft on the inside, with butter on the side. Caterina drank all the water and took a big bite of the roll smeared in butter. She wasn't sure if the owner was on his way driving here now or if he was driving somewhere else with the clues the hostess gave. At the moment, she didn't care. Thirst and hunger can take priority over any pending issue. She was enjoying the sustenance.

The waitress brought her wine, a very healthy pour in a clean, elegant wineglass. It was cold. Caterina was tempted to take a big gulp, but she wanted to wait for her oysters, so she just took a little sip. It was delicious. She observed her surroundings. This would be close to the end of tourist season for most cities; however, this felt unusually quiet. She had to remind herself that Ukraine was in the middle of a war, but it didn't feel like a war. She didn't know what a war felt like. Perhaps this was just a slow day at a restaurant.

Her oysters arrived, and the presentation was your typical display of open-shelled oysters with two sauce options: cocktail and mignonette. She stirred the horseradish into the cocktail sauce and did not squeeze the lemon on all the oysters, only the one she was about to eat. Through her YouTube education, she learned that lemons will "cook" an oyster, changing the flavor if left to sit. She loosened the adductor muscle that adhered delicately to the shell and slid the oyster into her mouth, savoring the tasty liquor surrounding the body. She washed it down with a big sip of her wine.

She didn't feel war at that moment. She felt peace.

"You have not tasted perfection until you try our oysters with a gin and tonic," stated a good-looking man who approached her with two drinks. He was wearing a crisp blue Polo shirt and jeans. His salt-and-pepper hair was styled in a slight pompadour. He placed the two drinks on the table and stood straight. "I am Matteo," he introduced himself, "and you must be the famous 'Pearl by the Sea blogger.' Welcome to Odessa."

"Oh, great, hi, yes," said Caterina awkwardly. "Um, thank you so much for welcoming me. Do you have time to sit?"

Matteo looked around and laughed a sardonic laugh, implying he, unfortunately, had more time than he wanted. He sat down and pushed the drink toward Caterina. "Our oysters have a strong essence of cucumber and melon, so the botanical aromas of this gin infused with rose and cucumber pairs nicely."

Caterina was intrigued. "Do you recommend the cocktail sauce or the mignonette sauce?"

"Hmm, excellent question. Myself, I like neither for my first pairing to get a true sense of blending both the oyster liquor and the gin liquor. For you, pick which you like best."

Caterina tried no sauce like Matteo, and they both scooped one into their mouths and followed with the gin & tonic, enjoying the experience. "Mmm," said Caterina, "excellent suggestion."

He picked up a napkin to wipe his hands and then held his drink for another sip. "So, Miss Pearl by the Sea, you are far from America. I'm surprised Odessa would be your next stop for your food blog."

His English was excellent, and his wise eyes and warm smile made Caterina recognize right away he was an educated man, self-taught or otherwise.

"Have you been to the United States?" asked Caterina.

"Yes, in my late teens and early twenties, I spent summers waitering in The Hamptons. Those were great jobs. I worked for catering companies and local restaurants. Back then, so many of us from Eastern Europe were hired for summer jobs. Now, of course, with the war, our young boys do not have the freedom to travel. I sent my own son on a train to Warsaw to avoid the draft two years ago, but I have not seen him since. I have been trying to get him to America through my friends in

New York, but it is very difficult."

"I traveled the same train just this morning. I came straight from the station here," said Caterina, embarrassed, comparing her experience to that of this father who had not seen his son in over two years. "How old is your son?"

"Mikhail is twenty-five," said Matteo sadly. "I miss him so much, but he is a lucky one avoiding conscription. Neighbors less fortunate than us have had their sons injured or killed in battle." He looked out to the embankment of the Odessa Sea over toward the Maritime Terminal. He spoke, not looking at Caterina but staring at the empty dock. "Before the war, we would have oysters delivered from Japan and other delicacies. This port was bustling with trade. Now, we have to get all our food locally, which, of course, is no problem. The local oyster farm is delicious, but I miss the excitement of a cosmopolitan seaport."

Caterina was struggling with the conversation. They were switching from young soldiers being killed to pairing oysters with gin, but this must be commonplace for areas of war. You just tried to go on living. "These are delicious. Where are they from?"

"They are grown in a local estuary called Scythian Oyster Farm. Scythian is the term for a nomadic people who migrated to Odessa over a thousand years ago. They were known for their blue eyes and dark hair. They dominated the Eurasian Steppes from the Balkans down to Mongolia."

Caterina thought of Peter and his piercing gray eyes. The most beautiful eyes she had ever encountered. Her thoughts were now back to her mission. Matteo sensed her change of interest from oysters to why she was really here. He challenged her a bit.

"Do you want me to take a picture of you for your blog? I hope you give us a good review. After all, we could use the business. I mean, our reputation must precede us for you to travel all the way during a war just for our delicious oysters."

"Um," Caterina laughed lightly, "I'm a bit of a weirdo, I guess. I get something into my head and just, you know, go for it." She waved her arm with her fist closed. "I sent you my letter about my arrival and the thumb drive just in case I lost my luggage. I always have the worst luck traveling. Um," she was stumbling, "I'll get pictures later, maybe tonight when the restaurant is busier and with the sunset. My blog has a lot of good alfresco dining places from all over the world, France, Japan, Canada, and other places."

"Yes," Matteo smiled, "you are quite the traveler. Excuse me one moment." He got up and walked into the building. She took a sip of water. Where was he going? Was he getting the police to arrest her for mailing Russian propaganda to his place of business? Was he upset that she tried to fool him by pretending she was a food blogger? Did he suspect she was trying to circumvent the internet and border guards with Ivan Kanovsky's paper on the thumb drive? It was a stupid plan, but what choice did she have? Her instinct to get his paper into the country proved prescient as here she was, empty-handed, when the Polish police took her thumb drives.

He returned with the small manila envelope she mailed

him several weeks ago, along with the handwritten letter. He placed them on the table, and she held her breath, waiting for him to speak.

He ate another oyster and drank his gin, studying her as she squirmed uncomfortably in her seat, trying her best to look nonchalant.

"I was curious," he began, "why this girl from Boston wanted to review my restaurant during a war. I saw your articles were all very recent. So, I naturally searched your name and saw some Boston news highlights of you protesting in your city for the release of Peter Geller. This made me curious, and I researched some more. I linked to your DuckGirl website, which also happened to be your food blog website. I was wondering, why did you change your hobby so quickly? Then I realized Geller is a local kid from Odessa, a couple of years older than my son."

Caterina didn't know if he was angry or disappointed in her lying to him. She glanced down at the manila envelope. "I'm sorry. I was desperate. I didn't know who to trust or how to help Peter. On our first date, he told me about this restaurant and how much he loved eating oysters and drinking chardonnay on the deck. I just wanted to come and experience it myself. I wanted to feel close to him again. He was arrested in April and deported back to Ukraine shortly after. I just wanted to feel something."

"I see, so, on this thumb drive is what? Restaurant reviews? Or did you try to place me in harm's way with your little stunt? Is this Ivan Kanovsky's paper?"

"No," she shook her head, taking the envelope quickly off the table and putting it in her backpack. "I mean, I honestly didn't think of the repercussions to you as a person. It was just the only landmark I knew of in Odessa. I just remember Peter saying Di Mare was his favorite restaurant. I'm sorry. Truly."

He pushed his drink away from him and breathed heavily. Then he rubbed his hand on his closely shaven beard. "I have been thinking a lot about this upcoming visit. I wondered if some girl from Boston who fell for a guy from Odessa would have the guts to follow through on her absurd mission to help a man she fell for. While working in The Hamptons, I fell for a pretty redhead from Long Island. She was fiery, and who knows what she would have done if I had suddenly disappeared? I want to think she might've fought for me. There's something romantic in your gesture, even if it's hopeless."

His words made her eyes tear up. He looked at her not as an idiot but as someone strong, trying the right thing for a man she loved. Perhaps seeing couples in love dine at his restaurant day after day turned this restaurant owner into something of a romantic. She studied him. She felt it was more than that, though. It was more than just warm memories of young love in America. It was evoking a strong emotion of missing his own son and hoping someone would fight for him if he were in dire straits.

"This war has changed my country," Matteo said sadly. "We used to be neighbors who didn't care what language you spoke, what church you went to, or who you voted for. We were all Ukrainians."

"That all changed two years ago?" asked Caterina.

"That all changed ten years ago. We had been sliding into this war for eight years before Russia crossed the border. You have to picture my country as a country divided into two parts. Eastern Ukraine voted for President Yanukovych, and Western Ukraine voted for another candidate who lost in 2010. Our capital in the west did not like how we in the east voted. I mean it. Look at a map of the 2010 election, and you will see the contrast. Every oblast in the east voted for President Yanukovych, and every oblast in the west voted for the gas princess, Yulia Tymoshenko. She lost, and Kiev would never forgive us Ukrainians for voting wrong. Ukraine is only a democracy if you vote the way Kiev wants you to vote. If their horse loses, then it is Russia's fault. We were vilified, all of us, and shamed for our views. Slowly, our churches, our language, and even our president, we are told, were not Ukrainian. Do you know how it feels to love your country and be told you are a lesser person because of how your family has lived and worshiped forever? It does not feel good."

Matteo continued, "Kiev won, of course. The citizens of the capital took to Maidan Square, demanding the president resign. They won, and he flew on a helicopter to flee our country. Your assistant secretary of state, Victoria Nuland, gave out cookies to the protestors and handpicked the interim successor to take Yanukovych's place. Then President Poroshenko was voted into power, but the wounds were getting larger. He could not repair the chasm that took place. Many oblasts in the east declared their independence and did not recognize America's handpicked puppet. Crimea, Donetsk, Luhansk, and other regions seceded. Poroshenko bombed Donetsk and Luhansk for years as punishment for their refusal to recognize him as their president. Over ten thousand people, most from the Donbass region, died in those eight years of civil war. America was silent about this war. Why? Because dead Donbass kids didn't suit the right narrative, just like dead Ukrainians that burned in the Trade Unions Building fire didn't matter either."

He leaned forward as if he were a teacher giving an important lesson. "Your boyfriend's brother didn't matter, and your boyfriend doesn't matter in the eyes of Kiev and Washington, D.C. They like maniacs like Dmitry Panchenko, who will do anything for them to fight Russia. Your friend is caught in the crossfire like so many Ukrainians. This is just how it is." Matteo took a sip of his drink and continued. "I didn't know any of the victims of the Trade Unions fire. I'm sorry for the death of Alexsei. There are so many senseless deaths."

She listened to his words thoughtfully. He was sympathetic to Peter. He clearly researched him and his brother Alexsei after learning about her mission. She wondered how his son felt living in Poland away from the war when so many of his classmates had been recruited to fight the Russians. The contradictions of emotions must be overwhelming. Her dilemma seemed small compared to a father navigating being the wrong type of Ukrainian in his own country. She sensed the heaviness in his heart.

Caterina spoke carefully. "Panchenko may be a war hero to Ukraine, but he also killed innocent people. His crimes have been covered up since 2014. Ivan's paper in 2014 proved he threw the grenade into the checkpoint and proved he threw Molotov cocktails into the Trade Unions Building." She continued. "Those crimes were nothing compared to what he did in Bucha, Ukraine, and what he did to Kanovsky, murdering him in Boston. He thinks killing Ivan and framing Peter will make his crimes disappear, but I won't let him get away with it. I can't, knowing Peter did nothing wrong."

Matteo answered. "It sounds like they moved the case to Ukraine after your publicity stunt in America. I'm sure they never thought you'd bring your one-woman show overseas," he laughed. "Peter must be a good Ukrainian for you to go to such great lengths. I know I was irresistible to that redhead in Long Island."

She laughed after his remark and relaxed her shoulders, knowing he was not angry about her lies. "So, what happened after Panchenko? Was President Zelensky the next president after him?"

Matteo smiled a sad smile. "Oh, President Vladimir Zelensky. Where do I start? We watched him play the president on a television series called *Servant of the People*. The show was in Russian, and his character promised the unification of East and West Ukraine. He was one of us with the same Russian language and culture. He formed a political party named after his show and ran for president in real life against Poroshenko, who became unpopular with his heavy-handed attacks on Donbass. No political ads were allowed within the weeks leading up to an election in Ukraine, but the owner of the television station that ran Zelensky's sitcom played his show twenty-four hours a day. We were saturated with his face and message that morphed him from a fictional character into an actual presidential candidate."

Matteo rubbed his chin. "Igor Kolomoisky, who owned the TV station, as you may or may not know, funded Dmitry Panchenko's far-right group back in 2014. He is a billionaire who personally financed the Azov Battalion with their black sun watermark behind two lightning bolts. Panchenko got away with his crimes back then. His private army marched into the very courthouse where Peter will be tried and carried him out to avoid punishment. Nothing has changed since that time. All the promises of peace by Zelensky ended up as empty words, and we are as divided as ever."

Caterina did not follow all the names and dates but understood Matteo's message. He was letting her know that the odds were not in Peter's favor. She understood that Panchenko was protected, and anyone exposing the truth would be silenced. Panchenko understood that Peter knew why Kanovsky was murdered. Panchenko was taking no chances that Peter would explain to the world what Kanovsky exposed. Would Peter? Caterina wondered. He didn't have a chance to do anything. He was arrested the very next day. Would Peter be brave enough to have challenged someone like Dmitry? Maybe not, if he was quiet about his brother, Alexsei, all these years. She remembered Peter saying he wasn't supposed to be happy. Perhaps he knew that even being a pacifist was not enough, that the war found you. All she knew was she loved him and wanted to fight for him no matter what.

"I'm sorry for your country, Matteo. It's not fair." She didn't know what else to say.

Pearl by the Sea

"One day, this port will be lively again. They will clear the Russian and Ukrainian sea mines that pepper the ocean. Ships will bring me oysters from Japan again. The world moves forward, in which direction I don't know, but it *will* move forward. They will rebuild buildings hit with Iranian-built drones and maybe even allow Odessites to place flowers at the Trade Unions Building fire site. We don't know what the future will hold. Godspeed to you, Caterina. I wish you a good life."

He stood up and tapped her lightly on the shoulder. She smiled, thanked him, and was grateful he gave her the thumb drive. She took a chance on a stranger, and it paid off. She could now continue her battle for Peter's freedom. The waitress came to clear her dishes and said the meal was on the house, but Caterina felt awful for taking advantage of such hospitality. She left four, five-hundred bank notes, equivalent to fifty dollars. She read that the average monthly salary in Ukraine was three thousand hryvnia a few years ago. Since the war, salaries have tripled to ten thousand hryvnia a month, but that still only converted to around two hundred and fifty dollars. This was a poor country. Returning from The Hamptons, Matteo must've been rich compared to what this waitress must be making.

She had no time for sightseeing, even though she would've loved to explore the area. She researched ahead of time an internet cafe. She bought some thumb drives at an electronics shop next store, made a dozen copies of Ivan's paper, and took a taxi to the front of the Odessa courthouse. She didn't have a dozen bodybuilders to help her spread the message this time, but she carried what she always has had . . . the truth.

Chapter 31

CATERINA STOOD OUTSIDE the Odessa Courthouse, observing the people entering and leaving the building. Some were dressed casually, and others were in business suits. Nothing seemed out of the ordinary, and no one looked familiar. She walked around the entire building, which took awhile, considering the back redirected you a long way around. She surmised the long route was there for security purposes when the judges came to work and left. The court system was notoriously corrupt, and despite many nongovernment agencies like the Anticorruption Task Force highlighting misdeeds, corruption continued unfettered. The hubris of someone like Dmitry Panchenko being able to walk out of his trial smiling smugly at the judge made Caterina's skin crawl. Imagine any scenario in America where a criminal could just have his friends escort him out of his case!

Caterina stopped looking over her shoulder for Panchenko. She felt the Rubicon, or should she say, the Dnieper, was crossed, and all caution was thrown into the river. She hadn't traveled this far to be intimidated, and for some reason, she felt more fearless this close to the case. Tomorrow was opening statements, and she would testify the following day. There was a definitive timeline that gave her strength. She couldn't understand how a case could be tried in Ukraine for a crime committed in America, but laws were different in different countries. Also, Ukraine suspended many of its laws to punish speeches that Kiev didn't like. There were numerous examples of civil rights being crushed, including the jailing of the opposition leader, Medvedchuk, the jailing of American journalist Gonzalo Lira, and even the canceling of the presidential elections, giving Zelensky another term without a vote. If trying Peter Geller for the murder of a Ukrainian murdered in America was unprecedented, well, so were the other examples.

Caterina sat on a bench across from a young man typing on his laptop. His cameraman was stretched out on the bench, sleeping with his baseball cap pulled over his face to block the sun. This was the first media she saw today, and she wanted to get her message heard.

"Anything exciting happening at the court today?" she asked in English, hoping he would understand. He looked up distractedly from his laptop to see who was talking to him and saw her sitting on the bench across from him.

"You are American?" he asked in excellent English. "Hi, I'm Chris Miller with the *Kyiv Post*. I'm covering a murder trial starting tomorrow. Anything that relates to America they assign to me."

"Hi, I'm Caterina from Boston. I am interested in the case too."

"Well, I didn't say I was interested. It's pretty dry compared to the war going on around here. Like I said, 'assigned.'" He rested his laptop next to him on the bench. "I'm from Chicago. I worked for *Huffington Post* in London until they had layoffs, and then I got this job. I've been at it for three years now, but I'm completely burnt out. I'm done in a couple of months and heading home, but who's counting the days?" he laughed, clearly enjoying talking to an American.

"What did they tell you about the case?" she asked.

"Well, since you traveled all the way to Odessa for the case, I suppose you know way more than me. All I know is it was a love triangle, and this guy got jealous and knocked off the other guy. My editor sent me down here, and I'm just trying to read about it now. I got no Wi-Fi on the train."

Caterina liked this guy. He seemed genuine, and she wanted to educate him about the trial. "Well, I'm a corner of that 'triangle,' if you get my drift. The bigger story is that it was not a love triangle at all, but an innocent man being framed."

"Well, you'll forgive me if I don't take your word for his innocence quite yet, but maybe I can get a quote."

"How about off the record since I'm a witness in the trial? I don't know how all that works. I still have to meet my lawyers. I just got here today."

"That sounds fine to me; give me the scoop. You'll save me some research time."

Caterina gave him the USB, which he inserted into his laptop. The cameraman moved to her bench so Caterina could sit beside Chris. She guided him through links to videos and Ivan's old paper that exposed Panchenko in the Trade Unions fire. She linked to Alexsei's death certificate, and the article of Panchenko getting marched out of the Odessa courtroom with the Azov Battalion flags being waved by his comrades. She explained that Peter was framed and even added the CCTV of Panchenko cornering her in the Life Time gym in Boston. She had all Ivan's evidence plus her own investigative work about Kanovsky's death. Chris listened and was curious and intrigued. His eyes closed, and he winced at the video of the Bucha executions by Panchenko.

"Are you sure that is Panchenko in Bucha? Are you sure Ivan's research is solid about the murders and the embezzling?" asked Chris.

"Do you think Dmitry Panchenko would murder him in cold blood if it weren't? Peter is Ivan's friend. Ivan showed Peter all his research because he knew Peter saw no justice regarding his brother's death. There is no motive for Peter to hurt Ivan. He respected him. Also, there was no love triangle because I only met Ivan once, the day of his murder."

"Holy shit." Chris rubbed his hands through his hair. "How do I not know any of this? How is this story not making headline news? Shit," he repeated. "Shit, I thought I was going to phone this story in. Now, I actually have a *real* story." He paused and rested his hands on his lap with his head hanging low. It was a lot. She dumped a big story literally in his lap, and he might not want the responsibility.

Caterina realized this was a lot to absorb. She thought back to the exposé of the American military gunning down the Reuter's journalist by accident. Democrats highlighted the story because it hurt the Republican President George W Bush. This time, the story just highlights the corruption to cover up a Ukrainian war criminal. "I-I don't know what to say. Let me call my editor and see if I can open this can of worms. The *Kyiv Post* is very pro-Zelensky, so they might want to bury the story."

"No problem, Chris. I will give you half an hour. I see another journalist over there who I'm sure will run the story. You keep the USB and share it with your editor. This isn't a pro-Russian story. This is about truth despite its outcome in the narrative. Isn't that what a journalist is supposed to do? Tell the truth and not try to influence a narrative?"

"Not in my world of journalism. Maybe in some alternate universe. Okay, I'll do my best."

Caterina stood up and walked over to a food truck selling coffee, just hot, and ordered some calzone with sausage and sauerkraut. A good meal on the go she could hold in one hand. It was warm and delicious. She walked around the area, returning to Chris in half an hour.

"He's interested, definitely interested, but I cannot guarantee it makes the paper. He won't commit. I'm sorry. I don't know if what I submit will make it into the *Kyiv Post*. This was supposed to be a filler story, not headline news."

"Your loss," Caterina said, trying to act more confident than she felt. She realized the enticement to an exclusive was not enough to persuade a journalist. She needed to just give the story to anyone brave enough to cover it honestly. She walked over to another bench and sat down, finishing her coffee. She was exhausted, and her backpack was getting heavy.

"Excuse me," said an older woman with a thick accent like Peter's. She spoke in English to Caterina. "I saw you talking to the *Kyiv Post*. Care to share with independent media?"

Caterina didn't know who to trust, so she cautiously guided the conversation. "Are you interested in the Geller case here tomorrow?" asked Caterina.

"Yes," replied the woman, adjusting her large, black glasses on her face. "I have a YouTube video that covers court cases. It's pretty popular, and I know this case will get some views. I do a video in Russian and English. The Russian-speaking video gets the most views. Many Odessites prefer Russian, even if they are discouraged from speaking their native tongue in public." The woman showed Caterina her YouTube channel and her other social media accounts. She would get over a hundred thousand views on a video.

This is precisely what Caterina hoped for. A brave woman not bound by her editor or a government official telling her she can't tell the story, although, maybe after hearing the story, the woman might get cold feet. If she still had a YouTube channel, she must not have pissed off enough people yet to get it removed.

"I'm Irina Krushova," the woman held out her hand.

"Caterina, Caterina Antonucci from Boston, and do I have a story for you," said Caterina. She gave her the thumb drive, which Irina uploaded to her laptop. Caterina once again guided someone through the story. Irina was a quick study, having been familiar with so many cases in Odessa. She had some vague memories of Panchenko but never thought about him in a negative light. Ukrainian and American media consistently lauded praise upon him. The more Irina learned, the more questions she asked. It felt good to Caterina to speak with a woman who was empathetic to Peter and the situation. She didn't know what to expect when coming to Ukraine, which was at war with Russia. She thought people would scream at her, saying she was "helping the enemy" like the Good Fella government employee yelled at her. Instead, she was being treated with respect, and people understood the nuance of the story and the possibility of Peter being innocent. She was flooded with new hope.

She stood up to stretch as the sun lowered in the sky and was now behind the courthouse. The lack of sunshine made the air chillier. She unzipped her backpack and threw on her fleece vest.

"Caterina?" a timid voice behind her said her name. "Caterina?" Then someone repeatedly grabbed her forearm excitedly. A couple who looked to be in their early sixties stood side by side, each taking a turn repeating her name. She looked back and forth at the husband and wife. She could see Peter in each of their faces. The man had Peter's strong chin and his same loving, crooked-toothed smile. The woman shared his beauty. Her eyes were the same gray coloring. "Caterina?" they repeated once more.

"Yes, yes, it's me. How did you find me?" asked Caterina. Their English was not as good as Peter's, and Irina helped translate. They went back and forth in conversation with Irina, filling in Peter's story with the parents emphatically crying that he was innocent. They clearly respected this American woman who flew to Ukraine to help their son.

Leonid and his wife, Anna, asked Caterina to stay with them. They also asked Irina to come along for dinner, but she wanted to get right on the story. They exchanged numbers. Although Caterina had no phone, she gave her phone number anyway. Caterina was touched that they came to the courthouse to look for her. In her letters to them, she told them she would arrive today but gave no other details. They all thanked Irina for her time and patience in interpreting their conversation, and then the Gellers and Caterina drove to their home.

The Gellers lived on Koblevskaya Street, which was close to the Spaso-Preobrazhensky Cathedral. Catherine the Great commissioned the Italian Ukrainian architect Frapolli to design and build the church in this new city named Odessa. The church was ruined during the Bolshevik Revolution, and a Stalin Memorial was erected in its place. After the fall of the Soviet Union, Odessites rebuilt the cathedral. Included in the construction were twenty-three bells donated from Greece. You can still hear their ring daily in the largest bell tower in Ukraine. The Patriarch Kirill of Moscow traveled a great distance to consecrate the cathedral. As they drove by, they saw chess players immersed in games and artists selling their works around the beautiful fountain in front of the church. It looked like an idyllic scene until you looked further and saw the large scaffolds surrounding the church to rebuild it again.

On July 23, 2023, a missile hit the Ukrainian Orthodox Church of Spaso-Preobrazhensky. The missile was one of nineteen fired by Russia on Odessa that evening, killing one person and injuring twenty-two. This was the Gellers' church, and Caterina heard Leonid mutter something angry in Russian. She assumed they were curse words toward Russia for bombing his cathedral.

They arrived at their apartment in no time at all. It was a short ride from the courthouse. It was a nondescript apartment building like most high-rises built during the Soviet Union era. The emphasis was on function and not aesthetics. It was a far cry from architects like Frapolli during Catherine the Great's time. The Gellers spoke little English, and Caterina knew no Russian, so they just smiled a lot and spoke in their own language to one another, neither understanding the words, but their respect for each other was apparent. Caterina was brought to the kitchen table and given tea and a piece of dark rye bread with butter while Anna heated up a meal. Caterina wished she had not eaten from the food truck as she had little appetite for her hosts. She thanked them and ate a small bite of the bread while drinking the tea.

Through Irina, she found out that the Gellers had visited Peter several times in prison, but how he looked, acted, and sounded were details that were difficult to ascertain. She had no phone for Google Translate, and Leonid's was set for Cyrillic, so she did not want to mess with his phone. It was easier without Irina just to smile and nod for communication. Anna set the table for three and served a type of pierogi called a Varenyky. It was potatoes and cabbage and a dollop of sour cream placed on the plate. The three ate while Anna and Leonid spoke to each other and to Caterina in Russian. Mr. Geller put on some music that was sung in Russian. A song came on that sounded familiar to Caterina, or at least the singer's voice did.

"Leonid?" said Caterina, pointing to the speaker. "Leonid and Friends? Is that the name of the band singing this? Peter and I would listen to them all the time. We were planning to see them in Boston in June."

"Yes, Leonid," said Leonid Geller, pointing to himself.

Caterina laughed, realizing how easy this was to misunderstand. She sang the Earth, Wind & Fire song she and Peter listened to, which the band Leonid & Friends covered. They still did not understand, and she laughed some more. "September, um, January, February, March . . . September." She was getting nowhere with her explanation. Mr. Geller opened his phone to Yandex translate and had her voice dictate her search into the English box, and the app translated into Russian Cyrillic. She said, "September cover Earth, Wind & Fire sung by Leonid and Friends Band." She was sure the translation would be disastrous, but Mr. Geller understood and punched the song into his phone to play from a YouTube video.

"Yes!" he smiled, and Caterina sang along as they enjoyed listening to the song for the first time. On the final chorus, Mr. Geller sang, "*ba di da*," and they all laughed. It felt good to have this connection with them and Peter. She understood why Peter was so likable. His parents had the same attributes. Mr. Geller typed the word *lev* into Yandex translate and read the English word, *lion*. He pointed at Caterina and said the word lion and then said, "Leonid and lion," several times. Caterina understood what he was saying. She remembered Peter said Leonid meant lion. She even remembered him going on and on about some Greek or Roman it came from. He was so learned and intelligent that it was hard sometimes to follow his mind. Mr. Geller called Caterina a lion, saying she was brave and strong like a lion. She smiled and thanked him for the compliment.

After dinner, Anna brought her to Peter's room, showed her how the shower worked, and gave her some towels and her own pajamas. She took Caterina's clothes to wash. The first day of the trial was tomorrow, and Peter's parents would attend, but Caterina was not allowed since she would be a witness on day two of the case. Mr. Geller called the lawyers and confirmed the logistics for her testimony on the second day of trial.

After her shower and snuggled into cozy pajamas, Caterina immersed herself in Peter's room. It was the bedroom of a serious person, not the remnants of toys from childhood. His bookshelf was filled with books, and she wondered if his books from Boston were shipped back here. She would have to ask his parents if they could retrieve his belongings. She remembered his apartment in Boston when she found his parents' address on the letter. Thank God she had the forward-thinking idea to search his place. His desk was neat with little clutter. There was a framed photo of him and his brother Alexsei with their arms around each other. Alexsei was about twelve and Peter ten. They were both grinning ear to ear and appeared very close. Alexsei was good-looking like Peter but had his dad's eyes and a softer chin like his mom's. She wondered how families endured the loss of a child. Now, the Gellers were facing the loss of their second child to life in prison for murder . . . a murder he didn't commit. Both tragedies involved the same man, Dmitry Panchenko. Did Peter's parents understand the villain in this story, or was Ivan Kanovsky's research not something they wanted to learn? Maybe it was all too much for them, and they just needed to take it day by day.

Caterina put the frame down, then saw the envelope with her name on it on the desk. Anna placed it there for her to read. She opened it up and became weak in her knees when she realized it was a letter from Peter. She stepped backward until she found the bed to sit on. Her hands were shaking, and there was proof of life he existed. Her eyes welled with tears, and she had to pull the notebook paper away to avoid it getting tear-stained. She rubbed her eyes dry until she felt they would not overflow again.

My Darling Caterina,

I have loved you for an eternity. Our love has no beginning and no end. It just exists beyond time. When I walked into your office, it wasn't love at first sight but meeting my soul mate again. There was a familiarity to you that just was inexplicable. All I know is that your love for me has kept me sane these past months. I think about you constantly; when I wake up, all day, at night, especially in the starlight. There, your warmth melts away any fear I have, and I feel at peace. There is no greater feeling than having you in my heart. You sustain me. When I die,

and the angels ask me what thrilled me the most, I will say "you." I remember you: yesterday, today, and always.
   Forever yours,
   Peter

"Oh, Peter," Caterina whispered, "I remember you too. I do."

Chapter 32

THE SCENE IN front of the courthouse was much different than yesterday. There were more reporters and camera crews. Peter's parents walked up the front stairs arm in arm with cameras snapping their picture. Chris Miller's cameraman looked a bit more lively today. He said Chris was inside covering the case, but no phones or cameras were allowed. Caterina assumed Irina Krushova was inside the courtroom too. She felt alone and vulnerable outside and desperately wanted to be able to see Peter. How did he look? Did he have to sit in one of those plastic holding pens she had seen on television as they do in Russian courts? Or was he allowed to sit with his lawyers?

She grabbed a coffee from the food truck stationed there yesterday. She desperately wanted an iced coffee and swore at herself for whining about the temperature of her coffee when her boyfriend was facing life in prison. She sat on a bench, closing her eyes and rereading his letter in her head. She knew it by heart and, with every word, felt his warmth envelop her. She loved him and all the efforts to get her to this day were worth it. She felt calm and strangely energized at the same time.

Inside the courtroom, the prosecution began its case. An older lawyer stepped forward in front of the judge and jury to deliver the Justice Department's case.

"We live in trying times during the Mordor of war with Russia. Mordor is a darkness, a peril, an evil that most men do not wish to explore. The United States of America did not want to explore this evil and sent it back here to Ukraine for us to deal with, but we will face this darkness as we persevere through troubled times. America laid out a scathing indictment of Petrov Leonidovich Geller for murder in the first degree. He was being charged with the brutal stabbing of a Ukrainian citizen, Ivan Kanovsky, in Boston, Massachusetts, far from our battles here at home. The motive is as old as time: love, jealousy, and revenge. You see, Peter's girlfriend, whom he had been dating since he moved to America, started dating his friend, Ivan Kanovsky. We have GPS data of her at Kanovsky's home and workplace. Caterina Antonucci tried to break it off with Peter many times. Finally, to show him that she no longer cared for him, she showed her love for Ivan by sailing with Ivan and Peter on the day Petrov Leonidovich murdered Ivan. We will prove that Petrov Leonidovich's cell phone data placed him at the scene of the murder. He was at Ivan Kanovsky's home from five to six that night. His DNA is on Ivan's backpack and his water bottle inside Ivan's apartment. Now, the defense has dreamed up some insane conspiracy theory involving war crimes in Bucha, Ukraine, by someone nowhere near the scene of the crime. Their defense is pathetic, and worse, they smear the good name of a Ukrainian war hero. Ladies and Gentlemen, it is times like this when we must prove to the world that we have a fair and legal justice system. It is times like this that we will find justice for the death of one of our own boys, Ivan Kanovsky. Thank you."

The jury remained stoic, and it was now the defense's turn to give their opening arguments. Peter was dressed in a suit, looking solemn next to his lawyers. He did not have to wear the dark navy blue jumpsuit he'd been wearing daily in prison. He seemed fairly healthy and tan from being allowed time in the courtyard. His hair was closely shaven, but it did not deter from his good looks. He did not look like a killer but appeared kind in nature.

A lawyer in a dark suit stood up and spoke to the jury and the judge. "Ladies and Gentlemen. My client, Petrov Leonidovich Geller, is innocent of this charge. America realized the case was not solid, which is why they closed it. Why the Ukrainian government is choosing to prosecute an innocent man for a crime committed on another continent outside our judicial guidelines is unclear. The Justice Department thinks they can suspend all our rights, citing the war with Russia as an excuse not to exercise judiciary prudence. Let me be clear. Petrov is innocent, and our evidence is rock solid. Tomorrow, you will hear from Caterina Antonucci herself and learn she was chased down by the killer, Dmitry Panchenko, on the streets of Boston. You will learn that Dmitry Panchenko killed Ivan Kanovsky to silence him for his academic work, and we have his paper as evidence to prove this. We are not here to try Dmitry Panchenko but to show that Ukraine arrested the wrong man for the crime. Our client is innocent. Yes, the motive is as old as time, but not in the way the prosecution states. The motive was power and greed. That is what drove Dmitry Panchenko to kill Ivan Kanovsky. We will prove Petrov is innocent. Thank you."

Outside, the cameramen were setting up their tripods, knowing that lunch break would come soon and that the journalists would give a one-minute summary in their cameras. There were maybe half a dozen media outlets set up. Caterina recognized the *Kyiv Post* from yesterday and also saw a Polish news team and a couple more Ukrainian reporters, but no Western media outlets. She saw Irina exit the courthouse, and her friend filmed her summary. She did not apply foundation like the other media personas did.

"*Well, we just heard opening arguments for the Petrov Leonidovich Geller murder trial in the brutal stabbing of Ukrainian professor Ivan Kanovsky. The prosecution says it was out of jealousy, but the defense team is using a complicated conspiracy theory, pointing the blame on the former head of SBU intelligence, Dmitry Panchenko—a bold move considering the sphere of influence Panchenko has in elite circles here at home and in America. Will this bold strategy pay off? Tune in tonight and tomorrow as we continue our coverage of the Leonidovich murder trial.*"

"Wow, Irina, that was great," said Caterina as the light was turned off on the filming. "How did Peter look? Did you see him?" Caterina wasn't sure if she was breaking any rules as a witness speaking off-record to someone in the media. She didn't care. She felt she had more power out here trying to influence public opinion than she did inside a courtroom. Wasn't that how she got the United States to bury and hide the story over here?

She saw Chris Miller from yesterday, pacing back and forth, who was speaking on his cellphone to someone. She could overhear the conversation. "I know, I know, okay. I get it," he answered on the phone. He hung up and walked over to Caterina. "I'm sorry," he said, not explaining his apology. "My editor just won't touch the real story with a ten-foot pole. I'm writing about the prosecution angle, nothing about the defense. It sucks, I know. I can't wait to quit this stupid job and this stupid war." Chris did look tired. It was clear covering war, killings, and casualties had put him under a lot of stress. The burnout must have been high covering the war.

"I'm sorry, Caterina. I don't know what to think about this case, but I know you want his story told. I just can't be the one. I know it's frustrating." Chris shoved his hands into his pocket. He let out a big sigh and spoke. "Hey, maybe when this blows over, we can get together back home. I think my next gig will be in New York City—nothing Russian or Ukrainian related," he laughed a tired laugh.

Caterina was so disappointed she didn't even know how to respond. "Chris, I needed a hero today, and that is not you. I'm sorry. I can't process this yet." She wandered off, not finishing her sentence. She felt numb to the push and pull of hope and disappointment. It was all so surreal that the man she fell in love with was close to spending the rest of his life in prison. He would die in prison. She felt that was certain.

She stood idling between reporters. She felt lost. "Caterina," said Irina. "Check this out. *Der Spiegel* just put out an article about the case." She handed her laptop to Caterina. "Here, you can use it while I'm in the courtroom. I'll be back out later."

Caterina read the article that she translated from German to English. She googled *Der Spiegel* and realized it was one of the most prominent newspapers in Germany. The article was long and detailed. The newspaper had access to Ivan Kanovsky's paper. It was repeating all the evidence that Ivan wrote about Panchenko's war crimes in Bucha and his embezzlement of money diverted to his luxury cars and condo in Dubai. It talked about his crime of throwing the grenade into the checkpoint in 2014 and even the charges of him assaulting Peter ten years ago when his comrades carried him out of this very courtroom. She couldn't believe it. Here was all Kanovsky's lifework summarized in one of the most prominent newspapers in Europe. She saw their social media linked to the article, which was being shared worldwide. The comments were piling up. People were sharing their own views on Panchenko and the Azov Battalion. Independent journalists in Boston and across America were now catching on to the story. They wanted to jump on the bandwagon of a viral story, particularly if it was a local murder.

She looked up from the laptop and saw people staring at her and some pointing at her. Irina's friend sat next to her on the bench as the media descended on Caterina, realizing who she was. She was being asked questions in Polish, Russian, Ukrainian, and English. Caterina didn't know what to do. She took out her remaining ten thumb drives and passed them around to the reporters. "Ivan Kanovsky's paper," she said repeatedly as she gave it to each reporter. "His paper." She let them all take pictures but answered no questions. She wanted to play it safe while navigating the trial. She pointed to the last USB in her hand, saying, "Ivan Kanovsky's paper," as if this would answer all their questions.

The afternoon flew by, and everyone emerged from the trial around three o'clock. Peter's parents answered no questions and drove Caterina to their home. She borrowed Leonid's phone and called Irina, who had a better pulse on the trial than the Gellers could give her with their limited English. "Wow, Irina, your YouTube video is blowing up."

"I know," answered Irina. "It's at 350,00 views—crazy. Things are buzzing. We spent most of the afternoon in the dark with the judge and the lawyers huddled together. I have a feeling something big is going to happen tomorrow. The prosecution looked shaken after lunch. I'm sure it was from the *Der Spiegel* article."

Caterina could hardly sleep. The next day, she woke up early and showered. She wore black pants and a conservative blouse of Anna's. She even borrowed a pair of shoes to match the outfit. By now, Anna would have given her everything she owned. She was so grateful for Caterina helping Peter. Caterina wished she could give Anna something in return . . . hopefully, her son. That sounded dramatic, but it was true. Caterina keeping the story in the public eye ruined the case in America, and her testimony today would be damning to the prosecution. They were ready. There were many more reporters and curious Odessites outside the courtroom today. The Gellers and Caterina separated once inside. Caterina stayed with one of the lawyers until it was her time to testify, and the Gellers were able to enter the courtroom. There were whispers and eyes cast to her as she walked the courthouse hallways. She settled into a small office off to the side, and her lawyer left her alone for long stretches. The bookshelves were lined with books in Cyrillic. There was little for her to occupy her time. It felt like forever waiting.

At eleven a.m., her lawyer opened the door. He was excited and bubbling with the news. His English was good, but his Slavic accent was even heavier than Peter's. "It's over—it's done!" He grasped her hands in his. What? She did not understand. How could it be over? She didn't give her testimony. There were no closing arguments. The jury didn't decide anything. Is this good or bad? Her body shook as she tried to process what he was saying. "What?" she repeated.

"It's over. It's done!" he repeated, then slowed his speech, still grasping her hands. "The government dropped the case in light of new evidence the defense wanted to submit. The case blew up." The lawyer dramatically moved his hands like an explosion. He was still smiling ear to ear.

"What? What does that mean? Can they do that?" she asked.

"Yes, the judge agreed in light of the new evidence that the prosecution was making the correct decision to drop the charges. It was you, Caterina. It was you. They didn't want you on the stand. They didn't want the name Dmitry Panchenko spoken in the courtroom. You had CCTV of Panchenko chasing you in Boston. The prosecution was hoping to bury that evidence, but now that it was in the defense's hands and you were an eyewitness to him robbing you, it was damaging to the government's case."

"Does this mean-does this mean that Peter is free? He's innocent?" begged Caterina for an immediate answer.

"Yes; all charges are dropped. He is free to go today."

Caterina covered her face and was overwhelmed with emotion. She hugged the lawyer tightly and thanked him for everything. He opened the door of the room and directed her back outside. The news of the case being dismissed had made its way to the front of the courtroom. She tried to find a familiar face, but it appeared that the family was still inside. A journalist she had never seen before shoved a microphone in her face.

"How does it feel, Caterina? How does it feel to have the charges dropped on Petrov Leonidovich?"

She smiled wide and just shook her head in bewilderment. Her expression said it all. The cameras flashed, and more microphones were pushed toward her. "Are you a private investigator from America? What do you have to say about the rumors circulating that Dmitry Panchenko is now persona non grata in America and has fled to Dubai? Did you help Ivan Kanovsky obtain the evidence of the millions of dollars embezzled?" Caterina did not answer the questions. She just shook her head at the events that were unfolding, straining to recognize anyone exiting the courthouse. The cameras all turned from her to the doors as Peter exited the court with his lawyers on either side and his parents close in the huddle. The security officers were helping form a barricade between the family and the press. Caterina was trying to inch her way closer to Peter. Her heart skipped a beat when she saw him. She was about to burst through the crowd when a woman grabbed her by the shoulder and spoke to her.

The woman wore a crisp white blouse under a thin black sweater with black pants and had a designer purse over her shoulder. She smiled fondly at Caterina and hugged her. Who was she? Caterina hugged her back. Maybe it was Peter's cousin or friend. The woman introduced herself. "Hi, Caterina, I'm Svetlana. Thank you, thank you for everything you did for my Peter. You are a very good person."

Caterina started to feel dizzy. "Your Peter? Who? Who are you?" She didn't want to say the words. She looked at her hand to see if she had a wedding ring. There was none. "Your Peter?" she said again. "Are you? Are you his girlfriend?"

"Yes," the elegant woman said confidently. "Thank you for helping my Peter. You are a good person," she repeated.

None of this made sense to Caterina. His girlfriend? Why would Peter call her his darling and soul mate? Why would Anna let her sleep in his bed and wear her clothes? Did they hide Svetlana away because his freedom meant more than anything?

Peter spotted Caterina from the stairs and shouted her name. "Caterina!" he screamed, and she turned and ran. She didn't know what else to do. How could she be such a fool and think this amazing, handsome man was hers?

Pearl by the Sea

Peter saw her run away and ran after her. His lawyers told him to stop to give a statement, but he broke through the crowd and ran after her.

Caterina ran through the crowded sidewalks toward the water. She came to the top of the Potemkin Stairs and ran down them as if she were in an intense aerobics class, all one hundred and ninety-two stairs. He chased after her, shouting her name. He followed her down the stairs and prayed she would turn around, stop, and run to him, but she kept going.

"*My Peter*," she could hear the woman's silky voice with its beautiful Slavic accent say his name. "*My Peter*."

"Stop, Caterina, stop!" Peter shouted. Caterina reached the bottom of the stairs and paced back and forth, deciding which way to run when she caught her breath. She ignored his shouts and could not turn to look in his direction. She took deep breaths and decided she'd run left toward Di Mare, the area she was familiar with. He grabbed her right arm hard and turned her around before she took off running again. Both were panting heavily from the chase. They stared into each other's eyes, breathing hard. "Caterina," he said breathlessly. "My perla," he said, pulling her close and hugging her tight.

She succumbed to his flesh. She panted into his chest as he pulled her in closer with her arms bent between his body and hers. He pulled her arms apart, and she hugged him tight, burying her cheek deeper toward his racing heart. They held each other, catching their breath, and then he kissed her passionately. It was exquisite, desperate, and needed. She was flooded with memories of being in his arms and wanted to stay in this moment forever. "Svetlana," she tried to say, but he silenced her.

"No, she is no one. I promise. We had some dates over Christmas break, but I knew she was not for me. We never even corresponded during my second semester at school. I figured she got the hint, but after my arrest, she came around again, hoping I changed my mind. I haven't spoken to her since last year. She sent me a couple of letters; that's it. Honest." He stroked her hair and kissed the side of her head, soaking in her physical presence. "Caterina," he said, kissing her hair and pulling her close for a hug. She believed him. She could feel his love for her was genuine. "Marry me, Caterina. Stay here with me forever. I love you."

She held him close and cherished his words. It felt so natural, his proposal. She loved this man with all her heart and soul. "Come to America with me, Peter. Marry me there," she smiled.

Her words pained him a bit as she was countering his offer. She added in a variable. "Surely, the United States will let you back in now that you are clear of charges. They'll let you come back."

He stared into her eyes, wanting to stay with her love forever, but the world was not just the two of them. He thought of his brother, Alexsei. "Caterina," he stroked her hair, "my parents lost one of their two sons and almost lost me. You gave me back to them. I could never hurt them by leaving again. Don't you understand? Even if America let me back, I could not leave them again."

Pearl by the Sea

His words stung, but she understood why he would choose his parents over her. Could she leave her family and live in Ukraine? Live where cathedrals were bombed, and mines littered the Black Sea? Could she live in a place so foreign, away from her family? These questions were not the questions she had been asking herself all summer. Her questions were about his freedom, not about what happened next. Maybe she didn't want to explore that possibility because she knew the answer. She loved this man . . . but was it enough?

They kissed long and hard, wanting to avoid the future. After their kiss, they hugged and stayed that way for a long time with their eyes closed. Finally, she pulled apart. "Peter, you ran. You ran when you chased me. How? You said you couldn't run since you broke both heels."

He laughed. "I couldn't run. I hadn't run in ten years. I guess I never really tried before."

She laughed. "You're in pretty good shape for a guy who's been locked up for six months." She became serious, suddenly realizing she had stated his terrible situation the past six months out loud. "I'm sorry for everything you went through, Peter."

"Caterina, you saved my life. You saved me. If it weren't for you finding Ivan's paper in his office and figuring out Panchenko tried to pull you into a love triangle by placing you at Ivan's house and workplace, I'd still be in prison. If it weren't for you being smart enough and brave enough to take on the United States government and the Ukrainian government in a cover-up of Panchenko's crimes, then I'd be spending the rest of my life in jail." He held her shoulders and spoke clearly.

"Caterina, you were meant for this moment. You were in the right place at the right time, and you were brave enough to save me. This might sound strange to you, but I have had a lot of time to think these past few months. I believe that maybe our time together this time around was meant to be fleeting . . . not our love, but our time. Maybe in Tahiti or on the Nile we were together a longer time. Our love spans lifetimes. I truly believe that when I say you are my soul mate."

It sounded weird, but she understood what he was saying. She felt it in a familiar way too. "Well, please, don't compare us to Catherine the Great and her emperor husband, Peter. And don't compare us to Cleopatra and her lovers. I'd like to think we were just ordinary people living in Egypt and Russia living happily ever after in our lifetimes."

He smiled and hugged her again. He loved her humor and intellect. Yes, that sounded better than kings and queens. "I was in prison, Caterina, and you set me free. Not just an actual prison, but even before that, I built up a fortress and didn't let anyone get close to me . . . until you. You taught me how to be happy. You taught me that I deserved happiness despite what happened to my brother. I want to carry that with me for the rest of my life."

Caterina thought about what he said. "I was the same. I was always competing and challenging people in my relationships and not just enjoying the person. You taught me to love too, Peter. No one has ever loved me like you have, and I never knew how to love like I did with you. You taught me that."

"Was it Tahiti? Or were we on the Nile? I remember you."

Peter sang softly while they ignored the world around them and swayed. "And when the angels ask what thrilled me most of all, I will say 'you.' I remember you. I do."

"Petrov," a journalist shouted, who was disembarking the inclined elevator that brought pedestrians up and down the Potemkin Stairs without having to climb them. He had his heavy camera and rode the funicular instead of trying to navigate the stairs with his media equipment.

Peter looked at Caterina. "C'mon, let's go celebrate my freedom. Where should we go?"

Caterina smiled. She couldn't believe they could go anywhere they wanted with each other at the moment. She was filled with so many emotions that it was overwhelming for her to have choices. "Well, we need to get a phone to call your parents so they can meet us somewhere. Let's go to Di Mare. Invite your parents. Let's all celebrate your freedom."

He asked the reporter if he could borrow his phone and then called his parents to meet him at Di Mare. "I'll give you a quote from me if you keep it to yourself where I'm going."

The reporter laughed. "Sure thing; go for it."

Peter cleared his throat. "I want to thank my wonderful friend from America, Caterina Antonucci, for always believing in me and going above and beyond what any friend would do to prove my innocence. She is the best private investigator I have ever met in my life. I am honored to know her. Thank you, Caterina, with all my heart." He placed his open palm over his heart, turning toward her, and she opened her palm, placing it over her heart, copying his gesture.

"Thanks, buddy, and congrats on getting the case dropped," the reporter said.

Caterina and Peter strolled hand in hand down the boardwalk toward Di Mare's. They ordered gin & tonic and several dozen oysters. Matteo hugged them both and put several tables together when his parents and friends joined the crowd. More drinks and food were ordered. It felt perfect. It felt right. Caterina leaned on Peter's shoulder, who had not left her side all evening. "You know, Peter," she said, slightly tipsy. "Svetlana is really cute. When I go home, I want you to date her. You have my blessing to continue being happy. You deserve it. You really do." They both knew that it was painful for the words to be said, to realize that she would not move to Ukraine, and he would not move to America. They weren't meant for a lifetime but had a lifetime of love in just a few short months.

He touched his head toward hers, and they both looked out over the sunset. "You too, Caterina. I wish you every happiness in the world. You will always hold a special place in my heart. Always and forever."

"Caterina," someone was shouting loudly on the boardwalk. "Caterina," it was repeated. They both stood up to see who was calling her. The voices sound familiar and foreign to Odessa. She saw her uncle Jimmy and her mom, Arlene, with cupped hands shouting her name in different directions.

"Mom, Uncle Jimmy!" she shouted and waved in shock that they were in Ukraine.

"Oh my God, thank heavens," her mother, Arlene, gasped.

Caterina had left a note for them that she was going to Ukraine after Kimmie's wedding, but never in Caterina's wildest dreams did she think her mother, of all people, would travel to a war-torn country to find her. Caterina was overwhelmed with love and emotion for her family.

"Hello, Peter," Arlene waved.

"Tell them to join us," said Peter to Caterina. "I want them to meet my parents and friends. They can stay with us as well."

Caterina thought about herself and her family smushing into the tiny apartment together, making her laugh. She felt this was a sign to go their separate ways now.

"No, Peter, this is goodbye. I'm going home. You are home and where you should be."

She hugged him and his parents and finally Matteo and left the restaurant.

She ran out to the boardwalk and hugged her family. She didn't know how they got here or how they found her. Maybe someone outside the courthouse knew where the party was. Whatever the circumstances, she knew it took her mom and uncle a lot of courage to travel here to retrieve her. She welcomed the love. They had a million questions for one another, but all she cared about at that moment was contentment. She had no regrets falling in love with Peter and helping him with his case. She knew deep down they would part ways as they would before his arrest. They knew that after his teaching assignment in Boston, he was returning to Ukraine. They both knew it but loved each other despite the ending.

Caterina strolled the boardwalk with one arm through her uncle's arm and one through her mom's.

When the push came to shove, her mom loved her unconditionally. Caterina didn't need to be what her mom envisioned for her. She was loved for just being herself . . . Caterina.

Chapter 33

"MY FELLOW AMERICANS. *I stand before you today not as a Republican but as a member of a unified Congress to ensure you that House Resolution 322 has passed with a strong majority in the House of Representatives. With strong Senate approval, the bill is now making its way to the president's desk to be signed. This will ensure continued aid to help Ukraine fight against the Russian invaders. Sixty-one billion dollars will go a long way to help the struggling nation. This is a lot of your taxpayers' dollars, we know, and understand your concerns about corruption, not just in our nation's capital but in Ukraine's capital as well. I assure you that we have strengthened our oversight and included more checks and balances to track the money flow.*

"Just this week, the head of the Senate Intelligence Committee, Senator Eric Mason, has identified areas of concern and passed this intelligence to the Justice Department, which will take swift action on any war profiteers who break our laws. The Financial Crimes Task Force has seized over fifty million dollars of property from oligarch Ihor Kolomoisky in America. His properties were seized in Dallas, Cleveland, and Miami. A close associate of Kolomoisky,

former head of the SBU Ukrainian Intelligence, is also wanted in Ukraine and the United States for embezzlement. Efforts to extradite him from the UAE are now underway by both countries."

House Majority Leader Mike Jones stopped his speech to sip water from a glass on his podium. He wore a dark suit with an American flag pin, and the United States and Ukraine flags were behind him. Members of the Ukraine Assembly stood with members of Congress in between the Speaker of the House and the flags. The speaker finished his speech with a closed fist, emphasizing his bullet points.

"We demand transparency and have the tools to ensure that our allies defend democracy as much as we do. Ukraine is on the frontlines to defend our freedom. If they fall, then we fall. We are proud of our brothers and sisters in their fight against Russian imperialism. We have joined forces with NAFO, AntAC, NABU, and hundreds of NGOs to ensure continued accountability with our allies. Together, we are stronger as a nation and a world. God Bless You. God Bless America and Slava Ukrainia. Thank You."

Arlene, Aldo, and Caterina watched the speech from Caterina's laptop on the kitchen table. They were finishing their coffee on a Sunday morning. Arlene and Caterina made breakfast together, and Aldo cleared the dishes. Arlene took a sip of her coffee. "I don't get it. He didn't even say the name of Dmitry Panchenko. He didn't even mention any of the bad stuff he did."

Caterina smiled. "Wow, Mom, impressive you just rattled that guy's name off your tongue. You're getting good at this."

"Well, it's not like we haven't heard them out of your mouth a hundred times. It's just not right that the poor BU professor got no justice in his murder."

Caterina sighed. "I agree, Mom. It's lousy. They can turn any event into a narrative to justify spending billions in a foreign country. It's not like the people of Ukraine see the money, either. Some of them are so poor over there."

"Yeah, well, some of us are poor over here too," said Aldo, who seemed to have reached his limit on foreign policy talk for the day. He lifted his coffee toward Caterina before taking another sip. "Except moneybags over here. I can't believe how much Peter's defense team paid you for research. I didn't even know you were on their payroll."

Neither did Caterina, which stunned her when she received the check in the mail for $125,000 for "opposition research." It looked very legal, and detailed itemized hours were on Latham and Watkins LLP letterhead. She was sure both the Kanovsky family and the Geller family were grateful for her efforts to solve the murder. Maybe other anonymous people out there had the funds to show their appreciation. She deposited the check before it bounced and will make sure to file with her income taxes for her private investigator company. Also, the five hundred dollars cash she got from Justine, aka Joan Barry, for hiring her to follow Ivan Kanovsky. She wanted to stay on the right side of the law.

Her private eye business had been booming since she got back from Ukraine. She took a few easy money cases but had to refuse most requests. There were simply too many.

Of course, her mother gave her ample time and attention

to indulge in her heartbreak. There were plenty of nights of tear-stained pillows and hugs of positive affirmation from her mom. Her mother was her rock through her grief. They became so close in those months since returning from Ukraine. Peter texted and emailed Caterina constantly at first, and she would respond with one-word replies or emojis. It wasn't that she didn't love him. She obviously did, but what was the point of prolonging their breakup? He was still sanctioned and not allowed to come to America, and she never wanted to move, no matter how gorgeous his gray eyes were. She was a Boston girl through and through.

"We are stopping off at Grammy's on the way to Tony's house today. Do you want to come along?" asked Caterina's father.

"No, thanks, Dad. I just saw Grammy Thursday, and I'll see Tony Tuesday night for Angela's soccer game. My niece is much more coordinated than her auntie."

Arlene answered. "Yeah, but she doesn't have that competitive streak like you did, Caterina. You were a wild child out there in the field. Lord have mercy, the gray hairs you put on my head when you were skating and running around . . . I never knew if we would end up at McDonald's for lunch after the game or the ER with another injury. I guess having four older brothers lit a fire in you to compete." Arlene made the sign of the cross, and her husband belly laughed, telling the same rehashed stories of her escapades in the emergency room. Aldo's laugh was contagious, and Arlene's colorful commentary made them laugh even more.

"Oh, Aldo, run down and get the salad we're bringing to Tony's. It will be cold enough in the car when we visit Grammy."

"I'll get it." Caterina jumped up and went down to the fridge. She remembered that day she thought Dmitry Panchenko was in her basement. She sometimes wondered how she dared to do some of the things she did to help Peter. She admitted to loving the adrenaline of the mission. That was why she went into private eye work. She was always competitive. She couldn't change that part of herself. She learned from loving Peter that she didn't have to compete with her family. She didn't win anything by trying to outskate her brothers or her stubborn streak with her mom, never letting her put a ribbon in her hair. Her mother wasn't trying to win a fight. She was just trying to love her daughter in the way she knew how. Caterina ran up the stairs and placed the salad on the kitchen counter. She hugged her mom with a great big bear hug and then her dad.

"I love you, guys," said Caterina. It was out of the blue and caught her mom by surprise. Arlene's eyes teared up a bit with the unconditional love only a parent could know. "We love you too, sweetheart, our perla."

Caterina was thankful to have the house to herself after her parents left. She had been so busy with her personal training and new private eye cases that she hardly had time for reflection. She had her moments of grief missing Peter, but they were less and less and unexpected. Sometimes, grief taps you on the shoulder to remind you they are still lurking, and you cry at the most inopportune times, but her crying subsided quickly.

Caterina checked her emails and texts. She received a reply

from Mike, Derek's dad, in Long Island, to let her know he was doing great in his first semester at Stony Brook College and living a clean lifestyle. Derek didn't miss Tufts or the Encore casino and was thriving living at home. Caterina thought wanderlust wasn't for everybody. Some people needed their parents' support more than others. To each his own. She was happy for Derek and his dad.

She texted Alda back and confirmed they were working out together tomorrow at 7:00 a.m. Alda was an early bird like Caterina, and she liked to get her workout in at the crack of dawn. Caterina was freelancing her personal training, so she had no set hours at Life Time. She liked Alda's gym and was picking up some clients there thanks to referrals from Alda.

Caterina and Kimmie were still trying to nail down a time to get together. It seemed like their schedules never aligned, kind of like when they lived together. That was okay. She knew no matter when the time came to meet up, it would be like no time passed in between. That's the beauty of lifelong friends; the bond would remain strong. She sent Kimmie a heart emoji and threw out another date they could work with.

Caterina hovered her cursor over her Spotify playlist of songs she and Peter listened to. Then she hit delete. She still only had one photo of him with his Starbucks coffee. There were pictures on the internet of him in his suit with his short haircut during the trial, but none of the two of them together. She scrolled his pictures in Google images, which were the same few photos: his Starbucks selfie from her website, his courtroom picture, and his college graduation photo. He had a VK page, the Russian version of Facebook, but no Western social media. She was tempted to make a VK profile to visit his page to see if there were any new pictures, but that temptation was also becoming less and less. She wished him happiness and hoped his page would be filled with pictures of him and Svetlana at Di Mare at sunset. She loved him enough to let him go and hoped he'd find a more practical love with the hometown girl. She clicked on her "Pearl by the Sea" website, which still attracted visitors, and the hidden comments were as eclectic as you could imagine. Comments about oysters, Peter Geller, and lately, more and more about her and her private eye business. Who knows? Maybe she will revamp her website again from *#DuckGirl* and "Pearl by the Sea" to "Caterina Antonucci, Private Eye over Boston." Who knows? It was a work in progress.

Caterina closed her laptop and grabbed the keys to her Honda. She had the money to buy a new car, but a used tan Honda blended nicely for surveillance jobs. It started right up on this cold November day. She had two stops today, and she hoped everything went as planned. Stop number one could not have gone smoother. She picked up the item to deliver to stop number two. This would be interesting. She emailed Sidar an apology for their awful Hinge date and said she would stop by to say hi. He still lived in Cambridge and was surprised to hear from his disastrous Hinge date out of the blue, but he was curious enough to say yes.

Caterina grabbed the pet carrier from the back of the Honda, paid the meter through her parking meter app, and then buzzed his apartment number.

"Who is it?" Sidar said through the lobby speaker.

"It's Caterina."

He buzzed her in.

He stood at the end of the hall with the door open, waiting for her to get off the elevator. He was wearing a black V-neck sweater with a striped dress shirt underneath. She remembered he was a nice dresser. She had a cream-colored turtleneck on with jeans and short brown suede boots, no heels. Her long, dark hair was straightened using her blow dryer this morning. She wore colored lip gloss, and she radiated freshness and health. He smiled when he saw her and then looked perplexed when he saw the pet carrier, but his eyes drew back to hers.

"Caterina, I must say, I was surprised by your call. I wanted to apologize for my outburst at the restaurant. I was going through a difficult time."

"Sidar, I want to apologize to you. I shouldn't have assumed so much from your ex-wife's lawsuit. It was very rude of me. I wanted to make it up to you." Caterina looked down at the pet carrier, and he heard a meow.

"Please, come in." He waved her through the door. "That is very kind of you, but my lease still does not allow pets. You remember, the 'no cat's clause.'" Caterina winced, recalling her joke about the cat having no claws. Therefore, it didn't break the "no-cat's claws" rule.

"I know. Yes, I know, but I spoke with your landlord. I told them I worked for the organization NAFO, North Atlantic Feline Organization, a nonprofit that helped residents with emotional support animals navigate the housing regulations. I showed him my card and everything." Caterina showed Sidar the NAFO card and her picture and name on the front. "*Caterina Antonucci, President of the Feline Organization.* I had my lawyers draw up the papers and had him sign them, giving you an exception to the no-pet clause. You just need your doctor to sign a paper for the emotional support animal. I know someone that will sign it if you need help."

Sidar sat down on the couch, becoming very emotional because of her efforts to help him out. He missed his cat, Mr. Bond, so much since the divorce when his wife kept his cat. He had Mr. Bond even before they were married. He had given up after a nasty divorce.

He looked at Caterina and the pet carrier. "This is an amazing and generous gesture. I'm truly thankful and, frankly, a bit surprised. I thought you'd want nothing to do with me after my behavior at the restaurant. I've been trying to control my temper with the work of my therapist." Sidar rubbed his hands together. "As much as I am thankful for the gift, I must decline. I only want Mr. Bond. He was my best friend and roommate before I married my wife. I could move to a pet-friendly apartment and get another cat, but it wouldn't be the same. I'm sorry. I hope you can return this cat," he said, pointing to the pet carrier.

"Sidar," said Caterina as she bent over to unzip the opening and allowed the cat to exit the carrier. "Sidar, this *is* Mr. Bond. I got him back for you. He's yours."

Sidar was in shock. He dropped to his knees to scoop up

the black-and-white cat. He had a white chest and white paws, and the rest of him was all black. He looked like he was wearing a tuxedo like James Bond. The cat rubbed his legs and purred before jumping on the couch and settling into Sidar's lap.

"How? I don't understand. How did she let you take Mr. Bond? Did you kidnap him?" He was now concerned because he didn't know this woman before him, and he looked a bit scared.

She laughed at his suggestion. "No, I simply gave her the same card and letter I issued the landlord. I stated that the North Atlantic Feline Organization was dedicated to returning the rightful owners of cats to the original caretakers. I explained that studies showed that it was humane to declaw a feline that was to live in a home, and some studies showed their happiness index improved with less anxiety in the stability of stable homes. I also kind of threatened her with a lot of legalese."

Sidar laughed, envisioning this conversation with his ex-wife. His ex had sued him because he declawed the cat, and the judge threw out the case, but the divorce judge gave her the cat. Sidar laughed again, picked up Mr. Bond by his front legs, and touched their noses together. Caterina got a kick out of how happy the cat made Sidar. She couldn't even imagine he was the same man she had a date with. He started talking a mile a minute about what he needed to buy for Mr. Bond and where he would put his bed and toys. He talked about what kind of cat food he did and didn't like. Finally, he tentatively stood up, shook Caterina's hand, and thanked her. He offered her coffee, and she accepted.

He put out some Egyptian sweet cookies that melted in Caterina's mouth. They were so delicious she grabbed a second one, wiping the powdered sugar off her sweater. "Mmm," she said after taking another bite.

Sidar was enraptured with her and Mr. Bond. He was again struck by her beauty, as he had been when he had seen her for the first time.

"You still remind me of Cleopatra, Caterina. And your name, Cat, that is what made me ask you out. It had nothing to do with your profile picture, which was horrible, by the way. I hope you have updated it and had better success than you had with me."

Caterina laughed at his remark. It was true. She put a blurry picture of herself with thick-framed glasses to avoid an avalanche of offers. She remembered how she used to just go through the motions of a date every few months to stop her mother's nagging. It seemed like ages ago now.

"Well, I did find love, but not on Hinge, and nothing everlasting. It didn't work out."

"Oh, Caterina, I know all about you and your Ukrainian friend. You aren't the only one who knows how to use Google. I have read your DuckGirl blog and your Pearl by the Sea blog. I was fascinated when you, a private investigator, investigated me before our Hinge date. Not at first, but I found it slightly amusing over time. Of course, at the moment, you triggered me in an awful way. Worst date ever," Sidar laughed.

Caterina joined him in his laughter. "You left before your drink and meal came. I drank your margarita and brought your meal home to my roommate."

They both laughed at their atrocious date. Mr. Bond continued curled up in Sidar's lap, purring away. Sidar stroked Mr. Bond's fur and scratched him behind the ears in a familiar way that he probably had done a thousand times before they were separated. Caterina felt happy she had done her good deed for the day. It felt right and like closure in the whirlwind of events set off last spring. She settled into her chair with her fingers wrapped around the hot cup of coffee.

"You know," Sidar began. Caterina was sure he was going to ask her out. She wasn't sure if she was ready to date. Her breakup was so recent. She would decline, but maybe in the future . . . She was open to possibilities. She remembered Kimmie telling her to keep an open mind the day before Peter walked through her office door. It stung to remember that moment, but it was bittersweet as well. She had no regrets. She would do it again without hesitation. She liked a life of adventure and risk. She was never one to take the easy route. It was just her competitive nature.

"You know," Sidar continued, "I have this cousin, Ahmed, who has been having the most difficult time with immigration. It is a complicated story with the most unfortunate circumstances. I believe he is innocent of what the government accuses him of doing. His wife and children are here in America, and he was forced to flee to Egypt. His import-export businesses are on the up and up. Still, there are Mohammed Morsi supporters in Washington, D.C., who have had a target on his back since he supported Hosni Mubarak and Abdel Fattah El-Sisi.

He would be eager for some good 'opposition research,' and I think he would pay handsomely for your services."

Sidar stroked Mr. Bond's fur as he spoke. His English was excellent, with a slight, soothing accent and nothing too harsh. His dark eyes matched his dark sweater, giving him a rich, cosmopolitan look. His full head of dark hair was styled nicely with a recent haircut. He picked up Mr. Bond, moved him over on the couch, walked over to Caterina, and picked up her empty cup of coffee.

"More coffee?" he said with a sparkle in his eye.

"I'd loved some," purred Caterina.

THE END

Milton Keynes UK
Ingram Content Group UK Ltd.
UKHW050622160724
445389UK00012B/546